Catherine Sedgeitar

This is a work of fiction. All of the characters, organizations, and events portrayed in this novel are either products of the author's imagination or are used fictitiously.

LUMPERS

Copyright © 2026 by Catherine Lamm

Cover design by Tyler Smith

Cover copyright © 2026 by Barcelos Publishing, LLC

All rights reserved.

Published by Barcelos Publishing, LLC, Sacramento, CA, USA

The Library of Congress Cataloging-in-Publication Data is available upon request.

ISBN 9798994231913 (trade paperback)

ISBN 9798994231920 (hardback)

ISBN 9798994231906 (ebook)

Our books may be purchased in bulk for promotional, educational, or business use. Please contact your local bookseller for more information.

First Edition: March 2026

Printed in the United States of America

Novels by Catherine Sequeira

<u>Josie Harjo Series</u>
If You Hear Hoofbeats
The Lady or the Tiger
When Pigs Fly
Follow the White Dog

<u>Stand-alone Novels</u>
The Before and The After
Lumpers

To those whom society chooses not to see.

CHAPTER
ONE

The three of us stood in a semicircle around the corpse, holding our pikes. Blood dripped from the end of mine.

The lumper was lying face down on the scraggly lawn, dark hair splayed around her head like a halo. Blood seeped slowly across the pink of her shirt. Her velvet, low-waisted track pants had inched down, and a cancerous mound stretched the tramp stamp at the dip of her back. The wings of the tattooed butterfly were lumpy and distorted; I couldn't take my eyes off the horrifying thing.

"We need to get her in the truck and get to Decon," Earl grumbled, all business. He dropped a body bag between us.

I still couldn't move.

"Look at this dude." Earl nodded his chin toward me and snorted. "Popped his lumper cherry on his first run, and he's standing there with his dick in his hand."

He studied me, a frown pulling at his mouth. After a beat, he sucked his teeth in disgust and headed to the truck, holding his pike and leaving Decker and me to take care of the lumper.

Decker gave me a single, sympathetic pat on the back. "Don't worry, man. It takes time to get used to it."

I wasn't sure I believed him. Sticking a pike through the chest of a lumper wasn't how I'd expected to spend the next ten years. But I'd fucked up pretty bad, and this was the only way to the other side of my sentence.

Decker leaned over and spread the body bag parallel to the corpse. There was a soft *zzzp* as he opened it. His gloved hands looped around the lumper's thin wrists.

He tipped his chin toward her feet. "Grab her legs."

The words were enough to shake me out of whatever mind-fuck I was swimming in. I laid my bloody pike on the ground and reached down. Her feet were bare, the bottoms dirty and torn from wandering in the yard for who knows how long.

I grabbed her ankles, feeling the bones through my disposable gloves. The pink of her manicured toenails winked at me, and I noticed that dainty white and yellow flowers had been meticulously painted on the nail of her big toe. My muscles locked up again as my mind tried to make sense of what I'd done to her.

"Ready?" Decker asked.

No, I'm not fucking ready. I'll never be ready, I thought.

I nodded, and looked up at Decker, waiting for my cue.

"One. Two," Decker started, and we lifted on the unsaid "three."

What everyone says about dead bodies is true: They're heavier than they look. But it was a short lift into the body bag. We tucked her floppy arms and legs into the bag, and a distant part of me wondered why she wasn't stiff like dead people were supposed to be.

Or does that take a while?

Decker gently swept the lumper's hair inside so that it wouldn't catch in the zipper and closed the bag. The pink toenails were the last to be locked away.

"The bags have handles," Decker said, gesturing to the black loops. "Would be a fuck ton easier if we had a gurney or some shit, but the suits at BCB are cheap as fuck."

I grabbed the two handles closest to me, adjusting my grip to make sure the hold was tight through the rubber of my gloves. I figured I'd be pulling most of the weight; Decker was a skinny-ass toothpick, and I was big enough to hustle a hundred pounds of rebar across a job site without breaking a sweat.

We lifted our ends, Decker grunting with the effort. He hunched, arms pulled straight, barely lifting his end enough to clear the ground. It was clear the guy wasn't used to working with his hands.

We shuffled to the pickup truck with the sagging body bag looped between us. Earl had already lowered the tailgate and stood to the side, pulling supplies out of the toolbox.

My muscles tightened as we lifted the bag. Decker's end knocked against the tailgate with a *thud* that could only be the woman's head.

"Careful," Decker said more to himself, eyebrows creasing.

"It's a body," Earl snorted from the side of the truck. "And she was a lumper before that. Doesn't matter."

"It matters," Decker said under his breath. "*She* mattered." With another grunt, Decker made one last try with his spindly muscles and lifted his end in.

We dug our heels in and pushed the bag enough to clear the tailgate.

The *click, click, click* of the bead in the spray can pulled my attention away. Earl's big frame now blocked the front door of the house. Short bursts of swishing sounded as he sprayed the paint on the door. When he stepped away, the door was marked with a bright red "L" wrapped in a circle. The date was slashed below, trails of red dripping from the numbers.

Ten days from now, people would be able enter the property.

No one was stupid enough to go into the place before then. The world had lived with lumpers long enough to know the rules. The occasional junkie might be jonesing enough to take the risk, break a window, and steal a stereo for a hit. But one open wound, and a week or so later, we'd be putting a pike through their chest, too.

Decker grabbed the pump sprayer. It was one of the cheap, two-gallon, plastic ones that could be bought at a Home Depot. But instead of spraying fertilizer in a garden, thumpers sprayed dilute bleach on blood splatters to kill lumper cells. I wasn't sure that something so simple could protect people from getting sick, but who was I to really say? I didn't know shit about the Lumps other than to stay the fuck away from the infected.

Decker pumped the black plastic handle of the sprayer and moved over to the pool of blood on the lawn. He pressed the thumb trigger at the end of the application wand. Disinfectant showered out in a fan shape.

"Would you wake your ass up, Bear?" Earl barked at me. "Go grab the pikes."

Earl's bulky frame was too close for comfort. My back stiffened, and my feet shifted to a defensive position without even thinking about it.

If Earl noticed, he didn't show it. He'd already turned away and dropped the spray can into the toolbox with a loud *clang*.

I took a deep breath, and the tide receded. It was best to let things ride. I had a long fuse, but when it blew, it fucking *blew*. I had to be careful.

Following Earl's orders, I moved over to the pool of blood and reached down for the pike nestled in the unkept grass. The pike was about five feet long, with a smooth wooden handle and a metal tip shaped like an arrowhead. The shiny silver end was now covered in dark-red blood. A fly danced across the tip.

I waved my hand to chase it away.

"Why are they called pikes anyway?" Decker asked conversationally. "Pikes are like fifteen to twenty feet long. Infantry used them against cavalry in the Middle Ages and shit. Had to be long to reach the dudes up on horses before the infantry got pounded into the mud."

Earl tossed Decker an incredulous look.

Decker stopped spraying and used the application wand to gesture to his discarded pike. "Look at that thing. That'd be useless against cavalry. The shit they got us using is more like a spear."

Earl snorted a laugh and shook his head. "Bro, you don't know what the fuck you talking about," he said, voice relaxed. "They're fucking pikes. Everybody calls them pikes. We *pike* a lumper. We don't *spear* no one. You *spear* a piece of pineapple with a tiny little stick to make one of your bougie kabobs, richie."

I didn't know fuck-all about old-school weapons. But the BCB manual sure as hell called them pikes, and so did the Ken doll in our training video. Being the new guy on the crew, I wasn't going to say shit.

Decker raised his eyebrows and shrugged his shoulders in a way that could only be interpreted as a "whatever, but I'm right" gesture. He gave me a knowing look, a small smile pulling at the edges of his lips. He might've been right about the whole pike thing, but it wasn't smart to act like a know-it-all. Guys like that had a tendency to get beaten to shit in prison.

Moving to the other side of the pool of blood, I picked up Decker's pike. He'd been my back-up, so the tip of his pike was as clean as a whistle.

Since I was the new guy, I'd had to do the piking on my first run; it was one of many unspoken rules of being on thumper duty. I wasn't sure who'd made it or why. Maybe it was to get the ugliest part of the whole thing out of the way. Rip the band-aid off. That kind of thing. I wasn't sure about all that shit.

Back at the tailgate, I tossed the pikes into the truck bed, where they clattered and landed in the shape of an "X" across the black body bag. The blood had started to clot on the point of mine, and it looked like a thick smear of acrylic paint.

I was just about to raise the tailgate when I noticed a trickle of blood leaking from the body bag. The red liquid oozed slowly down the ridges of the truck bed. The tailgate fell back down.

"Well, fuck me," Earl grumbled, noticing the mess, and slapped the side of his fist against the truck in frustration. "Fucking amateurs."

"Ain't our fault," Decker said defensively. "Bag's a piece of shit and probably has a busted seam."

Earl dug through the toolbox and pulled out a roll of absorbent padding. He closed the tailgate and stuffed it in the crack, mumbling the whole time about leaving a trail of blood back to Decon.

Having scorched the earth with bleach, Decker returned the pump sprayer to the toolbox. He pulled out a roll of red biohazard bags, tore one off, and handed it to me.

I flicked it open with a *swish* and hooked it on the side of the truck. We took off our flimsy plastic face shields, Tyvek suits, and shoe covers, careful not to roll any of the blood onto our clothes. Our gloves were last.

"Let's get this lumper to Decon, get the truck cleaned, and get back," Earl huffed. "I need a beer."

Yeah, a beer. Right. That'll never happen.

There would be no beers in our near future. We got a lot of perks serving our time on thumper duty, but we never got anything as sweet as a beer.

Piking lumpers wasn't a pleasant gig; that's why the BCB used convicts to pop the shambling bastards. But as fucked up as it was clearing a lumper from a district in lockdown, working as a burner in Decon was ten times fucking worse. Thumpers, like us, would get to wait outside, have a smoke, and shoot the shit while those guys had to clean the truck and burn the bodies. I'd take thumper duty over being a burner any day.

Being a burner was a risky gig; only the real baddies were put on that duty. I wasn't sure if the BCB called those dudes burners because they incinerated the lumpers or because they were disposable like burner phones. Whatever the case, burners were the worst of the worst, and they did their work under the firm fist of armed guards.

Burners definitely wouldn't be getting a beer.

Earl pulled the walkie off his waistband to call dispatch. "Team Four reporting. District 32 clear. On our way to Decon."

There was a crackle, and a woman's voice replied, "Roger that, Team Four."

With the target nullified, the lockdown would be lifted. But I didn't expect anyone to stroll out into their yard as soon as the all-clear went out. People tended to hunker down until the thumpers left the district.

Best to pretend like all that messiness didn't happen.

Thumper vehicles were like garbage trucks, rolling in to clean up other people's messes. The people living in those cookie-cutter houses didn't want to know how the sausage was made and were more than happy to sit behind their shuttered windows, streaming a movie until all the ickiness was carted away. And they definitely didn't want to be contacted by a tracer. After we left, those desk jockeys would move in, tracking down anyone who'd come into contact with the deceased and making sure the lumper—with her pink manicured toenails—hadn't spread that shit to anyone else. If the infected cells had jumped, District 32 would be back on lockdown, and we'd be back with our pikes.

Doing our time.

The three of us climbed into the truck. Earl took the driver's seat, Decker rode shotgun, and I sat bitch in the cramped backseat.

I was a big dude—always had been—and riding bitch sucked. My knees practically touched my teeth, and I had to hunch to keep my head from hitting the ceiling every time we went over a bump.

Earl started the engine and rolled the windows down. The light, warm breeze trickled in, brushing away the faint whiff of Decker's BO.

Killing lumpers was like killing sheep. They just kind of shuffled around and didn't come after you. I wasn't sure why Decker had started weeping nervous sweat over the whole thing. Maybe he was antsy about being that close to infected blood. Maybe he had an open wound somewhere he was hiding.

The truck thumped out of the sharp incline of the driveway. A couple of turns later, we headed south on Northgate Blvd. With a flash of Earl's ID card and a cautious glance at the black body bag in the pickup bed, the guard waved us through the checkpoint and out of the district.

CHAPTER
TWO

The drive to Decon was about ten miles, but it would still take twenty or so minutes. Thirty if we caught a bunch of red lights. Since we were riding with a dead lumper, the freeway was entirely off limits, and Earl had to stick to certain routes.

I shifted in the tight backseat, trying to get comfortable.

Earl took a hand off the wheel to fuss with the radio. He twisted the dial to the local rap station. "Squabble Up" poured from the speakers.

"Kendrick. Really, man?" Decker moaned dramatically. He ran a knobby hand through his scraggly blond hair. The short, greasy stands tumbled in the breeze.

Earl smiled, white, pearly teeth flashing from his dark grin.

Decker turned to look at me over his left shoulder. "Bear, you like this shit, bro?"

Decker's skin was pasty, and his cheeks were hollow. He was missing a few teeth. But his eyes were crystal blue and had a kindness about them. He was a druggie, and I knew I shouldn't trust the guy, but I couldn't help but like him a little.

I shrugged and didn't answer.

I wasn't big into Kendrick, but I didn't hate him either. Plus, I didn't want to make any waves. When a dude like me made waves, they tended to be the tsunami kind, and I needed to keep that shit in check.

Decker pursed his lips, snorted, and turned back around. "Fine. Whatever. Fuck, man. Can't we just listen to something else? I'd even listen to country right now. Anything but fucking rap."

Earl turned the music up.

Decker ran his fingers through his hair again. His shoulder twitched slightly, and he started picking at the scars on his cheek.

The songs shifted from one to the next as we slowly wove through the streets. The blinker went *tink, tink, tink* every time we turned, barely audible over the music. Earl hung one elbow out the window, lightly beating the rhythm on the door.

I wondered what Earl had done to get here. From the bits I'd gathered, he was washed up with a life sentence and no chance of parole. He'd be spending the rest of his life killing lumpers. Beyond that, I didn't know shit.

I studied the gray hairs poking through Earl's tight, black curls. What was it like for him, being incarcerated and knowing he'd be spending the rest of his life doing this? How could he not be crushed under the hopelessness of it all? I thought my ten-year sentence was a heavy weight to carry; I didn't know shit.

When I was transferred about a week ago, I'd only been a few months into my sentence. No matter where they parked my ass, I faced a long stretch ahead. Even though I wasn't a lifer, there were still moments when I felt like I'd never see the end of it.

My eyes shifted away from Earl; I wasn't ready to unpack that shit.

The breeze trickled in through the windows. A few small strands of hair escaped my braid and danced across my face.

On the other side of District 32's fence, people were out, and the streets were full. Cars rolled by. People texted on their phones. A couple walked down the street, hands loosely linked. A few people waited at a bus stop with bored expressions. Everything had a normal feel to it.

For a second, I could pretend like I hadn't just piked a woman.

But try as I might, I couldn't ignore the way people's eyes slid right over us. As soon as anyone caught the BCB logo on the truck, heads would whip away. I wasn't sure if they were too scared to make eye contact with the felons who were doing their cleaning up or too terrified to face what rode in back. It was probably a little of both. We were like Death, carrying a pike instead of a scythe; they knew why we were there, and if they looked away, maybe we wouldn't come for them.

The weight of everything I'd done today made my chest feel tight. I closed my eyes and rubbed them with the base of my palms. A flash of pink toenails filled my mind.

My eyes shot back open. I couldn't handle thinking about that right now. Or about the woman who'd put so much time into painting those little flowers. All that effort, and she'd died before the polish had even started to chip off. Watching the dismissive looks of the people out in the world was better than seeing mental images of the lumper. Anything was better than that.

I shifted my attention to the world outside. The truck passed through a half-dozen district checkpoints on the way to Decon. The gates separating the remaining districts were wide open, and we rolled right through with the other traffic. The guards didn't even bother to look up.

When Earl pulled into the driveway at Decon, my eyes darted across the looming industrial complex, taking everything in. This had been my first run, and I'd never actually been to the place before.

Right after my transfer, I'd gone through the bullshit they called training and watched the video that explained what happened in Decon. I'd thought I knew what to expect, but the place we were headed into looked nothing like the one in the video. The building in the video had a sterile, hospital vibe, like it was a place where people could go and come out feeling better.

The Decon in Sacramento looked like a fucking concentration camp. A BCB logo graced an innocuous sign out front. Beyond that, there was a ten-foot, solid metal fence topped with concertina wire. Guard towers capped each corner like a medieval castle. No one would come here unless they had to.

After a quick scan of our ID cards, the double gates rattled open one after the other, letting our truck pass through. A sprawling industrial complex spread out beyond the gate. The buildings were a cluster of gloomy gray stucco rising from a weedy asphalt parking lot. It was treeless and had a barren, depressed feel to it. Smoke rose in a thin plume from the far side of the complex, and a faint smell of metallic ash drifted through the air.

Earl pulled the truck into the large bay on the right, shifted it into park, and killed the engine. We piled out, leaving the keys dangling in the ignition.

The burners would take things from there. They'd clear the body from the truck bed and swab up any mess. The truck would reappear on the other side of the building, sanitized and squeaky clean.

In the meantime, we had to go through our own decontamination process. I knew the steps from the training video. But reality had turned out to be a little darker—and a lot rougher—than BCB had made things out to be. I wasn't sure what to expect inside those walls; they might end up spraying chemicals on us with firehoses.

Earl pushed through the building's side door with a clank. Decker and I followed closely at his heels. A cop shop sat on the right, and a bored guard watched us through the bulletproof glass as we moved into the vestibule. A buzzing fluorescent light blinked overhead. Our boots scuffed across the dirty linoleum floor.

"Team Four, checking in," Earl announced without looking up.

We each scanned our ID cards and moved through a set of double doors into the decontamination chamber. My feet carried me forward, but my body tensed.

The room was floor-to-ceiling cement, and it was the first time since being incarcerated that the prison showers actually looked like they did in the movies. The walls were a dingy off-white marred by scuff marks. The floor was gray, rough concrete with regularly spaced drains. On the left side of the room, there were two metal chutes poking out from the wall. On the right, there were three shower heads arranged in a row. Even though the room was likely blasted with bleach on the regular, the smell of mildew lingered. I wondered if it came from the drains.

The training video hadn't said fuck-all about what I was supposed to do next, and I hadn't actually read the 623-page manual. I paused just inside the door like a dumbass.

Decker gave me a gentle nudge. "Take your stuff off and dump it in there. Clothes on the left. Boots on the right. You'll need to lose the hair tie, too. Everything off except the charm bracelet." He pointed to his ankle monitor with a goofy grin.

All thumpers wore ankle monitors. For the BCB, it was a way to track us when we were out on a run. A way to make the normies feel safe when felons roamed beyond their cages and did the community a service. For us, the monitors hung around our ankles like chains. They were a constant reminder of who we were and what we'd done. A reminder of our place in this city.

Earl ignored us. He'd already pulled his boots off and tossed them into the chute. They tumbled down with a clunking sound. His fingers began working the snaps on the front of his coveralls.

Decker and I joined him by the chutes and pulled off our boots. The rubber was tight, and I had to struggle to work them off my sweaty feet. When I shifted to drop them in the chute, I caught sight of Earl.

He had already moved to the showers, scars arcing across his dark brown skin. There was even a small, puckered slash tucked just below his hairline that I hadn't noticed before.

I'd known the guy had seen some shit. He had this clouded look in his eye, like there were two parts of him, and one was locked tightly away with only a shadow peeking through. Those deep scars held a nasty truth. By the looks of it, another human being had done that to shit to him. Though that person had surely been a sick motherfucker, those wounds hadn't come from a lumper. Otherwise, Earl would've shambled right along with them before someone piked his ass.

I tore my eyes away from Earl's scars, only to have them land on Decker.

Decker was out of his coveralls. His shoulder blades were sharp razors against his pale skin. I could count every nub of his spine and each rib through the tattoos that were splayed down his back. The meth was written on every inch of his body.

I wondered how long he'd had to detox before they'd let him out with a pike. I wondered how long it'd be before he relapsed once his sentence was up. Killing lumpers weighed on the soul, and meth was an easy escape from it all.

A flicker of pink nails filled my mind, and I shifted my gaze away. I'd piked a woman today. Then, I'd stuffed her into a body bag and tossed her in the back of a pickup truck to be roasted by a bunch of burners.

I wasn't sure I'd ever get over that.

When I shifted my coveralls off, goosebumps brushed across my arms with the cold. I had nothing to hide on the outside. My body hadn't been slashed to ribbons by fuck knows what or ravaged by drugs. The shit I carried, I'd done to myself, and it was all a twisted mess hidden inside.

I yanked the hair tie off my braid, feeling the tug as a few strands were pulled loose. The hint of pain wasn't enough to help me focus. I bundled everything up and tossed it down the chute. A small, petty part of me wondered if I'd ever see the hair tie again.

I crossed the room to the shower and turned it on, shifting the handle to max heat. I thought the showers in here would be like the showers in prison: tepid water that felt like dribbles of piss. But the water was hot and the pressure was strong. It stung against my skin.

Palming the depressor of the soap dispenser on the wall, I filled my hands with the thick liquid. The lemony smell wafted through the air as we washed up.

I made sure to suds up every inch. There were cameras in the corners, and I knew they were making sure we followed the rules. I didn't know what would happen if we didn't wash up right. Would they just push us back into the showers for another round? Lock us up in quarantine? Or move us to burner duty for not following orders?

A buzzer announced the end of the mandatory three-minute wash. It came sooner than I expected. Part of me wished I'd had more time under the hot water. I wasn't worried about any infected cells still being on me. It was more about washing away all of the shit I'd done today.

We each shut our showers off and waited naked at the doors on the far side of the room, none of us bothering to cup our shit. After being treated like cattle, we just couldn't give a fuck anymore.

There was a buzz and then a click as the locks released. We passed through into a second, smaller room. Two guards waited for us at the far side. We each grabbed one of the scratchy towels stacked near the door, dried off, and dumped the towels in another chute before lining up against the wall for a nuts-and-butts search.

I'd been through so many that the humiliation had started to fade. When the first dour-faced guard finished, the second came by with a small pen light, checking for open wounds. If they found anything, we'd be sent to quarantine, and fuck knows what happened in that dark hole. I assumed it was worse than the SHU.

The guards stepped back, and the dour-faced one said, "Suit up, boys."

We moved to the racks of clothes and boots, searching for our sizes. They had underclothes and coveralls in XXL, but I was shit-out-of-luck when it came to the boots. I'd be suffering with a pair that was one size too small.

We dressed in silence.

The back of my coveralls soaked up the residual water from my damp hair. I itched to re-braid it, but my hair tie had gone down the chute with the rest of my shit.

Fully clothed, we passed through the doors, collected our sanitized ID cards, and moved outside to wait for the truck. Beat-up plastic chairs and a wobbly table sat on a weedy concrete patio facing a long stretch of asphalt.

We each took a seat.

Earl looked placid, one leg cocked forward and the other bent beneath his chair. His fingers folded together across his stomach.

Decker hunched forward, elbows resting on the arms of the lawn chair. "Man, I wish I had some smokes," he lamented. He wiped his hand across his face, sewing machine leg bobbing.

"Truck'll be out in a minute," Earl commented.

"Psht," Decker replied, shifting his gaze away, and started picking at his arm.

"Better watch that shit," Earl said, nodding to Decker's needling fingers. "They catch an open wound on you, and you'll be in quarantine."

Fear danced in Decker's eyes, and he switched to drumming his fingers on his leg. "You know, transmissible cancer was around way before the Lumps," he said offhandedly.

Earl snorted.

Decker straightened and turned to face him. "Seriously, bro. There's this disease in dogs. They get it from screwing each other. The cancer cells are from some wolf, like ten thousand years ago. Just like lumper cells going all the way back to patient zero. The cells grow on the host and then spread everywhere in the body."

"Whatever, bro," Earl scoffed and shook his head.

A hurt expression flickered across Decker's face. "It's a real thing," he sulked. "Even if people can't get it."

"Not my problem," Earl said, looking bored.

I agreed with Earl. I hadn't heard about a cancer that could move between dogs, and if it couldn't make me sick, it wasn't worth wasting energy over.

The Lumps was different; the worry about getting infected festered in the back of everyone's thoughts. We were always checking ourselves, making sure we didn't have any open wounds. The Lumps was scary shit. It only took a few cells to set up shop, and before someone knew it, their brain would be like that weird cheese with olives in it, and they'd be drooling on themselves.

A deep silence stretched between us as we waited for the truck, and my thoughts drifted back to the lumper with the pink toenails. All I could think about was how many times I'd have to do this. How many more lumpers I'd have to pop. I had ten years of this shit ahead of me. Part of me knew I deserved every single second of it, maybe even more. Another part of me figured I'd go crazy before my release date.

Ten fucking years.

Killing one person had gotten me in here. How many would I have to kill to get out?

CHAPTER THREE

Sometime later, one of the burners pulled the truck around to the exit point. He was an average-looking dude dressed in bright orange burner coveralls. He killed the engine, left the keys dangling, and slid out of the truck. His glance brushed right past, not really seeing us, and the dead look in his eyes made the hair on the back of my neck go up. He shuffled toward the back of the building and into the shadows that housed the burners.

"Let's go, boys," Earl said, ass out of his seat faster than lightning.

Even though he tried to hide it, I could tell being behind these walls agitated him. Hell, it made all of us a little twitchy. It felt too much like being in prison again.

Killing lumpers is just another kind of prison, a dark part of my mind whispered.

I followed Earl and Decker to the truck, keeping my head down. My hair had started to dry, and long black wisps dangled in my peripheral vision.

Earl yanked the driver's side door open with a rusty *creak.*

The truck was a piece of shit and older than dirt—like one of those super cabs from the seventies. The paint was faded blue on top and white on the bottom, and there was a bit of rust around the hood. The only thing sparkly new on the damn thing was the company logo that marked us as thumpers working for BCB.

The inside of the truck wasn't much better. It smelled like fifty years' worth of cigarettes and booze had been consumed, spilled, and maybe even vomited right there on the bench seat. The smell had stuck to the truck like a fly on a turd even through the ungodly number of rounds of chlorine dioxide in Decon. The seats were covered with dirt-encrusted canvas that chafed on my arms. The space in the back couldn't fit more than a flea.

Despite having about six inches and more than fifty pounds on the other guys, I folded myself into the bitch seat. As the new guy on the crew, there was no way in hell I'd be allowed to ride shotgun, much less drive.

Earl twisted the key, and the truck grumbled awake. He shifted it into drive and slow-rolled it to the gate. The truck's engine growled like a tiger waiting to get out.

"We should name her," Decker said, smiling at Earl with a grin, gaps winking.

"Huh?" Earl asked as he passed our ID cards across the scanner.

Decker patted his hand on the door through the open window. "The truck. We should name her. Maybe the new guy could do it." He turned his grin to me. "What do you think, Bear?"

A frown tugged at my mouth, and I shrugged.

I'd just killed a lumper, and I wasn't feeling like doing fuck-all, much less naming the truck that had carried her body.

Decker turned back to look out the front window. "Betsy," he proclaimed. "We'll call her Betsy."

Earl snorted before passing our ID cards back to us. A guard in the tower buzzed the gate open. Within seconds, we were out of Decon hell and back on the road.

Earl cued up his rap station. Decker looked over his shoulder and rolled his eyes dramatically, a smile tipping his lips.

"I hope we don't miss chow," Earl grumbled.

Decker ignored the comment, closing his eyes as the breeze stroked his cheeks and ruffled his hair.

The thought of eating right now made me sick.

I looked out the window and watched the world go by. Cars waited in line at a fast food joint. A truck rumbled by with a lawn mower and bags of garden trimmings in the back. A small van drove past with a stick figure family on the back. The normalcy of it all sucked the breath out of my chest.

I'd just killed a woman, and I was watching a barista hand a coffee through a drive-thru window to a waiting customer. It all felt surreal. Part of me wanted to get back inside our Home just so I wouldn't have to look at life plodding along around me. The drive wouldn't be too much longer, and I tried to hold it together.

My assigned Home was on the north side of the city, about fifteen minutes from Decon if traffic was light. There were a couple of Homes peppered around town, but I didn't know how many or exactly where they were located. Before I'd been sentenced, I'd been as blind to them as anyone else out in the world.

There was a designated route for the way back, and Earl stuck to it. Even though driving a truck might have given us a bit of freedom, we were still doing time. If we so much as stopped to have a smoke with our bros or kiss someone important to us, they'd move us to burner duty lickety-split.

The truck continued to rumble through the streets, invisible to everyone. At stoplights, people fidgeted with their phones, talked to the person next to them, adjusted their rearview mirrors—anything to not look at us. It was like we were lower than the bums begging on the corners. A necessary part of city life that had to be tolerated but could be ignored.

We passed the Midtown checkpoint and turned north on 16th St. One more checkpoint and a couple turns later, we pulled up to the gate surrounding our humble abode. Earl scanned his ID card. The chain link fence rattled as the gate rolled open; the concertina wire lacing the top wobbled with the motion.

Earl parked the truck in our numbered parking space, and we clamored out.

"Home, sweet home," Decker said with an edge of bitterness.

Earl grunted, palmed the keys, and slammed the door behind him.

The Home was an old elementary school shaped like a rectangle with sharp corners. Barred windows and drab, cracked stucco warned everyone to stay the hell away. The front office and library formed the front of the building. A courtyard squatted in the center. The classrooms rimming the edges had been converted into resident rooms. The chow hall, gym, bathroom, and laundry sat at the end of the building.

We pushed through the double doors in the front and stopped at the front desk.

Four guards lounged in the converted front office. One perched in front of monitors filled with camera feeds and ankle tracker data, obviously trying to ignore his chatty companion who sat next to him doing fuck-all. A third one sat behind the counter. The fourth eye-hustled us.

"ID cards," the guard behind the counter said in a monotone voice. She had blond hair scraped into a tight bun, accentuating her sharp features. Her eyes were hazel, and freckles dusted her pointy cheeks. I was surprised to notice laugh lines and wondered what could make a woman who looked so stern smile enough to create permanent creases. The name bar on her uniform said "Jones."

Earl handed over our ID cards and the truck keys. She scanned the laminated cards and passed them back. The keys went on a pegboard next to her monitor.

"They're ready for you, Jackson," she said, turning back to her computer.

There was a buzzing sound, and the fourth guard stepped into the waiting area. He strutted out like a dipshit, thumbs hooked on his belt. The kid must've been in his early twenties. His pale cheeks were baby-soft, and sparse hair formed the saddest mustache I'd ever seen.

"Stand in the circles and arms up, ladies," Jackson drawled.

We each stood in one of the yellow circles painted onto the scuffed linoleum. We spread our arms and legs wide.

Jackson started with me, patting me down. "Sure make them big on the rez, don't they?"

I tried to fight back the rising irritation.

When Jackson finished the pat-down, he faced me with a shit-eating grin, chomping on his gum. "Heard you took the lumper out with a single strike, Chief. Sticking someone with an arrowhead must be in them genes."

The slur washed right over me; what stuck was the fact that he knew it had only taken one hit. Did someone in Decon report over to the Home? Was that procedure, or was swapping stories some fucked-up thing the guards did for fun? All the residents in here piked lumpers; that was our job. Why did it bug me so much that Jackson knew the details?

"Heard she was hot, too." Jackson chuckled to himself, moving over to Decker.

My teeth ground together, and I took a deep breath, nostrils flaring.

"Such a shame, losing a babe," he tutted. "Bet her cholo boyfriend is missing that coochie."

An image of the lumper crumpled on the lawn flashed in my mind. I could see the tumor pushing through the tattoo on her back just above her track pants. Snapshots clicked through my brain like a view master. Her face pressed into the ground. Unwashed hair splayed across the lawn. Those pink toenails with little flowers.

Jackson was scrawny, and if it weren't for the damn tasers they all wore, I'd punch the fucker in the mouth and take the extra year on my sentence. Instead, I kept my eyes forward, staring at the wall, and lowered my arms.

Jackson looked up at Decker as he patted his legs. "How 'bout you, Mr. Twitchy? Get some good wanking material?"

Decker's throat bobbed, and he looked about ready to cry.

Jackson didn't even notice. He moved onto Earl, still chomping his gum and snickering to himself.

The rage swept over me. If he kept going, I wouldn't be able to hold it back.

Jackson must've sensed something in the air, because he made a half-assed pat-down of Earl and stepped back with a nervous laugh. "You guys are clear."

Earl gave him a scathing look before leading us out. We passed through the metal detectors without a squawk and through a second set of doors into the central courtyard.

"What a dick," Decker murmured under his breath. "Lumpers are people, too."

Earl sucked his teeth. "What makes you think he'd be saying anything different if she weren't a lumper? He's the type to sneak some Molly in a drink just to get his rocks off."

Earl looked over his shoulder at the cop shop. A deep frown pulled his cheeks into folds, and his eyebrows furrowed in anger.

In that moment, I knew if I'd lost my shit back there, Earl would've jumped right in with me to beat the hell out of the guy.

Earl turned back, not meeting anyone's eye. "Let's get something to eat."

Thumpers didn't work a set schedule, and a crew could get called out at any time of the day. Because of that, the chow hall operated a bit different than inside a traditional prison. It was open for a three-hour window, three times a day. The food was still shit, but at least we could get something in our bellies even if we'd been out popping a lumper.

My eyes danced across my new cage, mapping every inch. The walls were a drab tan, textured stucco, enough to take a bite of skin if you brushed against it. Scuff marks and unknown smears marred the surfaces. A leaky overhang covered the breezeways that formed an inner rectangle around the open halls. The courtyard was filled with scraggly grass, mismatched chairs, and rickety tables. Four dudes were sitting around one of them, playing a game of bones. There was some chatter and a bark of laughter. They didn't bother to turn around as we passed; a returning thumper crew wasn't much to look at.

The sun tipped over the far wall as we moved down the breezeway, passing the repurposed classrooms. The residents roomed in their thumper groups, three to a classroom. We had shitty cots with a thin mattress and threadbare blankets to crash on, but at least it was more space than a prison cell.

The chow hall sat at the back of the school. A meaty smell poured through the open doors and down the breezeway to greet us. My stomach rumbled even though I knew whatever they served today would taste like cardboard.

Decker inhaled dramatically. "Chili night," he said wistfully. "Maybe they'll have cornbread."

"Man, that glop they serve ain't chili," Earl grumbled, shaking his head. "It's worse than MREs. Back your shit up worse than them, too."

I hadn't been here long enough to experience chili night, whatever the fuck that was. But my stomach didn't care at this point. Putting a pike through that lumper had drained me, and I needed to pack some calories before my body started gnawing on itself.

We passed through the chow line, trays in hand. The cafeteria ladies—and they were ladies, just like back in school—slopped spoonfuls of food into the small sections on our plastic trays. They avoided eye contact with us, just like everyone else out in the world. It felt like we didn't even exist, and they were just moving widgets on an assembly line.

Our trays clanked on the tables as we clambered onto the benches. My knees pressed against the bottom, sticking to something that could only be old gum. I shifted my knee, not really wanting to know.

We slurped and chomped our way through our food. Decker grinned, crumbs of cornbread sticking to the sides of his mouth. Soon enough, our trays were empty, and we bussed them to the cart.

"Ahhhh," Decker said, patting his belly. "I love cornbread."

All things considered, I felt like I might start liking chili night, too. The meal didn't hold a candle to chili out in the world, but it was the best I'd had since they'd slapped cuffs on my wrists and sent me to prison. And even though the cornbread was a bit dry, it wasn't half bad either. A part of me wondered if it was my hunger talking, and the other part didn't care.

"Yeah, it might taste alright going down, but that log you'll be trying to push out tomorrow ain't no sweet thing," Earl snarked.

"Least I ain't as bad as Brent, man," Decker said with a grin. "That dude could burn holes in his sheets when he busted ass on chili night. It's like the Balrog lived in his colon."

"Fucking Brent," Earl said with a half-chuckle, shaking his head.

There was a millisecond of thoughtful silence. Then, as if a switch had flipped, both of their faces dropped. Decker's eyes grew shifty, and he started picking at his upper arm.

We made the rest of the journey to our room in silence.

Our cots were as we'd left them, but I wasn't expecting anything different. There was a second set of rules in the Home, a different kind of law that kept us in line. We all knew to leave another man's stuff alone. Things could get ugly fast if you sat on another guy's bed or rifled through someone else's stash. And if the guards didn't like a guy, they had a tendency to turn a blind eye when he was getting his ass whooped.

When I sat on my cot, it complained with a loud creaking sound. I pulled my tight rubber boots off, lay on my back, and rested my hands on my chest. The ceiling tiles were patterned with the stretching brown blooms from previous leaks. One tile had a hole in it, as if a rat had gnawed at it.

There was a nails-on-the-chalkboard *screech* as Decker opened the window. He pushed his head against the bars and made kissy sounds. I shifted to watch him from my cot.

"Cockroach," he cooed softly, followed by more kissy sounds.

Decker had long since pushed out the screen, and the bars were just wide enough to let a critter in. Within a minute, a slender cat slipped through and hopped to the floor, circling Decker's legs. Decker dropped to a crouch to stroke him.

The tomcat was mostly white, with spots of brown and black tabby, like someone had dripped bits of another cat on him. The tip of his left ear had a jagged edge, probably from when they'd lopped off his balls before releasing him again. His tail had an ugly kink, and there was a puckered, hairless scar on the top of his nose. Just like with Earl, I could tell Cockroach had seen some shit.

Decker pulled the piece of cornbread out of his chest pocket and fed the cat little bits of it. He looked up at me, a soft smile stretching across his face. "Cockroach likes chili night, too."

Earl sucked his teeth and shook his head, but he didn't say anything nasty. He slumped on his cot and pulled out his kit to roll a cigarette.

Being allowed to smoke tobacco in the Home was a perk exclusive to thumpers. In any other prison, cigarettes, lighters, and matches were considered contraband. Since we were doing the civil service of popping lumpers, maybe the folks in Central thought we deserved the right to smoke a stick every once in a while. It was a small act of kindness, and I figured someone with half a heart had squeezed it past the soulless dicks running the BCB.

I'd heard burners weren't afforded the same courtesy, and wondered why. Some of the crazies serving burner duty were just as likely to set someone on fire as they were to light a cigarette. But they cremated people for fuck's sake. Surely, letting them operate a damn furnace was riskier than letting them smoke a stick.

Cockroach snarfed his way through the cornbread. Decker moved to his cot and patted the space next to him. With a *merf*, Cockroach hopped up next to him and started purring so loud I could hear it from where I rested.

There was a *snap, snap, snap* as Earl flicked the lighter. He touched the flame to the end of the paper and inhaled deeply.

"Why you call him Cockroach, anyway?" Earl asked.

Decker looked up, smiling, eyebrows raised. "Because he can survive anything. Even lumpers."

Earl took another drag and blew the smoke out in a slow cloud. "Cats can't get the Lumps, stupid. Worst thing that can happen to them is their lumper owner forgets to feed them."

Decker pulled Cockroach onto his scrawny lap and wrapped his arms around him protectively. "Like I said. Cockroach is a survivor." It came out a bit defensive.

I slowly sat up, sensing the edge of a fight. The cot creaked as I rested my forearms on my thighs. My eyes bounced between them, looking for a hint of something ugly about to start.

Earl eyed me and took another puff of his cigarette. He shifted off his cot and tossed Decker a fresh stick. "Here."

Decker fumbled to catch it, all skinny arms and elbows. Cockroach ignored the fuss and sauntered off Decker's lap, curling into a meatloaf position on Decker's pillow.

Decker pulled a lighter from the ether and lit his cigarette. "Thanks, man. I've been itching for a smoke all day."

Before he sat down, Earl held out a third stick to me. "Bear?"

I shook my head.

Earl shrugged. "Your loss, man." He headed back to his cot, slumped back down on it, and leaned against the wall.

Earl's dark eyes considered me through the wisps of smoke. "What kinda name is that, anyway? Bear. Who names their kid that? It's a dog's name."

It wasn't the first time someone had given me shit over my name, and I ignored him.

Decker laughed nervously. "Earl ain't much better. Makes you sound like an old man with a cane."

"I'll beat you with that cane, motherfucker," Earl growled back. The smile that tipped the edges of his lips was discordant with his tone.

My eyes flicked between them, muscles tense. I didn't know if they were gonna start throwing fists or if they were just messing with each other.

"Looks like a bear, though. Don't he? How tall are you? Six-six?" Earl asked, his face unreadable.

I couldn't tell if he was baiting me or just trying to get me to talk. The muscle in my cheek bobbed again, and it took everything in me not to ball my fists. I could feel the rage, just on the edge, asking to be let in.

"Six-nine." I forced the words out.

"He speaks!" Earl said with a grin, like he'd won a round. "Fuck, man! Six-nine. How do you even fit in a bed, bro? Do your feet hang off the edge or what?" He chuckled as if it were a joke. He leaned back, closed his eyes, and took another deep drag from his stick.

"Bear Castillo," Earl drawled slowly, as if tasting my full name.

I waited to see what might come next.

He opened his eyes and flicked his cigarette. "You Mexican?" he asked casually.

"Nope." I tried to keep my voice even, but there was an edge of irritation to it.

I didn't have beef with Mexicans and figured Earl didn't either, but I also didn't like being called something I wasn't. With my light brown skin and black hair, people immediately jumped to that, as if someone who looked like me couldn't be anything else.

"Most tribes didn't use last names like Europeans did," Decker said absently. "They often took their last names from the colonizers. Since California was first explored by the Portuguese and Spanish...." He shrugged.

Earl was nonplussed and knocked the ash off the tip of his stick with a bored flick. Clearly, Earl was used to Decker spouting random facts and just ignored it.

It wasn't that easy for me. A part of me hated Decker for being spot-on with what he said. Another part of me couldn't get past the fact that a tweaker could just spew out smart shit like it was nothing.

Decker turned his attention back to Cockroach. One hand stroked the cat, and he smoked with the other. He held his cigarette with his thumb and forefinger, flicking the end with his middle finger nervously.

The tension bled away, and I rolled back onto my cot. I stared back at the ceiling, wondering how the fuck I ended up here and knowing why all at the same time.

Ten more years.

I lay there for ages before sleep finally took me. Then, I dreamed of pink toenails with flowers.

CHAPTER FOUR

The ringing of the morning bell woke me the next morning.

Since incarceration, the cadence of my life had switched from a series of cell phone alarm tones to the loud buzzing of the prison bells, and now, the eerie clanging of the school bell in the Home. It was weird having that wisp of a childhood memory running my life again so many years later.

I rolled over in my cot and stared at the brown spots on the ceiling tiles.

I'd been here about a week, and it still felt like I was wearing another person's shoes. It didn't help that I was sleeping in another man's bed. Even though all prison coffins had technically been slept in by a million other residents, this one felt different. I didn't know the circumstances under which Brent had left the Home, and it rubbed me the wrong way.

Earl and Decker weren't too forthcoming about their former roomie either, other than naming him Mr. Chili Balrog Ass. When I'd first arrived, they'd teased me a bit about picking up Lumps from his cot. I wasn't sure if they were just giving me shit or if the dude had really gotten infected.

Either way, I knew the cot was clean. BCB was cheap as fuck, but leaving a contaminated cot around was one step too close to being sued for negligence. Plus, the infected cells didn't live that long on surfaces. For the cancer to really set up shop, fresh blood or tissue from a lumper had to hit an open wound.

That's why lockdowns were lifted as soon as the lumper was cleared. Sure, they advised people to stay out of a place where a lumper had been popped for ten days. But most people thought that was a little over the top. At the most, one to two days was enough for any cells to die off in a place as hot and dry as California.

"Rise and shine, boys!" Earl barked like a drill sergeant.

I flipped the scratchy blanket back and shifted my feet to the cold floor. My lower back barked at me with the movement. Hauling a dead body had done something to it, and the shitty cot didn't help. I might as well have been sleeping on a piece of plywood for all of the support that thing provided.

Earl clapped his hands once and then brushed them across his sweats. The muscles on his back rippled, and the scars danced across his dark skin like snakes as he pulled a T-shirt over his head.

"Let's go, let's go," he chattered to the room.

Decker looked like he'd been run over by a truck. His hair was even more crazy than usual, and deep bags pulled at his eyes. He pressed a palm against his right eye like he was fighting a migraine.

"Seriously, bro?" Decker moaned, slumping his shoulders and draping his arms across his legs.

The PA system crackled loudly. "On the count," a deep, masculine voice said.

The three of us shuffled out the door and lined up just outside.

Life in the Home was far from what it was in prison. But there were a few things, like the morning and evening counts, that had spilled over. Part of me wondered why they even bothered since we all wore the ankle trackers. I figured they did the counts in case someone was able to get the tracker off.

Other guys slowly appeared from their rooms around the breezeway. Two guards started at the cop shop and worked their way left and right around the edge of the courtyard, each clicking a counter as they walked past.

I stared down at my naked toes peeking from the edge of my slips. My mind drifted to pink toenails and the woman I killed yesterday. Even though she'd been a lumper, I couldn't stop seeing the part of her that made her a person before she got sick.

Getting the Lumps was an ugly way to go. Smear some of the cells in the smallest cut, even a damn hang nail, and lumps would start popping up everywhere. Especially the brain. Those sneaky bastards loved the brain. That's when a lumper would go stupid; they were just shells at that point. The world had lived with the Lumps long enough to know the signs. These days, a lumper was reported before things got really bad.

We didn't get lumpers wandering into the street like an old person with dementia anymore. But lumpers were still stupid enough that we could walk right up and put a pike through them without a fuss. That's why I didn't mind so much that we had to use pikes instead of guns to pop them. They barely moved when you took them down; it was almost like killing sheep.

Of course, ragers were a different story. You'd need an Uzi to kill one of those motherfuckers. The lumps grew in just the right spot in the brain to turn an infected person into something fucking crazy. I'd seen shorts of ragers, but they were so damn rare it was like being worried about crossing paths with Bigfoot.

"I think I smell bacon, man," Earl said, dragging me from my thoughts. "We gotta get to the chow hall fast." There was a sparkle in his eye.

I inhaled deeply, testing the air. There was definitely a faint whiff of bacon. I hadn't eaten bacon since I was out in the world, and my mouth watered.

"Fuck bacon, man," Decker said. "I'm going back to bed."

Earl pulled an incredulous face that quickly shifted to a grin. "More for me!"

The guards had finished their circuit and conferred up front. The PA system crackled again. "Count cleared."

Earl practically jumped and fast-walked to the chow hall. I caught up to him, and we took our spots in line, careful not to bump the guys around us. I was big enough that most dudes tended to stay the hell away, but the last thing I wanted was any trouble in the chow hall line. Especially if the scent of bacon was real.

"This is fucking dope, bro." Earl flashed a grin over his shoulder. "We must've taken out a ton of lumpers yesterday. This feels like a reward."

A frown tugged at my lips.

There were six crews working out of this Home, and we could get routed anywhere in the city. I wasn't sure how many other Homes there were, but I figured we weren't the only ones. And chances were good that they wouldn't call out all of our guys without pulling crews from the other Homes, too.

A big dude behind me spoke up. "Our crew bagged one yesterday. Big John's group did, too. How 'bout you?"

I nodded, thinking of small flowers against pink polish.

The big dude nodded sagely. "I think all of us were pulled out yesterday."

Earl beamed. "See! It's a reward, man."

I did some mental math as the line inched forward. Most crews worked in shifts: one day on and then off the next. And even then, usually only one crew would go out on any given day. If, by some crazy chance, all six crews were out working yesterday, that meant six lumpers just out of our Home. That was a shit ton of lumpers, even for a busy day.

No way we took out six lumpers.

My mind wound back to the start of it all. We hadn't seen those kinds of numbers since the Lumps first sprang up. Back then, that shit spread like wildfire. People got infected before they even knew the person next to them had it.

We'd learned our lesson.

Now, lumpers appeared less frequently. Things like social distancing, staying home if you had a cut, and avoiding touching others had put the Lumps in check. The honeycomb system of the districts helped, too; most lumpers were put down before the infection spread to another person. But on the off chance that it made the jump, the Lumps would never move past the district checkpoints.

Earl and I had finally reached the serving station and grabbed trays. Sure enough, slices of crispy bacon winked at us from one of the serving pans.

"Fuck yeah!" Earl said, practically bouncing on the balls of his feet.

If you ever wondered how to get a Marine excited, put a tray of bacon in front of him after months of prison rations.

Earl's grin was infectious, and my lips tipped up to a reluctant smile. My stomach grumbled in agreement.

When we reached the end of the serving station, we each had two beautiful pieces of bacon gracing our trays, along with some powdered eggs, a fruit cocktail, and something that was trying to be hash browns but looked more like dog vomit. I planned on saving the bacon for last, like a dessert.

The guard at the end of the line spoke as we passed. "Good job, boys. Bagged a bunch of 'em yesterday. Get ready. With contact tracing, you may get pulled back out today."

I felt a jolt of surprise. After being sent out yesterday, I'd expected a day in the Home. I wasn't sure I was ready to go back out. Then, my stomach gurgled again, pulling me away from my thoughts and back to more important things.

Earl and I grabbed a seat, digging in before our trays had barely hit the table. Most of the food tasted like cardboard. But that bacon—that shit was fucking amazing.

Decker still hadn't appeared by the time we'd cleared our trays, so we headed back to our room. We found him curled up on his cot with Cockroach snuggled in the crook of his legs. The tomcat lifted his head, gave us a slow blink, and then tucked his nose back under his tail.

Earl stood over him. "Decker. You alright, bro?"

Decker moaned.

Earl nudged the cot with his knee. "Decker."

Decker pulled the pillow off his head, hair frizzing up with static. "What?"

"You good?" Earl asked.

"Yeah, man. I'm fine." He rolled on his back and rubbed his eyes.

Earl took a step back. "You didn't get any of that chick's blood on you or nothing. Did you?"

"No, man. Fuck. I'm just tired." Decker mumbled.

Earl sucked his teeth and sat on his cot. "You missed bacon, bro."

Decker stopped rubbing his eyes, and his eyebrows lifted hopefully. "Did you save any for Cockroach?"

"Fuck no!" Earl exclaimed. "I ate all that shit up."

Decker's gaze shifted to me with hope.

I shook my head apologetically.

Decker reached down to pat Cockroach. "Sorry, buddy. I promise I'll hook you up next time."

Cockroach stood and stretched, arching his back. He silently hopped to the floor, tracing his usual path up the empty bookcase, and then slipped through the open window.

Decker watched him from his bed and then looked at me again. "Hook him up next time? Will you?"

I didn't know how to respond to that. Feeding cats wasn't really my thing. I tossed a chin nod to Decker, hoping it was enough to keep the peace.

Decker seemed satisfied and rolled back over, turning his back to us.

We hung out in our room, each in our own world. Earl dug through his stash and pulled out a battered deck of cards to play a game of one-handed solitaire. Decker continued to snore away.

I pulled out my sketchbook, pencil, and eraser. Even though I often sketched the bits of prison life around me, feeling the pencil scratch across the paper somehow took me away from the brutal reality of incarceration. My pencil skated across the paper, creating a rough outline of Cockroach. I used the edge of the pencil lead to start shading in the details. The splotches of dark stripes on his white hair. The chunk missing from his ear. His kinked tail. All the scraggly messiness of him came to life on the page in front of me, and the muscles in my shoulders loosened.

After about an hour, Earl's voice pulled me from my work. "Wanna play Gin?" He pressed his cards into a tidy stack in his palm.

I shrugged and placed the sketchbook to the side of my cot. I stood and followed him out, leaving Decker to catch some more shuteye.

We claimed a rickety table out in the courtyard. The plastic lawn chair groaned under my weight. Earl did the honors, shuffling the deck with practiced ease and dealing the cards out.

The size and placement of the school's courtyard was designed by some idiot in such a way that the sun could never fully shine in, and it created a depressing gloom. I figured the kids who'd gone here before must've felt like they were in prison, too.

Tufts of grass struggled through the well-worn dirt. A sad, sun-starved tree was perched in the middle. It looked off-kilter, with leaves clustered along the top, reaching for the sunshine. The only other living things in this shithole were cockroaches and rats.

The murmur of conversation drifted through the yard. The cafeteria doors had been thrown open, and the space had shifted from being used as a chow hall to a gym. Sounds poured out: the dribble of a basketball, the squeak of shoes against the gym floor, and the clanking of weights.

After a couple rounds, Decker joined us, hands wrapped around his skinny arms. He hunched forward, like he was protecting his core. I knew the guy had to have stopped using since he'd been in, but he still looked like he'd tweaked last night.

He pulled a generic granola bar from his sweatshirt pocket. He took a bite, chewing with difficulty. I wondered what it was like to be missing so many teeth. His shitty life decisions were written on his face like gang tattoos.

"Deal me in on the next one," Decker mumbled, a few crumbs dropping from his mouth.

We played another round. Earl kicked our asses, which seemed to be the status quo. The cards hummed through a shuffle and then a rainbow: once, twice, three times. He sped the cards across the tables, dealing them out.

I looked up from my hand to see Earl studying me.

"You good?" he asked.

I wrinkled my eyebrows.

Who the fuck is ever good when they're in a place like this?

"I mean, after yesterday," he added.

My chest felt tight.

Decker's sewing machine leg started up, and his eyes darted from me and then back to Earl.

I couldn't tell if Earl was fucking with me, and I felt irritation start to seep in around the edges. Throwing my shoulders wide, I leaned back in my chair. My feet found purchase on the ground in case I needed to get up fast. I dropped one hand to my thigh, elbow cocked out. I studied Earl's face, trying to fight back the wave of defensiveness.

There was concern laced in the wrinkles around Earl's eyes. Even though the guy could be a real motherfucker, he actually seemed worried.

As if reading my thoughts, Decker mumbled nervously, "It's just hard after your first, is all. You never forget the person who popped your lumper cherry. Killing people...it never gets easy, but the first sticks with you." He picked at his arms through the cloth of his sweatshirt.

Earl closed the fan of his cards with a soft thump on the table and watched me.

"Earl's seen some shit. You know. Out in the world. Before all this. It takes a toll," Decker rambled on, unable to shut up.

Earl stiffened and flashed Decker a glare. He turned back to me. "You just gotta think of them like the enemy. They ain't people anymore, man."

I thought about the young woman lying face down on the grass, her bare feet streaked with dirt. She sure as hell felt like a person to me.

Then, I thought about the lump poking out above the waistline of her track pants. The thing that marked her as *other*.

"They're still people," Decker mumbled under his breath. His eyebrows furrowed with sadness.

"Bear," Earl barked harshly. "You good?"

Flowers on pink.

"Yeah," my voice scratched out. "Peachy fucking keen."

There was no other answer, really.

CHAPTER
FIVE

The day slugged by in a series of numbing routines. None of the crews got called out, and word around the Home was that the tracers hadn't pinged anyone off of yesterday's kills. All the guys seemed to relax a bit.

Except for me.

My mind was filled with a tangled mess of thoughts: the lump pressing through the tattoo on her back, her hair splayed out on the scraggly grass, her delicately painted nails. All of it was fucking eating me up. The casual conversations around the yard felt like claws on a chalkboard.

We switched from Gin to Spades when a dude from Room Two joined us. Bets were placed. Cards were dealt. Cards were passed. Someone won. Shuffle. Rainbow. Repeat.

It was fucking mind-numbing. I only lasted a couple of rounds before I couldn't take it anymore. Just as Earl was about to deal a new round, I held my hand up and shook my head.

"You ain't gonna play no more?" Decker wheedled.

I shook my head again and pushed my chair back to stand.

Earl tapped the cards into a tight pile and rested his hands on the deck. "Where you goin'?" he asked nonchalantly, but there was a flicker of something in his eye. Worry, maybe?

I wasn't sure how I felt about my roomie worrying about me. Brushing off the uncomfortable feeling, I tipped my chin up toward the back of the home. "Gym."

"I'll join you," Earl said.

I wasn't sure how I felt about that either.

"Ahhh, man," Decker said, looking put out. He threw his hands up dramatically. "Fine. Whatever. I'll see you bros later. I'm going back to the room."

I hadn't meant to leave Decker out. He obviously wasn't a lifter, but I'd only been thinking about myself. Bad thoughts were building in my head, and I needed to sweat it out before I did something stupid.

We all rose. Earl slid the cards back in their box and dropped them in his chest pocket. The guy from Room Two gave a chin nod to Earl, and they dapped before he headed to the rec. When I turned to leave, Earl followed close behind.

The gym was noisy, and the sound poured out of the open doors. The sound of hip-hop music spilled from a radio and echoed through the space. Four guys were playing half-court, and the tunes were interrupted by the irregular *thump, thump, thump* of the basketball as the guys moved around the space. They called out and jeered at each other.

One of the weight benches was occupied, and the clatter of the barbell was just another sound echoing through the large room. Earl and I claimed the bench furthest away from everyone else and took turns spotting each other.

I wasn't sure how many hours we stayed there. It had been long enough for my muscles to burn and my arms to shake. But it hadn't been long enough to sweat out the angst. I was still stuck, bouncing around in my own head, and couldn't stop thinking about the lumper I'd killed.

By the time the lunch bell rang, I was dripping with sweat, and the hairs that had escaped my braid were plastered to my head. As Earl and I dried off, Decker shuffled in to meet us.

"Let's eat," Earl announced.

I pulled my shirt back on and followed them into line. I felt lost, unable to pick up the threads of any of the conversations flowing around me.

We shuffled through and took our trays. Today's lunch was some sort of sausage roll with mashed potatoes and canned corn. My mind didn't feel like eating, but my stomach told me it was time.

The three of us took an empty table, and our trays clanged down. I spooned the food into my mouth, unable to taste anything, trying to fill the void.

Decker was unusually silent. His sewing machine leg bobbed, shaking the table, and his eyes nervously bounced around the chow hall. Earl ate slowly, watching me over his tray with sharp eyes. I had no clue what either of them was thinking. But Decker's jumpiness and Earl's eye-hustling pushed me closer to the edge.

I looked down at my food and tried to ignore them.

I tried even harder not to think about the color pink.

As we finished up our meal, Earl said, "Let's go to the rec."

I felt a distant hint of surprise.

Hanging out in the rec wasn't part of our usual MO. I'd passed by the rec when Earl was giving me the grand tour, but I hadn't spent any real time there. Granted, I hadn't been at the Home long. But still. There was a routine to life here, and Earl hadn't snuck TV time into his day since I'd arrived.

Part of me wondered why Earl avoided the place. The OGs tended to congregate in the rec, and Earl was definitely one of them. Was it because Decker and I were greenies? A part of me wondered if it was deeper than that, like maybe Earl wasn't ready to admit he'd be here until he died, just like the rest of the old dudes.

There wasn't much else to do other than follow him.

We bussed our trays and slipped back out into the breezeway. The air was just on the edge of being a tad too warm, and there was a dampness to it that suggested rain might be coming. A slight breeze tugged at my loose hairs.

We didn't have far to go. The rec was in Room Six, which was the first room on the corner where the cafeteria bordered the classrooms. The place was like any of the others: same paint, scuffed linoleum, ratty ceiling tiles, and buzzing fluorescent lights. A large TV mounted on the far wall played reruns of *Family Feud*. The audience cheer track bounced off the walls.

On the left side of the room, two old guys quietly played dominoes. A half-finished puzzle sat out on an adjacent table, and the surrounding chairs were empty. The puzzle had a picture of a handful of puppies arranged in baskets with fake flowers. Like the other dozen or so puzzles in the room, I knew from Earl that pieces would be missing. I wondered what it was like starting a puzzle that could never be finished, and why anyone would ever bother.

On the right side of the room, there were two more empty tables separated by a beat-up old rack of art supplies. Broken crayons were mixed together with fat colored pens, half of them missing their caps.

I considered whether a guy could kill someone with a fat Crayola marker, and figured if someone was mad enough, they probably could. But it would be a lot faster—and cleaner—to break a leg off of one of the plastic chairs and get it done that way. There were plenty of those arranged in the center of the room, pointed toward the TV.

A big dude with a shaved head sat with his back to us, facing the TV. He had broad shoulders that pulled at his T-shirt. His muscles weren't toned, but there was a solidness to him that might've made him strong enough to take me down. Tattoos traced up the light brown skin of his arms and peeked through the neckline of his shirt. There was a large patch that spelled out "NORTE" in Gothic lettering across the back of his neck.

Earl dropped into a chair one row behind and to the left of the guy. He leaned forward and said casually, "Yo, Al, change the channel."

I took the seat next to Earl, keeping my eye on the dude. This could go a couple of different ways, and I wanted to be ready.

"Alejandro," Earl said loudly but not unkindly. "Yo!"

The guy turned to look over his shoulder at us, dark blue tattooed tears dripped from the corners of both eyes. His eyes were glazed over, and he looked dead inside.

My chest tightened in shock.

I'd seen a lot of fucked up dudes in prison, but I'd never seen anyone look quite like that. With that look, I knew that he would paint me in a fight, even if I was bigger than him.

Earl reached across the chair in front of him and grabbed the remote.

To my surprise, the guy just let him take it. I wasn't sure if he was doped up or what, but he seemed five cards shy of a full deck. J-cats like that were scary as fuck; I never knew when they were going to fly off the handle.

Al turned his head back to the TV without saying a word. That's when I noticed the deep, puckered scar nestled behind his right ear.

"Is he alright?" I whispered to Earl.

"Yeah. Al's fine," Earl replied, not bothering to keep his voice down. He looked at the TV as he clicked through the channels.

Al didn't look fucking fine. His hand rested on his leg like it was trying to hold onto something that wasn't there. A part of me expected to see a line of drool dribbling down his chin.

Decker leaned over and murmured, "Al took a shot to the head. He's not all there."

Earl's head swiveled to Decker, eyes cold. "Al might not be able to hold a fucking conversation, but you stick a pike in his hand, point him in the right direction, and he pops lumpers ten times better than any other fucker in here. He's killed more lumpers than any of us. Now, shut your mouth."

"Sorry," Decker mumbled as he curled back into himself, hurt. His leg started bobbing, and his hand moved to pick at his cheek.

Earl clicked through the stations until he found a soap opera. He leaned forward over the row of chairs and placed the remote back in Al's hand. Al didn't move, and I wasn't sure if he even noticed the remote had been gone.

Earl sat back in his seat. He casually crossed his arms and tossed an ankle over the opposite knee. He looked relaxed. Like all this fucked up shit was normal.

I didn't understand how anyone could let their guard down. Even an OG like Earl. I was big, and most people left me alone, but I still kept one eye open. It didn't help that I was watching a soap opera with a dude who'd been shot in the head and somehow survived. A dude who had killed more lumpers than anyone else.

I tried to focus on the show and relax a little, but I could barely see the people on the screen. The actors' voices were a hum, and I couldn't follow what they were saying.

My eyes kept jumping back to the scar on the base of Al's head. What was it like to walk away from a fight with a bullet to the head? How much of who he'd been before had been lost with that single shot? Sure, he was sitting there right in front of me, breathing like a living person. And it sounded like he was more than able to pop a lumper. But what else was there?

Still. Even though Al had that dead look to his eyes, I suspected there was enough of him left that he knew his mind was jacked up. That something wasn't right. The whole thing was fucking tragic.

My mind drifted to the scars across Earl's back and chest. How many were from his time in the service, and how many were from before that? How could anyone go through shit like that and be expected to come out the other end in the right headspace to slip back into society?

Decker had his own scars: the missing teeth, the deep craters from picking at junkie acne, and the hollowness of his body. Could anyone see beyond those scars when they looked at him? Then, I wondered if anyone really even bothered to look at him in the first place.

As I sat there with the sound of the soap opera droning in the background, I thought about all the scars we carried on the inside. Those were easier to hide, but they'd hurt a lot more in the getting. How many more scars would we all get from our time in the Home? I knew I wouldn't be able to look at the color pink the same ever again, and I'd only served a sliver of my time. I still had a decade left to go.

My mind swirled in a sea of dark shadows until the buzz of the dinner bell dragged me back up. I broke out of my thoughts, gasping for breath like a person half-drowned.

CHAPTER SIX

The next morning, the school bell woke us like always, and my eyes blinked open to the brown stains on the ceiling tiles.

Another day. Another hashmark to count out the time.

Decker managed to crawl out of bed when we did, scooting through the cafeteria line, and squirreling away some food for Cockroach.

"It's not bacon," Decker said sadly. "But he'll 'preciate it."

Back in our room, Cockroach greeted us with a *meow* and swirled hopefully around Decker's ankles. Decker broke bits off of the stale toast and fed them to him piece by piece. A rumbly, wet purr echoed between bites.

I pulled my sketch book out from my stash and sat on the cot, leaning against the wall. The pencil scratched across the surface as I tried to quiet my head. This time, I drew Earl, trying to capture the haunted expression he always tried to hide.

Earl watched Decker from where he'd perched on his cot. A cigarette dangled between two fingers, and a trail of smoke spiraled up from the tip.

"He's getting crumbs all over your cot," Earl said thoughtfully.

Decker shrugged, not looking up. "Don't matter."

Earl sucked his teeth and flicked the ash from the end of his stick. "Why you feeding that cat all the time?"

Decker shrugged again. "He's got no one to take care of him."

"He looks like he can take care of himself," Earl mused and took a drag.

"You look like you can take care of yourself, but that doesn't mean you aren't worth being looked after once in a while," Decker replied.

Earl stiffened. His eyes locked on Decker through a beat of tense silence. I lifted my head, and my shoulders tensed.

"Plus, it's nice when he curls up next to me to sleep," Decker added softly.

"Hmm," Earl replied doubtfully and took another drag.

There was a *clack* as a baton tapped on the doorjamb, and one of the guards appeared at the door.

Garcia stood about six feet tall, with a thick build and light brown skin. The graying hair and wrinkles around his eyes put him in his mid-fifties. I figured he'd probably retire before my release date came around.

Garcia was one of the more chill guards. He didn't give us flak for bending the rules a bit. As long as we didn't stir up shit, he'd leave us be. That's probably why he didn't bat an eye over the fact that Decker had squirreled some chow and was feeding a stray cat in our room.

"Team Four," he said casually. "You're up. Let's go."

Earl sucked his teeth and stubbed out his stick.

"Really, man?" Decker sighed. "We just went out a couple of days ago."

Garcia ignored him, knowing we'd gear up no matter how much we bitched and moaned. He looked down at the cat, a slight frown tugging at his lips.

Everyone in the Home knew about Cockroach, despite the fact that Decker was the only person the cat would let get anywhere near him. Nobody seemed to mind. Even the ladies in the chow hall were cool with him because Cockroach helped keep the rats out of the powdered potatoes.

Still. No pets meant no pets. And if the warden ever deigned to show her face around here and caught wind of a cat in the rooms, she'd probably lose her shit.

Decker continued muttering under his breath, laying the last edge of toast on his bed and brushing his fingers off on his sweats.

Earl rose with a grunt. "Where're we headed?"

"Hell if I know," Garcia said. "Jones has the details for you."

I dug out a fresh pair of coveralls and traded them for my sweats. The starchy fabric pulled tight across my back. I rolled my shoulders, trying to stretch out the weave of the polyester. According to Earl, we rotated who was doing the piking, so I knew one of the others would be up today since I'd popped the last one. But I still didn't like the idea of being in a situation with my arms feeling like they were tied up in a straitjacket.

I pulled on my rubber boots. They were a bit too small, and the ends pinched at my pinky toes. Part of me hoped they'd have a larger size waiting for me on the other side of the Decon showers this time. But I wasn't going to hold my breath.

I combed my hair back with my fingers, toying with the idea of tying it back, and decided not to. I'd already lost one hair band going through Decon, and I only had two left. I couldn't imagine losing another.

The Home had a commissary that sat between Room One and the cop shop. It sold hair ties along with the standard junk food and hygiene products. If a resident had a stuffed commissary account, they might even be able to afford a set of earbuds. My commissary account had been at zero when I'd arrived, and I didn't have anyone to drop dough into it for me. I knew from training that I probably now had something in there from the lumper I'd put down; it was BCB's way of following state regulations and paying us a wage for our work. But any money sitting in my account was blood money, and spending it didn't feel right.

I decided I was fucked and left my hair hanging loose. I moved over to the door to wait with Earl.

Earl was already fully suited up. Being in the military had trained him to get shit done, and the guy didn't mess around. Even though the droop of his shoulders suggested he was relaxed, his hands were stuffed in his pockets, and his lips were pressed together. His eyes were locked on Decker, worry creases pinching the skin around his eyes.

Decker scrambled around, slightly panicked, and tried to find his shit. He twitched to the pile at one end of his cot and then bounced erratically back to the one stashed underneath his cot. It was like his brain was misfiring. When he finally found his coveralls, he pulled his shirt off. The bones rolled beneath his pasty skin.

I turned away.

Garcia glanced over his shoulder toward Decker. "Hurry up, Andrews. We don't have all day."

"I know, man," Decker said. He hopped to stuff his boots on as he shuffled to the door, practically tripping over his own feet.

Earl's lips dipped into a frown.

Garcia ignored the show, and as soon as Decker joined us, Garcia led our team to the main office. We slunk down the breezeway behind him.

A couple of guys were out playing cards in the court-yard. They paused their game, eye-hustling us as we walked past. I couldn't help but feel like they were considering who might make it back. I rubbed my face, trying to chase the dark thought away.

Garcia buzzed us through the doors to the main office. "Team Four," he announced, holding the door as we passed through, and then walked back out into the courtyard.

Jones was behind the counter again. "ID cards," she instructed in a monotone without looking up.

We obliged.

She scanned the cards before passing them back to us through the gap at the base of the bulletproof glass. Printed instructions and the truck keys followed shortly after.

"145 Seavey Circle. Off of 5th St.," she said.

Earl froze, hand hovering an inch over the truck keys. Every muscle in his body tensed.

Jones caught his hesitation and looked up at him. "That a problem?"

I couldn't tell if that was a sincere question or a warning. It was tough to know the difference with some of the guards.

"No, ma'am," Earl said stiffly. "Not a problem at all."

He pressed his lips together, and the muscle in his cheek bounced. He grabbed the keys, clenching them so hard his knuckles went white. He pushed his way through the door and out into the stark sunlight of the parking lot.

I tossed Decker a questioning look.

Decker shrugged, eyebrows furrowed. His hand rose to his cheek, and he started picking absently.

The sun hit my face, stopping me in my tracks. I closed my eyes and tilted my head to soak in the heat of it. Every time I stepped outside, I had to do this. It was the closest I could be to feeling free in the soul-sucking routine of our life in the Home.

"Come on," Earl barked.

My eyes snapped open, and I sighed as my shoulders sagged.

I headed to the car, a few steps behind Earl and Decker. Earl climbed into the front seat in a brooding silence. Decker took shotgun, his rubber boot slipping slightly as he stepped in. The door clanged close behind him.

My heart dropped a tad. I couldn't quash the hint of hope that Decker would feel sorry enough for me to let me ride shotgun. I grudgingly accepted the fact that I'd likely be relegated to the bitch seat for the duration of my stay with BCB. Once teams were put together, they stayed together, and I'd be the new guy until Earl or Decker was transferred, got out, or died. Since Earl was a lifer, he'd be driving forever.

My knees practically kissed my teeth as I folded myself into the back of the heap-of-shit truck.

I missed driving. The feel of the wheel of my Impala in my hands. The freedom to move through the districts as I chose. Being able to drive at night, the bright lights of the city flashing by as I cruised down Broadway. Stopping at Taqueria Maya's for a carne asada plate.

The sound of Earl clearing his throat pulled me back to reality. I shifted my weight and hunched my back, trying to give my legs a bit more room. My coveralls pulled tight across my shoulders, and I hoped they wouldn't tear.

Earl flipped to the second page of the instruction packet and sucked in a breath. "Oh, fuck no," he growled defiantly, eyes locked on the page.

Decker's head whipped around. "What is it?"

"Nothing," Earl snapped back.

It sure didn't sound like nothing, and I felt a tingle of apprehension. Earl had his head bent over the paperwork, but I didn't need to see his expression to know that someone had just yanked the carpet out from underneath him. His voice said it all.

Decker picked up on it, too, and his lips tipped into a frown. He ran his fingers through his hair. "Nah, it's something, bro. Spill it. I don't wanna walk into some crazy shit not knowing what's what," he pushed.

Earl turned to Decker, and his hands dropped to his lap. His face twisted in pain. "I know her," he replied, his voice almost a whisper.

"The lumper?" Decker asked aghast. "Fucking seriously, bro?"

Earl's eyes dropped back to the page. "She worked the after-school program at my school.... Always gave us snacks and shit." He shook his head in shock. "Fuck, man." The words came out in a horrible sigh.

A huge shadow enveloped the truck, and there was a tense beat of silence.

"Holy shit," Decker replied, his voice dripping with pity. "This must be so horrible for you."

Earl stared down at the page and clenched his jaw.

"Bear and I got this," Decker continued. "You can sit this one out and wait in the truck." He reached over to touch Earl's arm.

Earl flinched away, his far shoulder hitting the door. "Don't you fucking touch me!" he hissed. His nostrils flared, and he clenched his teeth. "Mind your own business, fuck-nuts."

Then, as if someone flipped a switch, a shutter fell over Earl's eyes, and he was suddenly somewhere else. A cool robot sat in the driver's seat, staring Decker down. The look in his eyes reminded me of Al.

Goosebumps trailed down my arms.

Decker curled into himself under the glare. "I didn't mean nothing."

Earl turned back to the paper and spoke in a firm, even voice. "Dolores Baker. Seventy-two-year-old Black female."

Decker shot me a nervous look.

I was right there with him. The change in Earl had been so immediate, I was still trying to figure out what the fuck just happened.

Earl ignored us and kept reading from the paper like a squad leader giving orders to his team. "She lives with her grandson. He was the one who reported her. According to him, she should be locked in their apartment. Here's her picture."

He held the second page up for us to see. In the photograph, Dolores smiled sweetly. Her short gray hair formed a wispy halo around her head. She wore a bright orange, patterned dress and clasped a small purse on her lap. There were blurred people in the background, and it looked like a party. A wedding, maybe, or a birthday.

"A grandma?" Decker said, sounding horrified. He started gnawing on his fingernail, and a deep furrow appeared between his eyebrows. "Man, I can't kill no grandma."

I couldn't help but notice that Decker's offer to cover down for Earl floated away like a fart in the breeze once he saw that kind old lady's picture.

"She's a lumper, man," Earl said matter-of-factly. "Doesn't matter what she was before. We have to pop her like we pop any of the others."

Decker shot me a horrified look.

Earl's cool detachment was starting to freak me the fuck out. It was like he'd locked the good bits of himself away. A secret part of me wished I could do the same thing. If I'd been able to section myself off like that when I'd made my first lumper kill, maybe I wouldn't keep thinking about those damned pink toenails.

Decker licked his lips and looked out the passenger window.

Earl returned the instructions to his lap. "The verification mark is a visible lump on the right side of her face near her ear."

"The verification mark," Decker repeated absently and started picking at some invisible fuzz on the leg of his coveralls.

"Yeah. The fucking verification mark," Earl replied gruffly.

At first, I thought Decker was in one of his tweaker loops when he'd parroted that shit. We both knew what Earl was talking about. That verification mark was how we'd confirm our target. A picture wasn't always an accurate representation of the current state of things, and we couldn't exactly be going around asking a lumper for an ID or their test results. The packet would always have a visual tag: a lump, a tattoo, something that we'd have to get eyes on before we pulled out the pikes. That being said, the whole process was still a bit rough and ready. If we happened to kill the wrong grandma, BCB considered it collateral damage.

A slow realization dawned on me. The chances of us killing the wrong grandma were slim to none in this situation. Earl *knew* this woman. He'd said she'd given him snacks as a kid. He wouldn't need a verification mark. And now, he was being sent in to kill her. Decker had picked it up faster than I had.

My chest grew tight.

There was a flutter of sound as Earl flipped to the next page with the address and driving directions. His lips twisted into a deep frown, and his shoulders tensed. He folded the instructions roughly and stuffed the papers into the crack of the seat.

"Do you need a map?" Decker asked cautiously, reaching for the glovebox.

Earl shook his head, eyes hooded. "Nah," he replied as he turned the ignition, engine roaring to life. "I know the place."

Those four words were heavy in a way I hadn't heard from him before. A part of me wondered if Seavy Circle was where Earl had picked up some of his scars. Another part of me knew that, after today, he'd be bringing a few more back with him.

CHAPTER SEVEN

It was a short drive to District 17, and an even shorter time to process the fact that we'd be killing someone Earl knew. Someone who'd cared for him in a way that left a mark some fifty-odd years later. I wondered what his childhood must've been like if he'd needed to bum food off the after-school lady.

I turned to the window, watching the world flicker by. I wanted to enjoy being out of the Home, but the way people's eyes slid right over us was just a reminder of what we'd have to do at our next stop.

A flash of the smiling old woman, clutching her purse.

All of these people were out, driving their cars, walking their dogs, filling their cars up with gas, or shopping at Target. People were everywhere, but it was like the three of us didn't exist. We were just a fixture in the city, like a sewage drain. Necessary, but uncomfortable to think about.

Within the next hour, we'd be driving with a dead lady in the back of the car. A dead grandma. And the world would just keep on going like it hadn't happened.

The radio was tuned to Earl's favorite rap station. But he wasn't hanging his elbow out the window, relaxed, tapping along with the beat. Instead, there was a stiffness about him. The Earl I'd gotten to know this last week was firmly locked away.

The truck turned onto 15th St., joining the thick one-way traffic. A slight breeze swept in through the open windows.

I closed my eyes, trying to clear my head. When I opened them again, Decker was fidgeting in his seat.

His eyes flicked to Earl, and he ran his hands through his hair. "Hey, Earl?" he started cautiously.

"Yeah?" Earl responded, keeping his eyes on the road and both hands on the wheel.

"How do you know this place?" Decker's voice was soft, and his eyebrows creased.

A muscle in Earl's cheek bounced.

"Did you ever stay with her?" Decker asked. "Dolores, I mean?"

After a beat, Earl answered coolly, "No. She didn't live in Seavy Circle back then."

Decker chewed his cheek and built up the nerve to ask, "So how do you know the place?"

"That's where I grew up," Earl replied without expression.

I tried to catch Earl's expression in the rearview mirror, but he was positioned just right so that only the furrows lining his forehead were visible.

Decker's eyes went wide. "You grew up in the same house? The one where she lives now?"

Earl sucked his teeth and flashed Decker an annoyed look. "Fuck no. I didn't grow up in no house, man." He shook his head and slowed the truck to stop at a red light. "What the fuck, bro? You think I'm one of them richies?"

"Sorry," Decker mumbled, curling back into himself.

Earl turned to him, and his hands gripped the wheel tightly. "They're apartments. Seavy Circle is public housing, bro. And, no, that wasn't my exact place. But I lived a couple buildings down from there."

I thought about what it would be like to go back to one of the places I'd lived as a kid, holding a pike to pop a lumper. A lumper who'd looked after me when I was little. I wondered if the specifics of it all didn't matter much. Killing people was killing people, and it sucked no matter where I was or who I was killing.

"Are you gonna be alright?" Decker asked. His tone was laced with a sincere pity.

Earl turned and gave him a scathing look. "Fuck you, man. I'll be fine."

A hurt expression flashed across Decker's face, and he quickly turned his head to look out the window.

I wasn't sure Earl was going to be fine, but I didn't know what the hell to do about it either. Adrenaline flooded through my body, and my pits started to sweat. I shifted in my seat, ducking my head to look out the window.

We passed under the freeway. A small mural sat on the building to the right. "Sacramento" was spelled out in swirling letters against a backdrop of orange poppies. The *clink, clink, clink* of the blinker sounded as Earl turned right onto Broadway. The short spire of the Tower Cafe sat off to the left. A line of people trailed outside, waiting to be seated for brunch.

It all felt so disgustingly normal. I hated it.

We passed several more stores and restaurants before crossing Riverside Blvd. The old cemetery sat to the left. I figured the property was worth a bucket-full of money but having the earth scorched by corpses was enough to turn off even the shadiest developer. No one wanted to be around dead people.

The truck slowed at the intersection of Broadway and 5th St., and Earl guided it to the left turn lane. The building in front of us had a large tower reaching to the sky, marking a local news station. The brick wall was painted with a montage of the city's iconography in bright 80s colors: the golden Tower

Bridge, a black panther, a lowrider, and half a dozen beaming people.

The smiling faces chafed, reminding me of a world where people like us weren't forced to kill people like them.

The mural swept by quickly, and the next block was bracketed by a small cluster of upscale condos. They had the neat and tidy look of a middle-class bedroom community. Beyond that stood a tall, sturdy fence that marked the edge of District 17. Once we crossed through those locked gates, there'd be a lumper waiting for us.

The truck rumbled up to the District 17 checkpoint, and my chest grew tight. Each checkpoint had its own flavor. Some looked a bit like a toll booth or a border crossing. Others were more solid-looking and housed more than one guard. The one outside District 17 was small and dingy. It screamed, "fuck off."

The guardhouse had just enough space for a chair and a built-in shelf to serve as a desk. The windows were thick glass, likely bulletproof, and a strong metal door locked the guard in. Another unique feature was a small window that would allow stuff to be passed through without the guard having to leave the booth.

An eight-foot fence stretched from both sides of the checkpoint. Unlike the other districts around the city, I could see where the fence turned in both directions, cordoning off a small section. I couldn't tell if the fence was trying to keep something out or keep something in. The look of it all set me on edge.

Earl turned the music off and pumped the window handle to roll it down. He frowned at the guard. "Team Four from BCB."

"ID cards," the guard instructed casually, punching something into his computer.

Knowing the routine, Decker was already passing his ID card over. Earl reached his hand back, and I pressed my card into it. All three laminated squares went through the window to the guard. There was a soft *beep* as he scanned each one.

Decker's leg bounced in a jerky motion, and his eyes danced around. "Why's the district so small?" he muttered, stretching his neck to see through the chain link of the gate.

The guard heard him and shrugged, eyes not leaving the computer screen. "That's the projects."

With our arrival posted in the system, the guard turned away from his computer and passed the ID cards back through to Earl. He leaned his elbows on the small ledge on the other side of the bulletproof glass.

"The homeowners in Land Park don't want to be on lockdown with those thugs," the guard added. "The Association pushed really hard for the extra district. One of the members forked up the cash for the extra fencing. Set up an endowment to pay for the guard post and everything."

Earl went still, and he clenched his teeth. The tendons corded tightly on his knuckles from gripping the wheel so hard.

"That's messed up," Decker said, frowning.

"Can you blame 'em?" The guard let out a disgusted snort. "They live like rats in there. Full of gangbangers and welfare queens. There're at least one or two murders a year in that place. Would you want that near your kids?"

I kept my eyes locked on Earl. If it had been my hood the guard was talking trash about, I knew the rage would've won over. I probably would have kicked the truck's door open, used the battering ram in the back to bust the guard's door down, and then bashed the guy's head against the shelf until a few teeth broke loose. The way Earl squeezed the steering wheel, I figured he was thinking along a similar line. I wondered how he managed to hold the tide back.

Decker's eyes bounced to Earl and back to the guard. "I'm sure not all of them are bad," he offered, trying to ease the tension.

The guard shook his head and snorted again. "Whatever." He turned away without as much as a toodle-oo and hit a switch.

The gate rattled open. As soon as the space was wide enough for the truck, Earl drove through, practically panting with fury. I wondered if the guard knew how close he'd been to getting painted right then.

"Fucking shiteater," Earl grumbled under his breath.

I knew that look and the anger that laced his voice; I'd been there myself many a time. It would be hard for Earl to walk it back without violence or the shakes from the unspent adrenaline. A small part of me worried about how his current mental state might impact the job we had to do in the next hour or so.

I dipped my head to look out the window.

Now that we were inside the fence, the tiny size of the district was even more obvious. Normally, districts were a couple of square miles, roughly matching the territory of the neighborhoods: Midtown, Curtis Park, Oak Park, Northgate, that kind of thing. This district was a tiny patch of land, with tall, angry fences separating it from the million-dollar homes just a ball-toss away.

Decker glanced around nervously. "The district is like four blocks," he said, echoing my thoughts. He turned to Earl. "What the fuck, bro?"

Earl finally spoke up, his voice heavy. "The richies don't want us here, but they can't kick us out neither. So they just walled us in."

I couldn't help but notice that Earl had used the word "us" and wondered how deep the bitterness went.

"Fuck, man," Decker said softly, shaking his head.

"They think they're better than us 'cause they got money. Even before the walls, we had to go to a different school," Earl added.

"That's fucking criminal," Decker said.

Earl's hands rhythmically clenched the steering wheel. "You have no idea."

The truck turned off 5th St. and into the parking lot of the development. A small ankle-biter of a mutt trotted between the buildings, giving us the side-eye.

Long, narrow buildings with red brick facings crouched in angled rows. Each building housed five or six units marked by a door covered with chipped, tan paint. Instead of curtains, everything from sheets to velvet blankets to cardboard hung across the windows for privacy. Cracked sidewalks snaked between the doors. Small patches of dying grass tried to eek a life out of dusty clods of starched dirt.

The only things that looked healthy were the mature oaks and sycamores that hung over the buildings like giants. They were an extension of the mature tree canopy from the Land Park homes. A sip of the good life. I figured the ancient trees may be one of the few nice things in this small community. I hadn't seen a single HVAC unit on any of the units we'd passed, and I figured the residents probably appreciated the shade in the broiling summers.

I wondered how the people in District 17 managed living so close to the mansions of Land Park without growing bitter with resentment. The fences kept them trapped, just like their poverty. The boot was on their neck, and the chances of any of them breaking out of the cycle were slim. I wondered if Earl had joined the military to escape this place, and what it must be like for him coming back as a felon.

With the mark of a felon hanging around my neck, my future wasn't too bright either. That ugly label would follow all of us forever: every job application, every move, every fucking step until we slid into our graves. I'd carry that baggage for the rest of my life, atoning for that shit even after my time was done. Might as well have it fucking tattooed on my forehead.

The truck rolled past the first row of apartments, and I was surprised to see a group of dudes kicking it on the porch outside one of the units.

Decker saw them, too. "What the fuck are they doing out during a lockdown? Are you sure we're in the right place?"

"Oh, I'm sure," Earl said.

Two of the guys lounged in mismatched lawn chairs. The third leaned against a porch beam. They were in their early twenties and clean-cut. The one leaning against the post was wearing a wife-beater, exposing well-muscled arms.

The guys had their eyes locked on us, heads turning as we slow-rolled by. Their faces were grim, their bodies tense. With just one look, I knew they were the real guards of the district, and they didn't look too pleased about us cruising through their territory. I wasn't sure if it was because we were outsiders or if it was because we were here to pike one of their own. It was probably a little of both.

My hackles went up, and the animal part of me growled in warning.

Most of us get that needling feeling inside, like a sixth sense, when we're around someone who has the potential to be violent. Like we know deep down that something is wrong with the person. Like we can smell it on them. It's like hanging over the edge of a cliff or stepping close to a fire; something in our body just tells us to step back before we get hurt. Those three dudes weren't doing anything but chilling on a porch, but my muscles stiffened anyway.

I suspected things could go sideways really fast in this district. If it did and those guys were packing, we were fucked. Fists and pikes didn't mean shit to a guy holding a gun.

Decker lifted a hand and gave them a nervous wave.

"Keep your fucking hand down, stupid," Earl growled under his breath.

Decker dropped his arm and frowned.

Earl was as tense as I was, which didn't make me feel any better. We were in someone else's hood, and we could feel it.

The three dudes eye-hustled us until they passed out of view.

Had any of those guys ever taken a lumper out? Part of me was certain this little district must've had to step up to take care of shit, especially in the early days. Even with the elementary school tucked inside, resources always seemed to follow the money and not the people who needed them. If it came down to an us-versus-them situation, BCB would be sending thumpers out to clear the downtown business district before they sent someone in here to save some kids.

With a flicker of worry, I wondered if one of those guys lounging outside was the grandson. I quickly brushed the thought away. Anyone living with a lumper went into quarantine until the house was cleared. They'd have told him to check into a facility as soon as he made the call. That is, unless he just decided to give BCB the old middle finger. I doubted anyone would bother rolling a SWAT truck in here to pull him out. As far as the city was concerned, these people didn't matter. And if another lumper popped because some guy in the projects didn't quarantine, so be it. BCB probably figured the thugs could take care of their own shit.

Decker read the numbers off the buildings as we drove by until he finally said, "There," and tapped his finger on the glass.

My chest grew tight as 145 Seavy Circle pulled into view. I'd been so distracted by those three guys breathing down our necks, a part of me had forgotten that we were here to kill a smiling old woman. Someone who Earl knew from before.

And we had to do it all without getting clipped by the local gang.

CHAPTER
EIGHT

Earl found an open space near the lumper's apartment and parked the truck. Our destination was a long stretch of a building, and the apartment in question was at the end closest to the parking lot.

He'd been unusually quiet, and an electric tension radiated off of him. The PTSD must've rewired his brain because a switch had flipped coming back to his old neighborhood. Knowing the lumper had most certainly triggered it, but the guard talking trash and the three thugs watching us roll in didn't help either. Now, he was wound tighter than a garrote.

Regardless of what set him off, Earl was acting weird, and it made me jumpy. A guy like that was unpredictable. He could be laser-focused and get the job done all business-like, or he could go ape-shit and pike everyone around him. Or he could freeze.

Freezing wouldn't be so bad with a lumper; they usually just sat there and stared into space. We could walk right up and put a pike through them without so much as a scuffle.

An image of pink toenails rose in my mind.

She'd just been standing in her yard, staring at a row of flowers like she'd come out to do something and forgotten what it was. She didn't even look up when we checked her verification mark. When the pike went through, she simply crumpled without a sound. It had been horrifyingly simple.

I wondered if all of them would be like that.

In some ways, having a lumper sit still and stare off into La La Land made our job easy. We could just get it done and get the hell out. But a part of me felt like killing something helpless like that was the same as crushing a baby bird.

I rubbed my eyes with my palms, trying to clear my head. If I didn't get my crap together, I'd be just as worthless as Earl on this run.

The creak of the truck doors opening was enough to light a fire under my ass. Decker and Earl piled out, and I followed along into an eerie silence. I was sure other people were hunkered down in the adjacent apartments along the path, sheltering in place, but I didn't hear a soul.

A squirrel skittered across one of the trees and barked, making me jump.

I missed the usual banter between Earl and Decker; their chatter had a way of taking the edge off. Without it, all I could do was keep winding myself up.

I watched Earl carefully as he moved around to the back of the truck to pull the gear out. If he flipped—and I had a feeling he just might—I didn't want to be in his cross-hairs.

As we pulled on our Tyveks, Decker turned to Earl and asked the stupidest question possible, "Hey, man. You okay?"

Earl turned to him, his eyes icy cool. It was like he'd shuttered his soul.

I instinctively took a step back. My fingers dropped from the zipper on my Tyvek. My arms hung at my sides with my elbows slightly bent. Without even thinking about it, my feet shifted for better traction.

Decker continued gearing up, oblivious. After a beat, he finally noticed the silence and looked up toward Earl. The blood fled his face.

Earl's eyes drifted away from Decker. He turned his attention back to his Tyvek and passed his arms into the suit's sleeves.

I couldn't help but feel like Decker had somehow escaped the hangman's noose. I risked turning my attention away from Earl and finished zipping up. I grabbed a pair of disposable gloves and squeezed them on over my fingers. After getting my face shield and shoe covers on, I waited.

Earl faced the house, unmoving.

Decker moved to stand next to me, slipping his face shield on. There was an awkward moment of silence as we waited for Earl to do his thing.

After what felt like forever, Decker asked carefully, "You gonna call it in?"

Earl frowned. He blinked a couple of times like he was trying to see straight again. He gave a low grunt and reached through the opening in his Tyvek suit for the walkie.

"Team Four reporting. Arrived at District 17. Heading in." Earl's voice was a low growl.

"Roger that, Team Four," a nasally voice replied.

Earl clipped the walkie back onto his waistband and zipped his suit the rest of the way up.

Decker reached into the truck to pull out the pikes. He handed one to me and whispered, "He gets like this sometimes. Don't worry."

Yeah, right. Don't worry.

"It's my turn to do the piking anyway," Decker added sadly.

We stood at the rear of the truck and waited for Earl expectantly.

I'd only been on one other run with these guys, but Earl was the de facto leader. He always told us how things were going to go down. Today, he only scowled at the apartment, both hands gripping his pike.

Decker gave me a look, shrugged, and fished in the back of the truck. He came back with the Halligan bar and held it out.

"You get the door," Decker said to me. His eyebrows furrowed, and his lips bowed into a sad smile.

It was an unspoken rule that everyone took turns doing the dirty deed. Decker would pop the lumper today. He'd also take the lead when we cleared the apartment. Since I'd put the woman down a couple days ago, I'd take the door down and follow right behind him. Earl would bring up the rear. Even though I knew my place, it felt weird not having Earl bark the orders.

Given his current state, I didn't like having Earl behind me with a weapon in his hands either. I'd feel a hell of a lot better if he stayed in the truck. But I was the new guy. Even if I said something, I wasn't sure anyone would listen.

My shoulders tensed, and I took the Halligan bar.

"Ready, Boss?" Decker nudged Earl with his elbow and gestured with his pike to the apartment labeled with the small, white metal sign reading "145."

The dead look was still in Earl's eyes, but he slowly rose from the shadows of his thoughts, back straightening, and said, "Let's get this done."

Earl pressed his lips in a firm line and stomped up the short path to the front door, with us following close behind. He pounded a fist against the door three times and stepped back.

"BCB! Anyone there?" Earl's voice boomed.

We waited for a response from inside.

I kept my eyes locked on Earl, watching for any wrong move. Every muscle in his body was wound tight. He'd tilted his body to the side like he was positioning himself to fight anything that might come flying out the door. His feet were solidly planted on the ground, and his right hand tightly clenched the pike.

If a thumper team came knocking, anyone in their right mind would answer the door with a nervous smile and explain that it was all a mistake. But if there was a lumper in there, they'd still be shuffling around aimlessly, acting like everything was normal and going through a shadow of their old routines. A rager was an entirely different story. According to the shorts I'd watched, a rager would start attacking the door at the sound. I'd be more than happy to go my whole life without confirming that, and chances were good that I'd never have to.

Earl waited almost a full minute, and when no one answered the door, he gestured to the Halligan bar with his chin.

Taking my cue, I leveraged the end into the doorjamb and gave it a heave. The wimpy lock popped like bubble wrap, and the door swung open.

We were met with darkness, and I couldn't see more than a few feet in. A stale, old-person smell laced with a hint of piss drifted through the doorway. I scrunched up my nose, trying not to breathe too deeply.

We stood quietly, listening for a shuffle or a bump. Earl stood still as a statue and watched the door. Decker shifted on his feet, chewing his cheek and looking flighty.

There wasn't a sound.

My eyes bounced up to the numbered panel next to the door. It still read "145." We were at the right place. I shot Earl a questioning glance, and he ignored me.

Earl pointed two fingers at Decker and then to the open door. He did the same to me, motioning me to follow Decker in. I did what I was told, but the hairs went up on the back of my neck when Earl stepped in behind me.

Decker held his pike in front of him, passing over the threshold into the dark room. I was right behind him and flipped the light switch with my free hand as soon as I crossed into the room.

Dull, yellow light filled the space. There was a well-worn brown couch with a crocheted blanket carefully folded in one corner. The wooden coffee table was peppered with halos of water stains, and a small bundle of lavender rested in a tiny vase in the center. A dark TV stood against one wall. Framed family photographs perched on every surface: Dolores with four kids, all of them aging between pictures until her kids had kids of their own. A small, distant part of me wondered which of the grandsons lived with her now.

"Clear," Decker said, voice laced with nerves.

My ears strained for any sound. I expected the scrape of feet on the floor or the bump of a body against a piece of furniture. The silence grated on me, and I felt the buzz of adrenaline race through my veins.

Decker passed down the hall and cleared the kitchen, switching lights on as he went. The smell of piss grew stronger as we moved through the house, and I was certain we'd find a lumper in the back room.

Or just an old lady with dementia who's peed herself. Losing one's mind happened way before the Lumps appeared.

I shook the thought away. Even though an old vegetable might fumble around like someone with the Lumps, all cases were confirmed by the BCB before they called us out.

At least, that's what they told us.

There's a lump near her ear. That's what the papers said.

My thoughts weren't very reassuring.

Decker cleared the first bedroom on the right, not bothering to check under the bed or inside the closets. This wasn't a police raid, and lumpers weren't smart enough to hide.

Straight ahead, the bathroom stood open and empty, leaving the bedroom on the left as the last room to clear. The door was closed.

Decker had started to sweat, and his breath came out in wild huffs. I knew he'd already had one or two jolts of adrenaline and was prepped to impale someone around every turn. He shifted his eyes to mine and then Earl's.

We felt the weight of the moment; it was go-time.

Earl pressed his lips into a firm line and gave us a nod.

I turned the handle of the last door, and Decker pushed in, gripping the pike with two hands. I followed right behind, flipping the light switch. Earl stayed just outside the room as back-up.

As soon as we took everything in, Decker and I lowered our weapons.

The old woman was lying on her back on top of the covers. A wet stain had spread across the threadbare blanket. Her head was turned toward the curtained window, eyes unfocused. Her chest rose and fell with shallow, raspy gasps. Her old knobby hands curled on her chest.

"Oh fuck, man," Decker moaned softly.

The woman didn't even register our presence. Her strangled breaths were the only sound in the hushed room.

"Confirm it," Earl said in a low, firm voice from the door.

Decker turned to me with his face folded in agony. "Fuck, man. She's just a granny."

She was definitely elderly. Deep creases stretched across the dark skin of her face. She was wearing a cotton nightgown with a scoop neck. I'd thought it was blue at first glance, but after a closer look, it was a white gown with hundreds of small blue flowers with pink dots in the center. A pink sleeping bonnet covered most of her ashy-gray hair.

"Confirm it," Earl repeated harshly. "Right side near her ear." He stood stiffly just outside the door, blocking our path out. His eyes were locked on the old woman.

The four walls closed in, and I felt trapped. Earl had a crazy look, and I didn't like having him so close to me. I moved further into the room, giving myself enough space to tackle him if I needed to.

Earl's nostrils flared. "Confirm it," he said a third time, his voice laced with warning.

Decker gripped the pike with both hands and gently slipped the metal tip between the old woman's cheek and the pillow.

She didn't even flinch, and her raspy breaths continued at a regular rattling cadence.

Using the point of his pike, Decker gently nudged her head to the other side.

A huff of air escaped as the woman groaned softly. Decker jumped back, practically dropping his weapon.

Her head flopped back down to its original position, right cheek kissing the pillow again. Her clouded eyes remained unfocused as they shifted back to the window. She'd only had her face turned for a second, but we'd still seen it: a purple lump the size of a quarter right next to her ear.

"Confirmed," I said, voice hushed.

"Fuck, man," Decker wheedled, stuck in a loop. His eyes filled with tears.

"Do it," Earl said, stepping into the room. "Put her down."

Decker froze.

Earl's eyebrows pressed down, shadowing his dark eyes. "Don't be a fucking coward."

Tears spilled down Decker's cheeks. "She's got the same jammies my nanna used to wear," he pleaded.

My eyes flicked back to the grandma.

"Put her down," Earl said, barking orders like a drill sergeant.

"I can't, man," Decker moaned.

Earl tensed, glaring at Decker.

"I can't," Decker repeated, this time in a whisper, eyes locked on the old woman gasping like a fish on her soiled bed.

Before I could blink, Earl flashed past me and shoved Decker aside.

Decker lost his balance and fell against the chair next to the bed, skinny arms and legs splaying out, and his eyebrows flew up in shock.

Earl double-fisted his pike and jammed it straight down through the woman's chest.

There was a loud "Urg!" and then a gurgling sound as the blood filled her lungs and bubbled out of her mouth.

Earl yanked the pike out, chest heaving. His eyes locked on her, making sure that one stab was enough.

It was.

Earl turned to Decker, blood dripping from the point of his pike and onto the ratty carpet near Decker's boot. There was a blaze in Earl's eye, and for just a second, I thought he'd put the pike through Decker for being such a pussy.

"Get the fuck up, asshole," Earl sneered at him. "You and Bear are on clean-up." He left the room in a cloud of disgust.

Decker shifted himself to sit on the old lady's chair. He looked at me, eyebrows furrowed. "I couldn't do it, man."

"I know," I said softly. "Come on."

"She looked like my nanna," he repeated.

"You gotta get up, man," I said.

We were lucky Earl had left. I'd seen the rage in his eyes, and I knew what could've come next. If Earl returned and found Decker sniveling like a schoolkid, it might be enough to push him over the edge.

Decker finally dragged himself out of the chair. He pulled his face shield off, wiped his tears with his upper arm, and pulled the face shield band back over his head.

Earl reappeared for just a moment to toss a body bag through the door. He snatched Decker's pike away without even looking at him. I handed Earl my pike as he left the room in a swirl of anger.

I laid the body bag parallel to the bed and unzipped it. Moving to the end of the bed, I looked down at the body, trying hard to avoid the lumper's lifeless eyes.

She was a big woman, and carrying her out was going to be a bitch, especially with Decker's scrawny ass hauling the other half. A part of me wished Earl had stayed back to help out, even if he was acting crazier than Travis Bickle. He'd known her before, and I figured he'd probably carry her out with the respect of a pallbearer.

But Decker had pussed out, and Earl had been forced to do the dirty deed. There was no coming back from that.

My gloved fingers wrapped around her puffy ankles. I looked up at Decker. "Come on," I said softly.

Decker pulled the old woman's nightgown down over her legs and closed her eyes with his gloved hands. He murmured something under his breath. Fresh tears streamed down his cheeks. He grabbed the woman's wrists and turned his head away from her.

We lifted without a count.

Pain arced through my lower back as the muscle I'd tweaked two days ago reminded me that I shouldn't be lifting dead bodies.

The old lady was so heavy that we had to half-drag her off the bed and into the bag. The blood from her chest seeped through her nightgown, leaving a smear across the bed cover.

We folded her arms into the bag and zipped it up. Gripping the handles, we lifted her, and it was barely high enough to clear the ground. I shuffled backward through the house, the weight tugging my arms at an awkward angle.

Decker's face was bright red, and his cheeks puffed out with each labored breath.

Just as I passed through the front door, Decker's arms finally gave out, and he stammered, "Wait, wait! I'm gonna drop her."

He quickly laid her front end down across the threshold. I rested her feet down, hanging my arms at my sides, and waited for him to catch his breath.

That's when I noticed we had company.

Earl faced the parking lot, his bloody pike held firmly in his right hand, the wood handle resting in the dry, cracked dirt. He had the other two pikes gripped in his opposite hand, hanging angled to the ground. Every muscle in his body was coiled and ready to jump.

About twenty feet away, three guys stood in a casual semi-circle. One had a joint pinched between his two first fingers, and the sour skunk smell of pot drifted over. He took a deep puff, eyes locked on Earl, and then flicked the ash on the lawn.

They were the same guys we'd seen outside earlier. Their faces were expressionless, but their eyes were locked on target. They were like a wolf pack, standing on the edge of the forest, watching us.

My hackles went up.

There was a tense silence as we measured each other.

"Let's go," Decker whispered nervously, grabbing the body-bag handles again.

I didn't want to turn my back on the guys, but I also figured getting out as quickly as possible was the best way to end this showdown. I lifted my end of the bag, walking backward to the truck and making sure the dudes stayed in my peripheral vision.

Earl kept pace with us, keeping himself between us and the other group. When we reached the truck, he tucked the pikes in the side of the truck bed before reaching down to help us get the woman past the tailgate and into the back. Thankfully, we were able to shift her in without bashing anything. I wasn't sure our audience would've appreciated that, and I figured that was a small win in this whole fucked up mess.

Earl was still wound tight, and he had a scary sharpness to his eyes. If those guys decided to start some shit, I wasn't sure who would come out the other side still breathing.

Watching them out of the corner of his eye, Earl grabbed the spray can and shook it as he headed back to the apartment. He closed the door as best he could after the wood frame had been crushed by the Halligan bar. He slowly sprayed a capital "L" on the door, drew a circle around it, and wrote the date underneath.

I closed the tailgate with a loud *clang*, making Decker jump.

"Fuck" he whispered, eyes wild.

Earl picked up the discarded Halligan bar and stomped back to the truck, head down. He seemed to be ignoring the group of guys, but I knew better.

Decker pulled the sprayer from the back and pumped the handle. The tears had made Decker's nose start to run, and he inhaled through a large clump of snot. He kept mumbling under his breath, all skinny elbows and knees, as he sprayed the path we'd taken from the front door to the back of the truck.

Earl popped open a biohazard bag with a snapping sound, making my eyes jump back to him. Over his shoulder, the dudes watched us, still standing at their makeshift guard post. I couldn't puzzle out why they were here, and I was on edge not knowing whether a fight was coming.

Decker returned and dropped the pump sprayer in the back of the truck with a *thunk*. Earl took off his Tyvek, and Decker followed suit. I was nervous keeping my hands occupied with those dudes standing there, looking ready to jump our asses. But I reluctantly followed Earl's lead.

The big dude in the wife-beater crossed his arms, muscles flexing.

Once Earl had all of his shit off, he rolled his shoulders back and stuffed his hands in his pockets. Ignoring us, he headed over to the group.

Decker turned to me, eyes puffy and red. His jaw hung open, and his eyebrows jumped up in surprise. A thumper talking to the normies in a district was a huge no-no. But then again, so was the normies standing outside watching us haul a dead lumper like it was no big thing.

I debated following Earl. I was big enough that they'd probably think twice about jumping him. But I also knew that going over there could also be viewed as a threat. There was still a chance we might make it out of the district without a scuffle. Even though I was wound tight, I leaned against the truck, forcing my body into a relaxed position.

Decker crossed his arms and started rocking, chewing on his lower lip. His eyes danced from me, to Earl, to the guys, and back. He was wound up, too. I wondered how he'd manage in a fight, then figured that brawling his scrawny ass was probably like wrestling a spider monkey: all nails and teeth and sharp pointy bits moving at lightning speed.

There was a hacking sound of a loogie, and I turned my attention back to the group. Earl had stopped a few feet away from them. There was a low murmur of sound. Too low to pick out any words.

One of the guys shifted his gaze over Earl's shoulder, taking us in. His face was stony and judgmental. The adrenaline rushed back in, sweeping through my veins and making my muscles tense. I shifted my feet and clenched my fists.

I expected Earl to hold up his hands in surrender and try to defuse the situation before they started shooting. Instead, Earl pulled a hand out of his pocket and gave the middle guy a dap. Joint guy came next. Finally, Mr. Muscles in the wife-beater reached out, and his palm met Earl's.

What the fuck is happening? I thought, my mind scrambling through the shock.

I strained to hear their conversation, unable to pick out anything. Earl held his arms casually by his sides, but he stood stiffly, and his shoulders were tense.

"Bear?" Decker whispered nervously.

"Shh," I hissed, keeping my eyes locked on Earl. The tension was thick in the air. Despite the exchange of daps, things could still explode.

Earl nodded his head back toward us and said something. The middle guy studied us coolly before turning back to Earl and responding.

Decker started biting at the nubs of his fingernails.

Earl looked over his shoulder and called over to us. "Decker. Bear. Come here," he commanded, his voice even and unreadable.

I hesitated. I was starting to trust Earl, but a part of me felt like I was walking toward a fight.

"Come on, bro," Decker said under his breath. He hugged his arms around his chest, forced a weak smile, and trudged over to them.

I reluctantly followed. Despite the flush of adrenaline, I tried to keep my expression neutral. I still kept my hands free at my sides, and when I reached the group, I positioned myself with enough room to jump in if I needed to. A part of me worried about how much traction my rubber boots would have on the scraggly grass.

Unable to stop myself, I quickly planned the fight in my head. Wife-beater guy would need to go first; he was the biggest threat. Earl could take the middle guy. I wasn't sure about joint guy; it would all depend on how Decker responded. If he didn't piss himself, he might keep joint guy occupied long enough that I could get to him when I finished with wife-beater dude.

Unless a gun came out. A gun would change everything.

All the worry was for nothing because as soon as I joined them, the middle guy said, "What's up," and gave us a chin nod.

We were all still tense as fuck, but it seemed Earl had negotiated a truce.

Earl pointed at us. "That twitchy guy is Decker. The big one is Bear."

They didn't bother with introductions on their side. Joint guy drew a long drag and studied us. Mr. Muscles stood firm like an unmovable mountain.

The middle guy tilted his head back and studied us through narrowed eyes. "Thanks for taking care of Ms. D."

The words were so unexpected, it took me a beat to take in what he'd said.

"Most times, BCB don't come out, and we gotta do it ourselves," he continued. "Would've, too. It's Ms. D and all. But since Isaiah got life for putting his brother down, we gotta be careful. Some of us got priors, and Acari's got a little boy." He nodded to Mr. Muscles.

They have families, I thought. Then, I kicked myself. *Of course they do.*

They weren't much different from us. They'd been dealt a shit hand and were trying to make do. Trying to protect their kids with the limited resources they had in the confines of a world designed to benefit the richies.

"She was a good woman," Earl replied solemnly. "Respect."

The middle guy nodded grimly. He looked at me and Decker, then gestured to Earl with his chin. "You just listen to how he does, and you'll be good. This homie knows his shit, bro."

He reached out to dap Earl one more time.

With an unspoken sign, the three guys turned away and headed back to their building.

Decker tossed me a wide-eyed look that channeled all of his fear, angst, and shock in one tiny twist of his eyebrows. And beneath it all, there was a thick layer of shame at making Earl pike the old woman.

As soon as the guys were out of sight, Earl's shoulders hunched over from the weight of everything. His face grim, he said in a flat voice, "Let's get the fuck out of here."

CHAPTER NINE

We left District 17 in silence. The dark cloud clung to us as we passed through Decon and back into the sanitized truck. Earl said a few words to the guards, but he didn't say fuck-all to us. He couldn't even look at Decker.

There was a stillness about Decker that was just as weird as his twitchiness. He'd curled into himself, and even though the tears had stopped, he still looked crushed. When we got back to the Home, he went straight to his cot and wrapped himself into a fetal position.

Earl caught my eye. "Come on," he said somberly. "Let's get something to eat."

With one last glance at Decker, I followed Earl to the chow hall. I didn't like leaving Decker that way, but I didn't know what else to do.

We scooted into the chow hall at the tail end of lunchtime. There was no line, and we swept right through. We claimed a spot, and our plastic trays clanged down as we took our seats.

I rested my forearms on the table and looked glumly at the meal. Two slabs of factory white bread with a slice of bologna, an orange, some dried, limp carrot sticks, and a sealed cup of red Jello. I was hungry, but it would be a fight to force the shit down after seeing the grandma get piked. I palmed the cup of Jello and slipped it into my chest pocket; it was the only thing worth a damn on the tray.

Earl was already halfway into his sandwich. He looked buried in his thoughts and a world away. If it wasn't for the sounds of him chomping, it'd be like I was eating alone.

A thousand questions swam through my mind. But Earl's fuck-off face was enough for me to keep them bottled up.

I had only been on two runs, but the one today felt wrong. I just didn't know enough to be able to puzzle out why. I had questions, and at the moment, the two guys who could answer them had shut me out. I figured they were busy dealing with their own shit.

When the judge had read my sentence, I didn't know where they'd put me: regular prison, in a thumper home, or with the burners. I'd fucked up pretty bad and could've landed in any one of those places. At the time, I was so messed up in the head, I didn't have a preference. I knew being a thumper was ten times better than being a burner. There was a freedom to thumping that the burners never enjoyed. Plus, I figured cremating dead lumpers on an endless loop was about as soul-sucking as things could get.

But I'd never been on a run before.

No one ever told us how hard it was to actually pike someone. When there was no anger or rage to it and our minds were actually working, we *saw* the people in front of us. The whole thing felt cold and calculated, like running animals through a slaughterhouse. I could understand how thumpers eventually have to shut a part of themselves off to make it through.

I studied Earl across the table, wondering at how he could pike a grandma and then wolf down a meal a couple hours later. I figured he had to tuck the good parts of himself away while he did the ugly work. The soldier would come forward and do what needed to be done to protect the good parts of him. Protect him from going crazy. When it was all over, the two parts of him would switch places again, and the Earl I knew would be back, snarfing down a meal.

I only had ten years; Earl was in here for life. I tried to imagine being a thumper until I died, and the thought was so foreign it slipped through my fingers like mist. Then again, I also couldn't imagine killing women with pink toenails or grandmas and still coming out the other side of my ten years being normal either.

I tried to force a bite of my sandwich down, but everything tasted like ash.

***

Back in our room, I stashed the Jello under my cot. The red glob jiggled as I slipped it under a clean pair of coveralls.

There was a *thump* as Earl lightly kicked Decker's cot. "Come on, man."

Decker was still in the fetal position, hands wrapped tightly around his arms, back turned to us. "No."

Earl kicked his cot again. "Come on."

Decker hugged himself tighter.

"You can't hide, man," Earl grumbled. "Here." He dangled a cigarette in front of Decker's face like a carrot.

Decker sniffed loudly and reached up to take it with loose fingers.

I thought it was pretty damn magnanimous of Earl to be offering Decker a smoke after Decker had left him hanging.

Earl stepped back and flopped down on his cot. A *click, click, click* sounded as he flicked his lighter and took a deep drag.

Decker rolled over, slung his feet over the edge, and hunched over his lap. His face was a shitshow: eyes swollen and splotchy red patches peeking through his acne. The unlit stick dangled between his fingers.

Earl sighed, stood again, and held his lighter out. Decker put the cigarette to his lips as Earl lit it for him. Decker took a couple of drags, and the musky smell of smoke seeped through the room.

Earl sat back on his cot and leaned against the wall. One leg was bent, his sock-clad foot perched on the bed, and his smoking arm rested on his knee. The other leg was tossed over the edge. Even though Earl had gone through the motions of eating a meal, he didn't look too hot either. His face was folded in a tragic frown, eyes dry and glazed over.

I lay back on my cot, one arm tucked under my head, and watched them. There was a silent tension between us. A shared trauma that none of us were ready to unpack yet.

Cockroach slipped through the open window and brushed against Decker's hand. A smile tipped the outer edges of Decker's lips as Cockroach settled into the space next to his thigh. Decker's posture relaxed. He leaned back and started petting him.

Someone had turned a radio on in the courtyard, and the sounds of hip hop drifted in. I looked up at the ceiling tiles. The spreading brown stains looked like a dried blood spill on concrete.

When Decker's stick had burned down to the fingers, he stubbed it out and rubbed his spindly fingers over his face. He made a sound that was half grunt, half moan. Cockroach ignored him, purring away.

Decker hunched over his thighs, putting his head in his hands. "I can't do this no more."

"The fuck you can't," Earl replied coolly. His eyes were locked on Decker, a fierceness raging behind his heavy lids.

Decker's eyebrows folded into canyons of worry. "Dude. That was a fucking old lady back there. You fucking piked a grandma like it was nothing. Someone you *knew*."

Earl's whole body tensed, and anger licked across his face.

I pulled my arm out from underneath my head, getting ready for whatever might go down.

Decker looked at Earl with despair. "I can't keep doing this," he whispered, eyes pleading.

Earl practically snarled at him.

A horrible silence stretched through the room. Even Cockroach had stopped purring and cautiously watched both men.

I slowly sat up, trying not to trigger anyone, and shifted both of my feet flat on the floor. My bare toes gripped the cool linoleum.

Decker chewed on his chapped lower lip, and his back bucked with tearless sobs. He'd already cried himself out, but his soul still ached. It was painful to watch.

"I took one for you today," Earl growled. "You ain't got no reason to be crying. Quit being a pussy and buck the fuck up."

Decker hunched further into himself, hiding his face. He ran a hand through his hair and left it cradling the back of his head, elbow resting on his knee.

Disgusted, Earl hit the wall with the bottom of his fist. He stood so fast his cot clattered against the wall.

My body mimed his, my full weight pressing down on my feet as I stood faster than lightning. Before I could step between them, Earl stormed out of the room without meeting my eye.

I dropped back down onto my cot, folding my fingers tightly, and tried to stop my racing heart. A heavy dose of adrenaline pumped through my veins. Without spending it, I'd soon get the shakes. I flexed the muscles in my arms and clenched my jaw, fighting it back.

Decker lifted his head to look at me. "Sorry," he whispered.

"Ain't me you gotta say sorry to," I mumbled.

I had mixed feelings about Decker. The guy wore all his emotions on the outside, and it was messy hanging out with him. Sometimes, I just wanted to bark at him to get his shit together and shake the pussy motherfucker. But another part of me knew he wasn't built for this. Killing lumpers was heavy in a way I hadn't expected, and it wasn't a load that most people could carry. He had a soft heart, and I felt sorry for him.

I wasn't too sure about Earl either; he was tough to read. I knew what he'd done today had been hard on him, but he kept everything locked deep inside. I wondered what those wild emotions looked like burning inside of him. I wondered what would happen if they ever spilled out.

Earl acted cool and detached. But there were occasional glimpses of a kinder man deep below the surface, like how he covered for Decker or shared his smokes. He'd had to shutter that part of himself away to survive growing up in a place like Seavy Circle. Seeing combat in the military had only toughened him. I wondered what he'd done to end up here and if doing time would squash what little kindness was left in the man.

I can't say that the weight was any easier for me to carry. What had popping the woman with pink toenails done to my spirit? Every time I tried to think about it, I had to push the thoughts back into a box so I could simply make it through another day. Ten years was a lot of time, and the bodies would keep stacking up. There was no way I could walk out after killing so many lumpers and ever be the man I was before.

CHAPTER TEN

By the time the next morning rolled around, a fragile truce had been silently brokered between Earl and Decker, but things still weren't right with the crew. No one had said a word about the grandma since shit had gone down, and her ugly death sat between the three of us like a festering wound.

We trudged to the cafeteria after the morning count and waited in line with our stomachs growling. The guys around us chatted about dumb shit, and I let my mind drift off as I wove through the line.

The staff served food into the different sections of our trays as we moved past. At the end of the line, Earl held out a plastic mug, and one of the ladies filled it with room-temp, brown water that was somehow called coffee. That shit was more like coffee's ugly step-cousin, and I wondered why Earl bothered. He wasn't usually a coffee man.

Decker and I each took a small carton of milk instead.

The chow hall in the Home was different than in prison. Instead of self-sorting by race, residents sat with their thumper groups. Depending on when guys came into the chow hall, there might be two thumper groups at a table. The only guy who broke the mold was Al. He sat by himself, spooning food slowly into his mouth and not talking to anyone else.

"Trade you?" Decker asked, holding his yogurt cup out to me.

My eyes bounced down to the precious strawberry flavor cupped in his hands and back to his eyes. I continued slowly chewing my rubbery, powdered eggs and lifted an eyebrow.

Decker shrugged with a goofy grin. "Cockroach prefers plain vanilla." He nodded his chin to the yogurt cup sitting on my tray.

With a grunt, I swapped yogurts with him.

Decker practically bounced in his seat. "Thanks, dude. Cockroach is gonna shit when he sees this."

We didn't get yogurt often. It wasn't as precious as something like bacon, but it was a hell of a lot better than some of the other shit they gave us.

The expiration date on the lid told me all I needed to know. It was probably donated by some grocery chain as a write-off. I hoped it would still be okay even if those numbers said it was a couple days past being good.

Decker glanced around nervously and stuffed the plain yogurt in his chest pocket. The guards in the Home didn't bat an eye if someone took stuff back to their room, but old habits die hard.

I was glad to see Decker's energy was back; all that twitchiness was now reassuring. I figured he was one step closer to getting back to his old self. A hint of a dark cloud still hung behind his eyes, but I could give the guy a pass. Yesterday had been ugly.

"Man, these eggs taste like shit," Earl grumbled, pulling my focus. There was a clatter as he tossed his spoon on his tray with a disgusted look. "Fucking bullshit." He switched to the yogurt with a glower.

Despite his bitching about breakfast, Earl was looking better, too. He was still broody, but that volcano fire I'd seen behind his eyes yesterday had simmered down, and he seemed less likely to explode. He was also barking orders again, and in the short time I'd known him, I learned that was a good sign.

I took a bite of the potato slop in the section next to the eggs and was equally unimpressed. It was time to try the yogurt. I peeled the metal film back and took a cautious sniff. The color was right, and it smelled okay. After a hesitant spoonful, there was a strong burst of artificial strawberry followed by the tang of the yogurt. It was utterly delicious. I scooped it into my mouth, savoring every bite and licking the spoon clean.

Just as I was enjoying the moment, the energy at the table shifted.

Decker hunched his back, stuffed his hands in his lap, and looked down at his tray. "Hey, Earl," he said as if he was testing the waters.

Earl leaned his arms on the table, practically mantling his tray, and looked up at Decker. "What." The word came out flat, like a statement.

"I..." Decker started. His eyes bounced up to Earl and then back down again, unable to meet his gaze. The table started shaking with the bouncing of his leg. "Sorry for losing it yesterday."

Earl grew rigid.

Part of me felt like Decker owed Earl an apology and then some. But when Earl went stiff like that, I started to doubt myself. Sometimes, receiving an apology was just as hard as dealing with whatever mess had led to it. Part of me felt like Earl was trying to bury that shit, and Decker wouldn't let him.

I slowly put my yogurt cup down, watching them both carefully. The mumbled conversations of the other guys in the room and the clank of the utensils on the trays filled the silence.

"I didn't mean to make you do it," Decker added, fumbling. "I feel like a fucking asshole, man. And I'm sorry."

"You *are* a fucking asshole," Earl deadpanned.

Decker instantly went still. His head shot up, his expression filled with hurt.

There was a twitch of a smile at the edge of Earl's lips.

"Well. I owe you one," Decker stammered, looking at Earl hopefully.

"Fuck yeah, you do," Earl replied. He leaned back on the bench and scooped another bite of yogurt into his mouth.

We studied our trays for a beat. The silence wasn't tense, but it wasn't relaxed either. It was like we were all thinking about heavy shit, and it was just too ugly to share.

Decker's eyes grew wide, and he grinned. "Be right back." He pushed himself up and made his way back to the chow line.

Earl shot me a confused look. "What the fuck is he doing?"

I shrugged, a bit surprised myself.

Earl shifted in his seat so he could look over his shoulder at Decker. No one else seemed to notice, and the chatter continued around the chow hall. The guard posted in the hall was equally unperturbed.

Earl glanced back at me, an incredulous look on his face. "There ain't no seconds here."

"Maybe he's just asking them a question?" I offered.

Earl shook his head in disbelief. "Stupid tweaker."

Yeah, but he's our tweaker, and you know it, I thought, reading the trace of affection in Earl's expression.

Earl turned back to his yogurt, scraping the last of it out of his cup.

My eyes were stuck on Decker. There was no one in line anymore, and the staff were cleaning up. Decker went right up to one of the ladies, bold as brass, and started talking to her. She shook her head. There was some discussion, and Decker put his hands together in a pleading gesture. One of the older ladies walked up and passed something across the top of the glass cover with a friendly wink. Decker palmed it, grinning.

Less than five seconds later, he was back at the table. He plopped a peach yogurt right in front of Earl. "Here," he said proudly.

Earl looked up at him. He swept the shock off his face so fast, I almost missed it. "This don't make up for shit, you know," he grumbled, snatching the second yogurt and peeling the lid back.

"Yeah, I know," Decker replied, smiling.

My shoulders relaxed.

Decker sat back down and prattled on about how much Cockroach was gonna love breakfast. Earl licked the peach yogurt cup clean; his face relaxed like all was right with the world. And I finally felt like our crew was back in working order.

After finishing up, Earl stood, grabbing his tray with the half-eaten eggs congealing like barfed-up cottage cheese. "Time to bounce."

Decker and I followed close behind. We bussed our trays, and I took one last swipe of the empty yogurt cup with my tongue before dropping it in the bin. I wished I had another.

As Decker scraped the stuff off his tray into the trash, he asked, "What was up with those dudes in District 17 yesterday?" His eyes darted nervously up to Earl and back down as he set the tray down on the cart.

My muscles tensed, unsure how Earl would respond. I wanted to swat Decker for asking the question. We were finally starting to get back to normal, and he had to prance right back onto another landmine.

To my surprise, Earl just shrugged.

"Did you know them?" Decker hazarded.

"Nah, man," Earl said. "I left that place before those bros were even born."

"Hmm," Decker said, keeping his eyes down.

They waited for me as I cleared my tray.

"But they Oak Park Bloods," Earl continued, like it explained everything.

Decker and I waited for him to fill in the blanks.

Seeing our confused expressions, Earl sucked his teeth. "When I was growing up, Seavy Circle was neutral territory, but I rolled with the OPBs," Earl added casually.

"You were in a gang?" Decker said, slightly aghast.

Sometimes Decker behaved like a child, and a small part of me wanted to smack him for being an ass. Based on the way Earl's eyebrows twisted and his lips turned down into a frown, I figured he felt the same way.

Decker caught the look. "Sorry," he mumbled and hugged himself.

I dropped my tray on the stack with a *clang*.

"All that die-by-the-sword gangster shit…that's just another way of smoking yourself," Earl said grimly. He gestured to Decker. "Just like drowning yourself in meth."

"Huh?" Decker replied.

Earl shook his head sadly. "See, bro, they got nothing to lose. They ain't got nothing better going for them. They either gotta go on living and fight, or they gotta give up and get jumped in. Then, they end up getting shot or going to prison. It's a slower kinda death, but it's still suicide."

"Fuck, man," Decker whispered. "That's dark."

Earl grunted. He tipped his mug back, finishing the last sip of his coffee, and tossed it into the dirty dish bin. He moved out into the breezeway, and we followed.

"It's fucking life in the hood, bro," Earl said bitterly. "Only reason I made it out to the other side was 'cause of the Marines."

I wondered how he could possibly consider killing lumpers for the rest of his life as having "made it out to the other side."

I figured he was referring to the fact that he was physically alive rather than having a life worth living.

"The military helped you?" Decker asked.

"Fuck, yeah, they did," Earl replied. "Gave me three meals a day, a bed to sleep in, and socks without holes in them."

"But you still had to shoot people," Decker murmured, looking up at Earl carefully.

Earl pressed his lips together. "It's different in the military," he said firmly.

A part of me doubted it. Killing people was killing people.

Decker cleared his throat uncomfortably.

Earl looked at him, eyes steely. "The Marines were good to me," he said. "If I hadn't been medical'ed out, I'd be living on a military pension right now. Wouldn't have had to do what I did. Wouldn't be in this fucked up place."

Decker folded his lower lip in and turned his head out to the courtyard. A few guys were already settled in, shooting the shit and playing cards.

"Looks like no one's been called out," Decker mused. "Maybe we'll get a break."

I could tell when a man was trying to change the subject, and so could Earl.

Earl snorted. "It's still early. Don't get your hopes up. Let's go see what's on TV," Earl suggested, nodding toward Room Six.

Decker's eyes shifted from the rec room to our humble abode. "I gotta give Cockroach his breakfast," he said and picked at a scar on his cheek.

Earl pursed his lips and studied him.

"I'll meet you guys in there," Decker promised and then skittered off across the courtyard.

Earl turned to me, shaking his head, and said, "Come on."

I stuffed my hands in my pockets and followed him. Watching soap reruns was a million times better than thinking about all the fucked up shit we'd had to do this week. It might also give us a bit of healing so we could somehow hold it together when we had to go back out and do it all over again.

CHAPTER ELEVEN

We found Al in the rec room, lounging in his usual chair and holding the remote loosely in his hand. His shoulders were relaxed, and he had a numb look about him.

If I didn't know any better, I would've guessed he was high. But if drugs had worked their way into the Home, Decker would've been the first one to sniff them out. The bullet to Al's head might've been enough to give him that empty look; it was either that or piking lumpers for fuck knows how long. For all I knew, I might have that same vacant expression when my time was up.

Earl and I slid into the row behind him.

From the TV, a competitive cooking show host shouted at some poor sod who was trying to slice onions faster than a speeding bullet without chopping the tips of their fingers off. The sniveling contestant looked like they were about to piss themselves. The way the host used his power to make the cooks feel small made me sick. Just because the host had money and fame didn't make him better than everyone else.

"Yo, Al. Find us the soaps, bro," Earl said, and I could've hugged him. I didn't want to watch another second of that cooking crap.

Al was operating on enough power to oblige. His thumb pressed slowly on the remote, clicking through the channels at a snail's pace. Within a couple beats, Sami Brady filled the screen.

"Whoa, whoa. Stop there, bro," Earl said and leaned back in his chair.

My gaze drifted to the "NORTE" on the back of Al's neck. I knew enough to recognize it as a gang tattoo, but I had no clue what neighborhood he was from.

I didn't know much about gang culture. Where I was from, it was all domestic violence and alcohol abuse more than anything else. The men tended to beat this shit out of their families instead of other men. Every once in a while, some asshole would smoke his wife; that had happened to a friend of mine in middle school. But those guys never pointed a gun at another man. Everyone was quick to cast stones at a thug for shooting another thug, then close their eyes to the screaming next door when a drunk guy beat his wife to the edge of death. Seemed to me that killing a family member was worse than killing someone who chose to be a thug.

Even though I hadn't grown up around heavy gang shit, a part of me knew that Earl and Al were from rival sets. In prison, that meant all sorts of bad blood. In the Home, who the fuck knew what that meant? Since they were both OGs and didn't fight over the TV, I guessed the gang stuff didn't matter here.

I shifted my eyes to the TV, trying to lose myself in the show. Sami and Lucas were arguing about EJ, and it was just stupid enough for me to get swept away. A few commercial breaks later, Decker walked in. Two OGs and a younger guy named Mateo followed close behind and set up at the domino table.

"Oh! *Days of Our Lives!*" Decker said cheerfully.

Decker grabbed a seat next to Al and gave the hand holding the remote a fist bump. "What's up, Al?"

Al stared at the TV like a zombie.

Decker looked over to me and grinned. "Thanks for the yogurt, man. Cockroach loved it. Licked it clean."

My lips tilted in a slight smile.

On the TV, Sami's rival had just walked in. The claws were out, and I could feel a fight coming.

A catcall whistle sounded from the door. "Gabi! Woo-ee!"

I turned to see two of the guys from Room Nine walking in. The one who'd called out had a shit-eating grin stretched across his pale face. He grabbed his shit and made kissy faces at the woman on the TV screen.

The guys flopped into a couple of chairs in the same row as Earl and me. The dude grabbed his balls again and turned to leer at us.

Revulsion washed over me. Even though being in the Home sucked, Earl and Decker weren't bad roomies. I thanked my lucky stars I didn't have to share a room with that fucker. A small part of me was also glad his team hadn't been called to pike the chick with the pink toenails. I didn't want to think about all the nasty stuff he would've said about her.

She didn't deserve that.

The younger guy playing dominoes called out, "Hey, Mike, they send anyone out yet?"

The ball grabber turned to look over his shoulder, still wearing that stupid grin. "Nope. Why? Looking for some action?"

The guy frowned, and his lids dropped down over his eyes. "No, man. Just askin'."

"Ignore that fuck face," one of the OGs muttered to the young guy without looking up.

Mike's eyes narrowed. His nostrils flared with a deep breath. He hadn't shifted out of his relaxed pose, but the muscles in his neck were tense.

I pressed my feet flat on the ground, feeling a small bump of adrenaline.

After a tense beat, Mike snorted and turned back to the TV, spreading one arm over the empty chair next to him. He slid his legs out, lounging like a tiger.

"Another day stuck in the Home," Mike whined dramatically to the room.

"Yeah. This sucks," Mike's buddy chimed in. He seemed like an ass-kisser.

"It's better than out there," Decker mumbled under his breath from the seat in front of me. "At least you don't have to kill nobody in here. They feed you, too. The Home ain't so bad."

"Pfft," Mike snorted. "You don't know what you're talkin' about, junkie. I'd rather be out there." His hand folded around an invisible gun pointed at the screen. "Pop! Pop! Taking those lumpers down."

Decker turned to look over his shoulder at Mike with a horrified expression. "You'd rather be out there killing people?" he asked quietly.

"Fuck yeah!" Mike said with a laugh. The dude next to him chuckled right along.

Mike shifted in his seat to see Earl further down the row. "How 'bout you, OG? You like takin' them down? Take you back to 'nam and shit?"

"I didn't serve in Vietnam, dumbass," he replied coolly. "I wasn't even born yet. And no, I don't like piking lumpers, but I don't want to be stuck in no regular prison neither."

I thought about Earl behind the wheel of the BCB truck with his rap music playing. He looked natural there. Settled. Like he was in his happy place, even if it was just a ten-minute drive. The only other time he came close to that was when he was playing one-handed solitaire with a smoke dangling between his fingers.

"We're still killing people," Decker said in a hushed voice, eyes cast down, picking at the back of one of his arms.

"We're killing *lumpers*," Earl corrected him, absently.

Looking bored, Mike turned back to the TV, soaking in the ladies with a grin like a cat lapping up cream.

Decker wasn't letting it go. His eyebrows furrowed, and he looked at Earl with a forlorn expression. "They're people, man. It's just like Duterte killing drug addicts. It's still murder."

"What the fuck you talkin' about?" Earl said. His mask had come down, and he was visibly irritated now.

I kicked the leg of Decker's chair, trying to get him to shut up. He ignored me.

"I...um..." Decker stammered. "Duterte? The leader from the Philippines? Crazy motherfucker who's like the Filipino Hitler? Dude. Really?"

Earl shook his head, not sure what to do with the facts spilling out of Decker's piehole.

"He was connected to the Davao Death Squad; they killed kids and shit," Decker continued. "Then, when he was president, he ran this anti-drug campaign where it was legal to kill junkies. *Legal*, bro. He killed something like seven thousand drug addicts. Seven thousand *people*. It was genocide, bro."

Earl's eyebrows popped up.

I also felt a bit knocked off my rocker. I didn't know who the hell this Duterte guy was, and honestly, I didn't give two fucks. What startled me was that, for the briefest of moments, there was a flicker of intelligence behind Decker's eyes. It was like when he said that shit about pikes versus spears or when he was talking about cancer in dogs; that was some "um-actually" shit if I'd ever heard it. I wondered what he could've done with his life if the drugs hadn't swallowed him up.

Earl turned away without a reply.

I couldn't imagine what it must be like for Earl, knowing he'd be spending the rest of his life piking lumpers. How did a guy even begin to unpack something like that? I figured he probably didn't. He probably stuffed it all away. That would explain the scary, faraway look he'd had after popping the grandma. It explained those moments of joy he eked out when he was behind the wheel or eating bacon; sometimes the small stuff was all that got us by.

I was sure Decker going on and on about lumpers being people only made shit worse for Earl. I didn't understand why Earl put up with it.

A loud whistle jerked me out of my thoughts.

Things were getting heated on-screen, and Mike was grabbing his junk again.

Decker scowled at him and shook his head.

I watched Earl from the corner of my eye. He crossed his arms and stared down at the ground, muscle still bouncing in his cheek as he clenched his jaw. I wasn't sure if that conversation had erased Decker's earlier apology or if Earl would simply brush it off.

Regardless of how things landed in Earl's head, the conversation ended, and there was no more talk of Duterte. From there, the day seeped by like spilled cherry Kool-Aid on concrete. We watched TV, played cards, and showed up at the chow hall at the right times.

Dinner was some kind of hash, a stale roll, canned green beans with the texture of mush, and a final splat of something white and soft. A tentative jab with the spoon had me guessing it was pudding, but I wasn't entirely sure.

We ate because we were hungry, and there weren't a lot of other options. We couldn't exactly hit a food truck when we were out on a run. We had to eat the slop they gave us or not eat at all.

The only other option—and I use the word "option" in the loosest sense of the term—was commissary. But the junk food gracing those shelves was never really a possibility for most of us. Unless we knew a rich person who felt sorry enough to drop some money in our commissary account, we were out of luck. Most of us in the Home didn't know anybody with real money; that's half the reason we were in here in the first place. For the rare few who come from money, their families were often too ashamed to even acknowledge they knew someone in here, even if it was something as simple as dropping cash for commissary.

I spooned a bite of green beans in my mouth, mashing them against the roof of my mouth and swallowing without chewing. They were flavorless, and the texture was weird enough that I just wanted to get it over with.

Decker gestured to the stale roll perched on the edge of my tray. "You gonna eat that?"

If I'm forking these shitty green beans down, you can bet your ass I'm gonna eat it, I thought.

I locked eyes with him and nodded.

"That's cool. That's cool." He held up his free hand in surrender. "Just thinking about Cockroach. He's looking a little skinny."

"Fuck that cat," Earl barked, mouth half full. "You need the calories more than he does."

I looked at Decker sitting across from me, thin muscles stretched across bulging bones. There wasn't an ounce of fat on the guy. His thin, pasty skin looked about two shades away from healthy. Along with the damage from all the meth, I bet he had some sort of nutritional deficiency thing going on.

His eyes said he didn't need that roll. His eyes said he needed to take care of something and have something love him back more than he needed the food.

I tore my roll in half and handed it over.

Decker's eyebrows shot up. "Really, man? Thanks!"

Earl sucked his teeth and leaned back on the bench, placing a beefy palm on his thigh. He nodded his chin at Decker. "Once this scrawny piece of shit gets out, you know we'll be stuck with that damn cat."

I shrugged.

"I got sixteen more months," Decker murmured. "A lot could happen between now and then."

Earl huffed a laugh. "Yeah, like you knifing a guy in the yard and getting extra time," he said sarcastically.

Decker's eyes went wide. Then, he realized Earl was messing with him, and he said, "Fuck you, man."

I wondered who'd replace Decker when he finally got out. He was a tweaker, but he was *our* tweaker. I didn't have to worry about him jumping me in my cot or stealing my shit. And even though he'd pussed out yesterday, he usually pulled his weight when doing chores around the Home.

I hoped we didn't get some asshole like Mike.

We slurped down the rest of our meals and headed back to our room. Cockroach was waiting for us, sitting on the windowsill, tail swishing.

"Hey, Cockroach," Decker cooed. His face was soft, and the worry lines had relaxed.

Decker pulled a roll and a half out of his pocket, crumbs dusting out on the floor. He flopped on the cot and patted the blanket next to his thigh.

With a soft *meow*, Cockroach dropped to the ground and sashayed over to Decker. He brushed against Decker's leg and then hopped up next to him. He crouched at his side, taking each piece of bread Decker tore off for him.

I leaned back on my cot and pulled out my sketchbook. The pencil scratched across the paper as I drew the outline of Decker's profile, using the side of my pencil to shade the hollows in his cheeks.

"You treat that cat better than some mommas treat their babies," Earl snorted.

Decker ignored him. Cockroach was his entire world right now, and the rest of us could just fuck right off.

Earl smirked. He fished around under his bed and pulled out his stash to roll his evening stick. I didn't know where he got his seemingly endless supply of tobacco and rolling paper. He'd been in here so long, I figured he had his ways.

Cockroach made quick work of the bread. When he finished, Decker brushed the crumbs off his bed and sat on his cot, legs crossed in an easy seat. Cockroach curled up in the center, purring so loud it rumbled across the room.

I felt a sliver of jealousy. I wasn't sure if it was because the cat had eaten the food I would've been more than happy to eat myself, or if it was because Decker had something cuddling him. The jealousy turned to anger, and I felt the low burn of rage that had always gotten me into so much trouble. I flicked my eyes to the ceiling, staring at the stains. I let my mind drift, taking deep breaths.

"I used to have a dog," Earl said in a surprisingly contemplative voice.

My head jerked toward him.

People didn't talk much about their lives before incarceration. Other than bragging about the pussy waiting for them, they didn't say shit. It was as taboo as talking about why we were all here in the first place.

Earl took a drag and blew it out. "Brindle pit bull. Big, blocky head. He looked like a badass, but he was a softie."

"What was his name?" Decker asked.

Earl gazed out into the room, draping his wrists on his thighs, lit cigarette dangling between his knees. "Sausage."

Decker burst out laughing.

Earl tensed, eyes locking on him.

"Sausage?" Decker asked, slightly incredulous.

"Yeah, Sausage," Earl said, voice cool.

The muscles in my back tensed.

"Got a problem with that?" Earl barked, shooting eye-daggers at Decker.

Decker's belly bucked with barely controlled laughter. He shook his head, a shit-eating grin spread across his face. "And you give me shit about calling him Cockroach."

Earl's lips pressed into a thin white line. His free hand clenched. "Naming a dog Sausage ain't nothing compared to calling a cat Cockroach. Cockroaches are fucking nasty, man. Sausages are tasty. Everybody eats sausage."

That got Decker laughing even harder. "Everybody...eats...sausage," he repeated back around guffaws.

I wasn't sure what nerve Decker had unintentionally plucked, but I could tell Earl was about to blow. Decker was oblivious to the impending whoop-ass.

"I had a dog named Patricia," I chimed in.

Both of them turned to me, slightly shocked.

"Called her Patty."

Like Pattycake, I added in my head, shifting my eyes back to the ceiling.

Now, both of them were roaring with laughter, the sounds echoing out of the room and into the yard.

Once Earl finally caught his breath again, he asked through gasps, "What kinda dog was *Patricia*?"

I shrugged, lowering my eyes locked on my sketch book. "Some kinda mutt."

My hand continued sketching as I watched Earl from the corner of my eye.

Memories clicked through my mind like shorts. Throwing the ball for her out in the field, and her bringing it back, dropping it at my feet, covered in slobber. Her tongue hanging out of her goofy dog grin, chest heaving from the run. Her putting her paw in my hand when I'd say, "Cake." Her sleeping by my bed, and me hanging my arm over the edge to run my fingers through her thick coat. Her licking the tears from my face when things got really bad.

Another loud bark of laughter brought me back into the room.

"Bro. Your momma named you Bear, and you named your dog Patricia," Earl teased, grinning ear-to-ear.

"I didn't name her," I lied.

I let their laughter roll right over me. I was glad Earl was getting that pent-up energy out by laughing rather than laying a beat down on Decker.

"No more giving me shit over naming him Cockroach, you motherfuckers," Decker said, pointing between us through the last bit of a snicker.

Earl sucked his teeth, but a slight smile still tipped the right side of his lips.

"I wonder if I can take him with me when I get out," Decker said, his voice turning serious.

My eyes bounced over to Decker. Cockroach had ridden out the heavy laughter on Decker's lap, and Decker stroked his hair. When Decker sat like that, petting his cat, it was the only time he wasn't twitching like a rat on a live wire.

Earl took a drag of his stick and tilted his head back against the wall. He blew the smoke out in a long *whoosh*, a heavy sigh pushed behind it. "Where you going when you get out?"

Earl was treading into no-man's land, and I shifted uncomfortably.

"I...I'm not sure," Decker answered, eyebrows scrunched together.

Earl's eyes shifted to Decker. "Ain't no halfway house gonna let you bring a cat. Plus, you can't keep him locked up. He needs to roam."

"I can't leave him here. No one will take care of him." Decker looked down at Cockroach sadly.

Earl flicked his cigarette. "There's plenty of rats running around. He'll be fine."

Decker pressed his lips together. "Maybe my mom will let me come back for a little while...." His voice trailed off, and he flinched slightly, like he hadn't meant to say the private thought out loud.

Earl studied him and gave his cigarette another thoughtful flick.

A family might let a felon back in, but a druggie was different. Most people wanted to pretend like the junkie in their family never existed. I didn't know what Decker's life was like before getting locked up, but I'd bet money his mom wasn't going to let him anywhere near her home. He'd chosen meth, and that had closed off all of the doors back home. Forever.

I wondered what was worse: being stuck in here for life like Earl or being pushed back out into the world with nowhere to go like Decker. It seemed like both of them were fucked.

CHAPTER
TWELVE

There wasn't a day of rest in the Home. If a lumper was confirmed, a crew went out to pop them, no matter what day of the week it was.

But if a resident was lucky enough to have someone who wanted to see their ass, visitors came on Sunday. Anyone who wasn't out popping lumpers would get a chance to kiss ole moms on the cheek. Maybe even get a snack or a soda from the machine.

Visiting days could make a man feel like a person again. Even something as simple as a brief hug was enough to give a man a bit of hope. Make him feel seen. Make him feel loved.

It was easy enough to set a visitor up: just a quick form giving someone permission to drop by. Of all the things to give residents control over, that one always felt a little weird to me. We were forced to be around dudes who might beat our ass or rape us, and yet we were allowed to refuse a visit from family. I guess some family members were as abusive as the assholes in prison; whether it was a mind fuck or a real fuck, family had a way of getting us where it hurt most.

We all had our dark days, and some guys didn't always feel like chatting it up with someone out in the world. After killing lumpers, I'd have a hard time looking my mom in the eye. I'd be too afraid she'd see those scars inside me. See the people I'd killed. Sometimes I was grateful my mom was long dead; that way, she never had to see who I was in this place. I didn't expect anyone to visit me in the Home, and no one did. So, all that thinking and worrying was for nothing anyway.

I hadn't been at the Home for very long, so I didn't know what the situation was like for Earl and Decker. When we woke up Sunday morning and went about our business as usual, I assumed they weren't expecting anyone to visit either.

We ate a boring breakfast, played cards in the courtyard, and tried to ignore another crew getting called out.

Around mid-morning, the visitors arrived. At the Home, we didn't have thick plastic windows separating us from them. We didn't have to hear their voices through greasy, crackly phones. We got to sit at actual tables in the library and hold their hands. I wondered if any of the guys could ignore the ID cards dangling from their chest pockets long enough to feel normal with their families, even for a second.

Earl, Decker, and I sat at one of the tables toward the rear of the yard. My back was to the front entrance, but when I heard people talking, I snuck a quick peek over my shoulder. One of the guards led a handful of people—maybe five or six of them, including a kid—to the library. They'd already signed in and passed through the metal detectors. Now, they'd find their assigned table and wait until the residents were called up.

I turned away quickly. I didn't want to be an eye-hustler and gawk at the normies as they filed in. If I were honest with myself, I also didn't want to see what I was never gonna have.

About a minute or so later, the school intercom clicked on. "The following inmates are to report to Room Ten for visitation: Jerome Jackson, Tony Lee, and Decker Andrews."

When they said Decker's name, he froze. His eyebrows furrowed, and his eyes went wide like saucers.

Earl patted him on the back playfully. "Looks like you won the lotto, my friend!"

Decker didn't look like he held a winning ticket. In fact, he looked like he was going to toss his cookies all over the table.

Earl grinned and gave his chair a light kick. "Go on now."

Decker hunched over like a turtle. He laid his hand on the table and slowly slid his chair back. "Um...I guess...um," he stammered. He hesitated, eyes darting between the entrance to the library in the far corner and our table.

"Andrews!" Garcia called out across the yard. "Visitor!"

"Be right back," Decker murmured and then shuffled to the library.

I tossed Earl a questioning look.

Earl shrugged. "No clue, bro," he answered. "He ain't had a visitor since he arrived."

Earl swept up our cards and shuffled. The cards thrummed as they slapped down, first with a pile shuffle and then back to a neat square with a rainbow. He dealt us both a fresh hand, cards sliding across the table to me as he counted them out.

I took stock of the courtyard.

Visiting day hadn't pulled nearly anyone away. Of the twenty-four residents in the Home, only three had been called up for visitation, and one team was out on thumper duty. The place still felt busy.

There was the low murmur of a few guys shooting the shit in lawn chairs on the other side of the yard. In the gym, several guys worked out, the low music interrupted by the *clank* of the metal weights. From where we sat, the rec room was pretty busy, too. We were just passing the time. None of us had anyone willing to make the trip out to see us.

Most of these guys had to have people out in the world. But between the low visitation rates and the measly stack of letters at mail call, I wasn't sure those people wanted to hear from the guys inside. Were their families too busy? Or was it too hard to see these guys locked up? Did people stop loving these guys when they went in? It was like the people they knew from before just wanted to block this part out, wait to see them on the other side, and pretend this never happened. I didn't have any family left to know what it felt like.

I figured the fact that we killed lumpers didn't help matters. There was something about being a thumper that made people's eyes slide right over us. I wondered why we got put in a separate box from cops and soldiers. They killed people, too; it was just part of the job. Maybe it was because we killed grandmas and women with pink toenails instead of an "enemy."

I swiped my hand across my face, trying to press the thoughts away.

Earl grinned. "Got a shit hand, eh?"

He'd totally misread me, but I wasn't gonna correct him, so I nodded and smirked dramatically at my cards.

Actually, I had a pretty good starting hand for Gin. I only needed two more cards, and I'd left my options open. We sped through the deck, slapping our discards down into a pile. Earl rambled about dumb shit, like the merits of Cholula over Tapatio or how the deodorant sold in the commissary didn't do fuck-all to keep the stank away.

He avoided talking about the visitors, and I appreciated him for it.

The time bled by, and we'd played several hands before visitation time was up. I'd have liked to say it mattered who won, but it didn't. Nobody won in this fucking place.

"Decker is on his way back," Earl said casually, looking down at his cards.

Unable to help myself, I glanced over my shoulder. The residents had filtered out first, just the three guys trailing out of the library. Two of them were smiling, throwing their chests back with pride. Not Decker.

Don't get me wrong, Decker was a tweaker, and looking like a bag of ass was normal for him. But when he walked out of the library, he looked like a pile of shit that had been run over by a truck. His hands were stuffed in his pockets, and he was folded into himself. His normally bouncy, jittery steps were sluggish. There was a dead look to his eyes. It was the look of a man who was about ready to jump in front of a bus, and part of me worried about him having access to the safety razors.

Earl picked up on it, too. "Fuck," he murmured under his breath. He laid his cards down and leaned back in his chair, elbow cocked back with his right hand on his upper thigh. His eyes tracked Decker across the yard.

Decker slid into the empty chair at the table, head cast down, and wild hair covering his expression.

"You alright, bro?" Earl asked. His tone was neutral, but worry was etched in every wrinkle around his eyes and in his frown.

Decker nodded, still not looking up.

Earl swept the cards into a pile and put them back in the box. He slid his chair back and stood. Waving to the chow hall, he said, "Come on. Let's get something to eat. The lunch bell is gonna go off any minute."

Decker followed him silently, with me taking up the rear. My eyes bounced from Earl's straight, muscled back to Decker's hunched shoulders. I wondered how two guys with completely different lives ended up here, each with their own set of baggage and both handling it their own way. Two guys just trying to get by. Not really living—just existing. Like all of us were. What other choice was there?

Earl's body clock was on the fucking nose. As soon as we crossed into the chow hall, the lunch bell rang. We were the first in line and had our trays within a minute or two.

We sat in silence at our usual table, eating the bland food and getting calories without a whiff of enjoyment.

The chow hall soon echoed with chatter as more dudes drifted in, and the silence between the three of us started to get uncomfortable. I kept my eyes on my tray, not wanting to set anything off with a look.

After spooning my way through the food, I came up for air and saw that Earl had kept pace. Decker still picked at his lunch, bouncing his spoon over the canned corn. He might've eaten a soggy tater tot or two, but all of his chicken nuggets still sat in a sad little pile.

In an uncharacteristic show of consideration for the cat, Earl suggested, "Wanna save those nuggets for Cockroach?"

Decker looked up at him, surprised.

I did my best to keep my face neutral, watching them.

"Come on," Earl nudged. He reached over, palming four of them.

Decker turned his head down and palmed the rest.

We rose together and bussed our trays.

Back in our room, Decker pulled a washed Jello cup out from his pile and dropped the nuggets in. Earl added his and then brushed his hands on his sweats.

Earl flopped on his cot, leaning against the wall and watching Decker.

I kicked my slips off and followed suit, sitting on my cot with my back to the wall, legs stretched out and crossed in front of me. I leaned over the edge of the cot to pull my sketchbook out and started doodling.

With Cockroach MIA, Decker slipped the cup of cold nuggets under his bed and swiped his hand across his face. I knew he needed to talk and that he was almost there. We just had to give him a few more minutes of space to get his misfiring thoughts in order.

Earl pulled out the deck of cards. He shuffled the deck on his lap a couple times, the sputter of the cards filling the empty space. Palming the deck, he flipped three cards over and started a game of one-handed solitaire.

Keeping his eyes cast down and voice neutral, Earl asked, "Who came today?"

There was a long stretch of silence, and I could barely breathe.

"Psht," Decker finally replied and rubbed his palm across his forehead again. "My mom and my nephew."

"Hm," Earl said in a tone that was impossible to read. The cards slid through Earl's hands as he sped through the game.

According to Earl, it was the first time anyone had come to see Decker at the Home. I couldn't help but think about Decker's life before coming here. Had his mom always held him at an arm's distance? Or did she push him away after he started doing drugs? Maybe it didn't happen until after his conviction? I wondered why she'd come to see him today.

Decker started biting at the nubs of his nails, gnawing on each tip.

"Was your mom that posh lady with the kid?" Earl asked, his tone was nonchalant. His eyes flicked up to pierce Decker before jumping back to his cards.

Posh lady?

Now, I wished I'd watched the visitors closely. A part of me wanted to see what Decker's mom looked like. A part of me wanted to see how she looked at him.

I'd never really thought about Earl and Decker beyond the two guys sitting in front of me. It was weird filling out the life around them. The life they had before this mess. The life they might be lucky enough to step back into when they got out. Well, for Decker to step back into—that wasn't an option for Earl.

"Noah ain't a kid. He's fifteen." Decker's reply came out slightly defensive.

Earl sucked his teeth. "He's a fucking kid."

It was easy for Earl to call the dude a kid; he was in his fifties, and everyone looked like a kid to him. Hell, I was in my twenties, and if it weren't for my size, he'd probably be calling me a kid, too.

I pictured Earl sitting on a porch with a forty in his hand, shouting at kids to get off his lawn. They'd probably all whisper to each other about how mean he was. They might even tell stories about how he used to kill people to scare each other. Of course, even if a scene like that had played out in the past, it sure as hell wasn't going to happen in the future. Not with a life sentence.

"How you have a fifteen-year-old nephew?" Earl said to Decker, pulling me out of my thoughts. "Ain't you like thirty or some shit?"

Decker looked annoyed. "I'm thirty-three. My brother is six years older than me."

Unable to help myself, I did the mental math, and everything checked out.

"Hm," Earl replied, lips pressed together.

Decker ran his hands through his hair and paused, cradling the back of his head.

"Why did your nephew come to see you?" Earl asked, pulling cards out of his hand as he played the game.

Decker didn't respond and kept his eyes cast down.

"Did he come to show off an award? Make the varsity team? Win a robotics competition? Some fancy la-dee-dah shit like that?" Earl asked.

It was a mean thing to say, given Decker's current mental state. My eyes jumped to Earl, trying to pick out what bug had crawled up his ass. He wore an unreadable expression.

My gaze flicked over to Decker, and I noticed a real, hot anger twisting his features. I slowly placed my sketchbook to the side, unsure of what was going to happen next and wanting to be ready for anything.

Decker's lips folded in. His face fell, and his hands wrapped around his arms. He started slowly rocking back and forth.

"Mom wanted to make an example of me," Decker mumbled.

Earl stopped playing his game and his head shot up. "Huh?"

I was just as surprised as he was.

"Garrett got caught sneaking some of my brother's Scotch."

Earl barked a laugh. "Sheee-it," he interrupted, drawing the word out. "Fifteen ain't nothing for a first sip of booze."

"He's on track to go to Stanford. Pre-med," Decker offered as a way of explanation.

Earl sucked his lips. "I thought rich people had no problem with a splash of alcohol or a line of coke. What's got your mom's panties all in a bunch?"

Earl was back to flipping his cards, cool as a cucumber. He didn't catch Decker stiffening or the swirl of emotions that danced across his face.

When Decker didn't reply, Earl looked up, and the movement of cards paused. He rested his hands on his lap and studied him.

Decker shook his head slowly. He reached with both hands to scratch through his hair and then slowly ran them down the front of his face. The tips of his fingers caught his lower lip before they dropped down to his lap.

"She doesn't want him to turn out like me." Decker's words came out in low agony.

The statement sat in the room like a stinky fart, and all of us held our breath. I wondered how many families felt that way about the residents in the Home.

Earl broke the stretch of silence, a thread of anger lacing his voice. "You telling me your mom came here just to point at you and scare this guy clean? First time she's come to visit your ass, and she does it to use you like a public service announcement?"

Decker nodded slowly. "Yep," he said sadly. He clenched his hands. Then, in a mocking, shrill voice, he said, "Look at Uncle Deck. Do you want to be like him? He can't keep an ounce of weight on, he picked his beautiful skin to pieces, and he's missing *teeth*."

Earl froze, as surprised at Decker's performance as I was.

Decker continued in that horrible voice, "He had a spot at UC Berkeley to study business, and he blew it all away." He brushed his spindly fingers back and forth through the air. "Now, he's in here with *criminals* and has to kill the *infected*."

He said the last word like it was too dirty to even speak, and I was certain that was exactly how his mom had said it.

Decker took a deep breath and shook his head. "It's like I wasn't even there," he murmured, voice back to his normal tone.

"Fuck, man," Earl replied, still frozen.

"Yeah, fuck is right," Decker said sadly. He rolled over onto his side in a fetal position, with his back facing us.

Earl turned to me, lips pursed and eyebrows raised.

Not knowing what to say or do, I shrugged.

Earl folded his lips in and frowned. After a beat, he lifted the hand holding his cards and went back to playing his game, the frown never leaving his expression.

Everything Decker had said bounced around in my head, and I felt an itch to move—to leave this room and escape these thoughts. Without a word, I rose from my bed and headed to the yard.

Hands stuffed in my pockets, I walked the square of the breezeway, doing laps and trying to clear my head. On my fifth lap, Earl appeared at the doorway to Room Four and leaned against the doorjamb.

"Wanna go lift some weights?" he asked.

I nodded once and continued down the breezeway, following the clanking of metal. We both needed to get some of the anger out and work through our shit. At the Home—in this cage—lifting was the only way we had to do it.

CHAPTER
THIRTEEN

The next day started like the others. A school bell woke us up. We stood outside our room for the morning count. We ate a bland breakfast. We hung out. We were just three guys going through the motions, not seeing what waited for us around the corner. Not wanting to even *look* around the corner.

It was raining, and everyone had been pushed inside. The raindrops pattered on the ground in the courtyard, turning it into a muddy slush. There was that sharp, fresh smell in the air that always hits right after a new rain. That smell had a name, but I couldn't remember the word for it. I bet Decker knew it with all of his fancy schooling—or, at least, he knew it before the meth had fried the wires in his brain.

Most of the guys were either in their rooms or lifting weights. The four walls of our room felt cagier than usual, and none of us felt like fighting over a bench at the gym. That left us with the rec room and the library, and Earl wasn't much into printed books. As the leader of our team, Earl made the decision and led us to the rec room to play cards.

When we arrived, the only other guy in the room was Al, sitting in his usual spot and holding the remote in his limp hand. The fake cheers from *The Price Is Right* blurted from the TV.

"Yo. What's up, Al?" Earl called out and picked a table near the door.

Al stared blankly at the screen and didn't respond.

I took the seat facing out the door, watching the rain drip from the edges of the breezeway cover.

When I was a kid, I used to like watching the rain. I always felt like it washed everything clean. But seeing the water drip down into brown, smelly puddles in the courtyard felt like the rain just made everything dirtier.

Mateo walked in a few minutes after us, scanning the room for a spot. He looked to be fresh out of high school. His skin was dark brown, and his head was shaved with a tidy fade. He held himself like he knew how to fight, but his eyes were soft. I wondered if he'd been put on a team with the OGs so they could look out for him, and then I immediately brushed the stupid thought away. BCB didn't care enough to put any thought into team composition. Residents were just slotted into open spots when one appeared.

Earl glanced up at Mateo. "Want me to deal you in?"

"What you playing?" Mateo asked.

"Well, with four, it'll be Spades," he answered.

"Sure," Mateo said, grabbing a seat. "I can play until my crew comes in. Watchu got to lay out?"

The question didn't surprise me. When just the three of us played cards, we never gambled. But most of the guys in the Home did. I wasn't sure why. Maybe it was the hope that luck would give them something better. Or maybe it added a bit of excitement to the life-sucking routine.

"I got sticks," Earl answered. "I'll cover these two with the same," he added, pointing to Decker and me.

Now, that last bit did surprise me. It was pretty damn nice of Earl to spot us. If I won, I'd definitely share back, and I figured he knew that. He had a knack for sussing out the odds.

"How 'bout you?" Earl asked, studying Mateo.

"I got a Cup-o-Noodles and a couple of hot sauce packets," he replied. "All in for five sticks?"

"You're on," Earl said.

The cards sped across the table as Earl dealt them out. We all swept our hands up and studied them.

"What's the deal with Al?" Mateo asked in a half-whisper, nodding his chin toward him. "Elijah and Jorge won't tell me."

Earl shrugged, keeping his eyes on his cards. "Bro took a bullet, man. Give him a break."

I watched Mateo out of the corner of my eye. He kept darting glances at Al, and I couldn't tell if those looks were driven by fear or curiosity.

"Did he get shot on a run?" Mateo asked.

"Fuck, no," Earl said, shifting a few cards around in his hand before passing one down. "We felons, man. You think they let us get near guns?"

The guy looked a bit chagrined. "I meant...like...did a lumper shoot him?" he stammered.

Earl rested his hands on the table, eyes finally lifting from his cards, and gave the guy an incredulous look. "You fucking serious?"

This was met with silence. Mateo shifted in his seat, unable to meet Earl's laser death gaze.

Decker's eyes bounced between them, and he picked at his cheek. His back hunched as he folded into himself. He looked like he was expecting a fight and was rolling in a fetal position to protect his gut.

I watched the others over my cards, pretending to consider the one Earl had passed me. I selected one and passed it to Mateo.

"I just want to know if I'm gonna get shot on a run and turn into something like meatloaf over there." Mateo swept the hand with his cards toward Al.

Earl pressed his lips together. His nostrils flared as if he were trying to keep his shit together. Finally, he said, "Lumpers are dumb as rocks. They can't hold a gun, much less shoot one."

"Was it a guard?"

Earl's eyebrows shot up. "If Al had done something bad enough to get shot by a guard, he'd be on burner duty, not in here with the thumpers." He looked down at his cards and added, "Shit happened a long time ago. Before he came to the Home."

Mateo worried at his lower lip. He studied his cards, then passed one to Decker. Then, his eyes bounced back to Al. He leaned forward and asked quietly, "Is he actually able to pop any lumpers with...you know...?" He tapped the base of his skull with his free hand.

Every muscle in Earl's body tensed, and he looked ready to snap. "Yeah," he replied, coolly. "He pulls his weight just fine. How 'bout you, motherfucker?"

Earl looked like he was going to beat the guy to a pulp. With more than fifty pounds and several inches on Mateo, I was pretty sure he could do just that. Since Earl was a lifer, there wasn't much keeping him in line either.

Trying not to draw any attention, I pushed myself back from the table a bit and planted my feet, getting ready to step in between them if it came to that. The whole situation teetered on the edge of getting really ugly.

Earl kept his ass in the seat, staring hard at the dude. Part of what kept Earl from flying out of his chair and painting Mateo's ass was the small privileges, like being able to smoke and getting bacon once in a blue moon. That and staying off burner duty.

Mateo leaned back in his chair and held his free hand up in surrender. "Hey, bro. I'm not judging."

"Leave Al the fuck alone," Earl growled, eyes dancing in anger.

Decker passed a card to Earl and put the rest of his cards face-down on the table.

Mateo laughed nervously. "Sure, bro. Whatever."

Earl was as rigid as a cat ready to pounce. A silent tension started to build as he ignored the card Decker had passed him and kept his eyes locked on the guy.

"Team Four. You're up. Let's go," a voice barked from the door.

Decker flinched, and his head shot up.

I jumped, too. I'd been so focused on what was happening between Earl and Mateo that I'd totally missed Jackson coming in.

Earl didn't move a muscle. He still had his eyes locked on Mateo across the table, and no one dared make a move.

"Team Four!" Jackson repeated.

Earl stood up so fast his chair wobbled, almost tipping over. "Yeah, we're coming," he said. He leaned over, swept the cards up, and turned to leave without giving Mateo so much as a "fuck you very much."

I was so relieved to have avoided a fight that it wasn't until the rain started soaking through my socks from the puddles in the breezeway that the reality of the situation started to sink in.

We were going back out.

Jackson followed us down the breezeway to our room so we could get changed. "Hurry up, boys," Jackson snapped. "Lumper ain't gonna wait all day."

He turned his back to us and waited at the door as we slipped into our gear.

"Thanks for sticking up for Al," Decker said quietly to Earl as he pulled on his coveralls.

"Fuck Mateo. He don't know shit," Earl grumbled. "Al's popped more lumpers than us combined. And what's going on up there"—he tapped his temple—"is more than being shot fifteen fucking years ago."

Earl zipped his coveralls dramatically, like he was drawing a line at the end of the conversation.

Decker cast his eyes down and let it go.

"You boys getting your hair done in there or what?" Jackson snarked. "Let's go already."

We filed up at the door, and Jackson escorted us down the breezeway to the cop shop. Every so often, there'd be a brush of wind, and the rain would mist in. The thin fabric of my coveralls already felt damp around the legs. I hunkered in my sweatshirt, trying not to shiver.

Jackson buzzed us into the office. He held the door for us and announced, "Team Four."

Jones was behind the counter again. She waved us over, scanned our ID cards, and passed Earl the information packet.

"District 3," she said matter-of-factly. She clicked the computer mouse a couple of times, looking at the screen. "I don't have an exact address for you. The location is on Broadway between Franklin and Alhambra under the highway."

Earl's head jerked up from the paperwork. "Huh?"

Jones smiled apologetically. "It's a homeless camp."

"Fuck me," Earl muttered under his breath, flipping through the paperwork. After a beat, he asked, "All we got is a tent color?"

She passed him the truck keys and then rested her forearms on the counter. "Sorry," she said, and I got the impression that she really meant it.

Earl let out a noise that was half sigh, half grumble, and swept up the keys.

"Come on," he said to us.

We trudged after him, the rain pattering against our heads. We climbed into the truck and waited for Earl to debrief us. The rain made tinkling sounds on the metal of the roof and streamed down the windows.

He stuck the keys in the ignition and read from the paperwork. "The lumper is an adult male. No name or race given. Reported by someone else in the camp. Verification mark is a lump on the back of his hand."

Earl flipped through the measly packet and then dropped it to his lap with an exacerbated sigh. "And no fucking picture. Great." He looked out the window, taking a few deep breaths.

Decker picked at his face. "How are we going to know who he is? What if we whack the wrong dude?"

Earl pressed his eyes shut and clenched his jaw. Another deep breath later, and he looked back down at the paperwork. "All we got is that he's in a brown tent in a camp and that he's got a lump on his hand. We're just gonna have to go and see how things play out."

"A homeless camp? Like with a bunch of other people? How are they locked down? What if he's wandering around?" Decker rattled the questions off in a nervous flurry. The scab he'd been picking at finally came off, and there was a small streak of red on his cheek.

Earl's eyebrows furrowed in anger, and he turned on Decker. "I don't know, man," he barked. "This is all I got." He slapped the papers against his leg. "We just gotta go down there and see."

Earl tossed the papers to Decker, who fumbled to catch them. He twisted the key in the ignition, and the truck rumbled awake. He angrily shifted the truck in gear and backed out, grumbling under his breath.

A tense silence fell over the truck as we weaved through the streets. The windshield wipers streaked across the glass.

The rushing sound of the defrost filled the spaces between the squeak of the wipers. The windows slowly fogged up anyway. I found myself wishing that Earl would put on some music; any kind would do.

We stopped at the District 3 checkpoint on Broadway and 19th. The guard huddled in the post, shying away from the rain.

Earl passed him our ID cards. "Team Four from BCB."

The guard scanned them and asked, "Know where you're going?"

"Kinda," Earl said. "Underpass between Franklin and Alhambra."

"Yup," the guard said with a nod, passing the ID cards back.

"Is it just the one tent or a camp?" Earl asked.

"It's a camp," the guard said, frowning. "The Response Team tried to clear them out a couple times. The homeless shitbags keep swarming back in like cockroaches." He shook his head in dismay. "Smells like ass over there. Watch out. They leave turds on the sidewalk. And needles, too."

I was getting a real bad feeling about this. I didn't like going into this without more details, and I knew Earl was right there with me.

"How many people would you guess are there now?" Earl asked.

The guard pursed his lips and looked up, considering. "Maybe five? Ten? They're squatting on both sides of the street. Three or four tents plus people just sleeping on the sidewalk. It's hard to tell with all the trash piled up everywhere."

Earl looked over his shoulder at me. This was going to be a shitshow, and he knew it. I could see him building a battle plan in his head, trying to figure out how to pop the guy and get him in the truck without stepping on a needle, slipping in shit, or getting swarmed. All while trying to make sure we popped the right guy in all that mess.

He turned back to the guard. "Alright then, we best get to it."

The guard nodded and pressed the button to open the gate. With a grim face, Earl rolled his window up and drove through.

I turned my head to look through the back window, watching the gate rattle closed behind us and feeling a tight ball forming in my gut.

CHAPTER FOURTEEN

The traffic lights blinked green, yellow, and red on their timers, oblivious to the fact that Broadway was empty past the checkpoint. Earl rolled right through the reds at a smooth thirty miles an hour, not bothering to stop. The district was on lockdown, and nobody was supposed to be out driving.

Broadway was a wide, four-lane street with a large turn lane squatting in the center. Bright green bike lanes crouched on the edges. The road widened and slunk back down as bus stops and parking lanes popped in and out on the edges.

I was used to lockdowns; we all were. But it was weird driving through such a busy part of the city when it was shuttered up like a ghost town.

Six lanes of freeway loomed ahead, rising over Broadway like a cross mark on a "t." About a block down, that sweep of asphalt would intersect with two other major highways, connecting the south side of the city to midtown and the north. It was also one of the few ways to get over the river. That section of the overpass was a major thoroughfare and was always packed with traffic.

Today, not a single car passed overhead. Normally, the freeways coursing through a district would stay open during a lockdown, and the empty section bugged me. Was it the fact that the camp perched at the bottom between the freeway ramps? Was it because the lumper was homeless and could be shuffling around anywhere?

But a lumper wandering onto the freeway wouldn't be much different than a large deer. They couldn't exactly yank open a car door, and they wouldn't try to bite someone like a zombie. Maybe it had more to do with the possibility of a lumper getting hit. A lumper could be easily avoided in the usual stop-and-go traffic that crept across that stretch. But running over a lumper at sixty or seventy miles an hour would trash the car, and infected blood would be splattered everywhere.

I thought about the city posting lumper crossing signs, and a bitter part of me laughed. I tried to blink away the images.

Just past Franklin Blvd., the road narrowed as it passed under the freeway. Earl pulled over to the side of the street in front of a U-Haul store about thirty feet away from the overpass. He shifted the truck into park, ignoring the bright red signs telling him it wasn't allowed, and killed the ignition.

"What a shithole," Earl grumbled.

I leaned forward and peered through the streaks of rain on the windshield, taking in the camp. It was dark and gloomy beneath the overpass. Clusters of tents hunkered on the sidewalks, and mounds of trash spilled into the street.

"Aren't you gonna pull forward a bit?" Decker asked nervously.

After Decker mentioned it, I also started to wonder why Earl had decided to park so far away. We usually liked to get as close as we could to pop someone. Carrying a corpse to the back of the truck was hard work. The shorter the distance, the happier our backs would be.

Earl flicked a hand toward the camp. "You wanna park the truck next to that animal den? Who knows what those crazy motherfuckers might steal from the truck while we have our backs turned, dealing with this shit."

"Dude. They're just as scared as we are. If they're even in those tents, they ain't coming out." There was a pleading edge to Decker's voice that I didn't quite understand. "Just pull up a bit. They won't hurt us."

Earl turned to Decker and narrowed his eyes. "I ain't scared of no loser bum."

"That's not what I meant," Decker said, looking down at his lap.

Earl scowled at him. "Quit being a pussy and get your ass out of the truck." He kicked open the door and climbed out. The door slammed behind him, making Decker jump.

I couldn't blame Earl for being a bit prickly. I'd faced down all kinds of dudes and could hold my own in most situations. Bums were a different story. Most of them had nothing to lose, and half of them were fucking crazy; I never knew what they were going to do. The unpredictability of the situation put me on edge.

Earl pounded the side of the truck with the bottom of his fist. "Let's go!" he shouted, his voice muffled through the glass.

Decker and I did as we were ordered and slipped out into the rain.

Earl pulled the walkie from his belt. "Team Four reporting. Arrived at District 3."

There was a crackling sound and then a responding, "Roger that."

It was just drizzling now, but it was enough to be uncomfortable as we pulled our Tyvek suits on and gloved up. Within seconds of putting them on, raindrops ran down our face shields, and our shoe covers were soaked with brown water.

Earl shoved a pike into Decker's hand. "You're up today. Don't puss out."

Decker wrapped his fingers around the handle of the pike, clenching it with both hands. He hunched his shoulders. His hair was limp from the rain, and he looked up at Earl through the dripping clumps. His face was white as a ghost, and deep purple bags sagged below his eyes.

Earl turned away from him and stomped toward the overpass.

I lifted my eyebrows in question to Decker.

He responded with a weak smile. "I won't chicken out. I know it's my turn. I gotta make up for last time. I'll be fine. Promise."

I wasn't sure about everything being fine.

Turning to the camp, a thread of anxiety knotted in my chest. We were walking into a seriously messed-up situation. We didn't know what the guy looked like, where to find him, or what state he'd be in when we did locate him. We also didn't know who else was around or what they'd do when we walked in with pikes.

Plus, it was fucking raining.

I followed Decker down the sidewalk, watching his back.

"Uck. Fucking nasty." Earl grimaced and held the crook of his elbow up to his face shield as if to cover his nose.

The odor hit me a millisecond later, and my stomach turned. It was the smell of damp garbage, human shit, and burned plastic. And if that wasn't enough, there was an undertone of the dusty musk that seemed to hang around all the camps. It wasn't the tangy smell of dudes working out in a gym; that was almost too clean for this place. The smell that leached out of the heaps of trash was a different kind of body odor, like the sweat that seeped into their unwashed clothes was as unhealthy as they were.

Earl stopped just under the shelter of the freeway and dropped his arm. He turned to us, frowning. "They're all fucking brown."

"Huh?" Decker asked.

Earl gestured with his pike toward the tents. "They're all fucking brown, man."

The muscles in my back tensed as I took in the shitshow spread out before us. I imagined a guy with two teeth dangling from his mouth, raggedy clothes dripping from his skeletal body, and a top hat sitting askew on his head. "Come on down!" he'd cackle.

The three of us stood there, frozen with our pikes in our hands.

Earl pursed his lips, and his eyebrows shrouded his eyes. The muscles in his jaw bounced. After a heavy sigh, he shook his head and said, "We got to clear them all just like rooms in a house. Decker, you're on the pike. Bear, you back him up."

Adrenaline dumped into my system with the first step forward, and my heart started to race. I swiped the raindrops off my plastic face shield.

Earl approached the first tent. He tapped the butt of his pike on the fabric of the tent roof, and the whole thing shook.

"BCB! Anyone there?" he called out.

Earl took a few cautious steps back as he waited for a response.

I didn't blame him. I'd seen tweakers get triggered by the weirdest shit. Once, I saw a woman yelling at a grocery store clerk, thinking he was a doctor trying to sterilize her and saying she would send her pimp out to smoke him. Another time, I saw a crazy lady push a little Asian kid down, thinking he was her Black drug dealer. Hell, just a couple months ago, a crazy motherfucker ran after an old guy toddling along on his bike and chopped him to death with a machete. We never knew what might set them off, and it was best to move slow and quiet.

Thankfully, no one flew out of the tent in a rage after Earl had tapped it with his pike. There weren't any sounds coming from it either. Earl tipped his chin to Decker and nodded to the closed tent flap.

Decker folded his lips in and wiped his free hand on his hip. Leaning forward, he grabbed the zipper handle. He tugged it open in a single, quick jerk and jumped back. The tent shook with the motion, but all of the trash mounded inside kept it from tipping over.

Decker stumbled back, and in a shaky voice, he said, "Clear."

Earl peered in. "Disgusting."

I was just as revolted. Inside were mounds of stuff: a wadded-up blanket with suspicious stains, a pile of dirty clothes, wrappers, cans, a bike wheel, and some other random shit. The smell was a concentrated version of the stench that hung over the camp.

I fought a gag.

"Next one," Earl barked.

We stepped over piles of trash, avoiding a haystack of used needles, and positioned ourselves outside the second tent.

The next tent hung open. We swept our eyes over the garbage inside, and Decker said, "Clear."

Next to the second tent was an unsheltered mound of fabric, tarps, a milk crate filled with who knows what, a broken broom, and a pile of cardboard that was half melted by the rain. To one side, there was a person-shaped rise covered by a dirty blanket that could easily be a gorked lumper.

Decker used his pike to lift up the folds. "Clear," he said.

Earl turned his attention across the empty street. Two brown tents sat on the opposite side. There was a makeshift fire pit sitting between them. To the right, there was a pile of bike parts. To the left, a heap of broken furniture lay next to a blue tarp and a mound of trash.

We made our way across the street, shoe covers swishing across the wet asphalt. We stepped over the center divider and onto the opposite sidewalk. Our bodies formed a loose circle around the door to one of the tents.

Earl approached and pushed his pike against the fabric. "BCB. Anyone there?"

The only sound was the soft patter of rain hitting the ground on either side of the overpass. Earl sighed and stepped back so Decker could do his thing.

Decker moved forward. He clasped the zipper and swished it along the half-circle in a single, quick motion. After a quick peek in, he instantly straightened and stepped back. He looked at us, eyes wide.

"There's someone in there," he said, voice hushed but panicky. "I think he's sleeping."

"Is it him?" Earl asked, keeping his voice low.

"I don't know, man. He's covered in a blanket, holding a stuffed animal," Decker replied in a whisper. His eyes shifted back to the tent flap, and he chewed on his lower lip.

"Lemme see," Earl said.

Decker stepped back, giving us a clear view of the inside of the tent. There was definitely a person-sized lump with their legs pointed toward us. The form was almost entirely shrouded by a blanket. And sure enough, the tip of a pink plushie was visible near a mop of dark hair at the far end of the tent.

Earl stepped back and looked hard at Decker. "Take the blanket off."

"Huh?" Decker wrinkled his eyebrows.

"Take the blanket off," Earl repeated. "We need to confirm it."

"What if it's just some guy sleeping?" Decker said, agitated.

"Seriously, bro? Are you kidding me?" Earl gestured to the tent. "You think some normal dude would let us yank open his tent and talk shit right outside without rolling over or nothing? Pull your head out of your ass and get that blanket off him. Confirm it."

Decker hesitantly leaned over and grabbed the end of the blanket with his gloved hand. With a quick tug, it spooled out of the tent.

A startled "Oh, fuck!" slipped from Decker's lips. He stumbled over the edge of the curb, arms flailing, and almost landed on his ass.

My heart started thudding in my chest. I shifted my feet and repositioned my hands on the pike. Earl took a cautious step forward and bent over to peer in. The muscles in his back tensed with a flinch. I couldn't see in, but I knew something terrible waited for us in there.

Earl slowly straightened and turned to Decker with a grim face. "Confirm it." His voice was low and stern.

"Fuck, man," Decker muttered nervously and, in a slight breach of safety protocol, swiped a gloved hand through his hair. "Look at him! Fucking confirmed, alright?"

"Then, do it," Earl ordered.

The blood whooshed from Decker's face.

Earl clenched his free hand into a fist. "Don't be a fucking pussy, man. Do it!"

Decker started panting, and his eyes darted between Earl and the tent.

"Decker," Earl growled.

I didn't like piking lumpers, but the tension crackled under that damp, smelly underpass, and I was just about ready to step forward to put the dude down myself. It was Earl's look that stopped me. Decker needed to do this. If I took the initiative to end it, that'd be two strikes for Decker, and there might not be any coming back from that.

I bit down hard on the inside of my cheek.

"Fucking put him down, man," Earl said. This time, his voice was icy cold, and I knew he was about two breaths away from losing his shit.

Decker must've sensed that Earl was at the end of his rope, because he closed his eyes and took a deep, shuddery breath. He lunged forward in a messy whirl of bony elbows and spindly legs. With his eyes squeezed shut, he blindly stabbed through the open tent flap. The repeated *shuck, shuck, shuck* of metal scraping through cloth and into flesh forced goosebumps across my arms.

Decker kept going, head turned away, eyes shut, stabbing through the open tent flap. Small arcs of blood splashed onto the insides of the tent, forming shadowed flecks.

Earl finally laid a hand on Decker's back. "Stop," he said, low and serious. "It's done."

Decker stepped back, chest heaving. The bloodied tip of his pike sagged and tapped the concrete just outside the tent with a soft metal *clink*.

"We'll do the rest," Earl grumbled. "Go sit down before you pass out, asshole."

Looking numb, Decker obliged, half-collapsing onto the dirty, wet curb.

Earl's eyes flicked to me. "I'm gonna grab the body bag. I'll be right back. Keep watch."

My eyes lingered on his retreating form as he headed to the truck, and I wondered what I was supposed to be watching for. I swept my gaze across the gloomy camp. It looked empty, and probably more importantly, it felt empty. I shifted my feet and adjusted my grip on the pike.

Earl was back before I knew it and tossed the bag on the sidewalk. He gestured to the tent. "Grab his feet and pull him out."

I laid my pike on the ground to the side of the tent. I tipped my head through the flap, trying to avoid the blood splatters even though I was wearing my Tyvek. That was when I got my first real look at the guy.

He had a lump on his hand: the same one mentioned in the packet. I felt a small sliver of relief that we'd popped the right guy. My eyes drifted past the bloody mess that was his chest and over the rest of him. Bile rose in my throat.

There were more lumps than the one on his hand. *A lot* more. He looked like a mutant monster in a B movie from the fifties. Masses pushed through his unshaven beard. One sat on the edge of his nose, nudging it to the side. Smaller lumps traced down his arms. I'd bet more lumps were scattered underneath his clothes.

He was curled in a fetal position, and his face was buried against a pink axolotl plushie, like he'd tried to find comfort there in his last moments. The plushie had a stitched black grin that stretched from gill to gill. One of the beaded black eyes was missing, and the cheap, pink hair was matted.

It was one of the most tragic things I'd ever seen.

"Come on, Bear," Earl directed in a patient, even voice, bringing me back.

I took a deep breath, fighting the nausea. Even with gloves on, I hoped I wouldn't have to touch any of the gross mounds. The feel of those firm masses might be just enough to send breakfast shooting out of my nose.

From over my shoulder, Earl said quietly, "Can't believe they let him get that bad."

I thought the same thing myself. Usually, the infected were reported at the first sighting of a lesion. The guy had been growing this shit on his body for at least a few weeks, if not more than a month.

Why didn't anybody call it in?

As if reading my mind, Decker responded in a half whisper. "It's 'cause he's homeless. No one wants to see him, so they don't."

I knew he was right. Regular folks avoided looking at bums just like they avoided looking at druggies shooting up on the street. Their eyes brushed right past them like they did with us when we were driving around, keeping the streets safe for their prissy asses.

I fought back another surge of bile as I took the rest of the scene in. His death had been messy. Bright red blood soaked through his shirt and pooled on the pad beneath him. His shirt was shredded.

I closed my eyes for a second, trying to get my crap together. Clenching my teeth, I reached down and grabbed his ankles. Dirty, olive green socks sagged around his feet. As I started dragging him out, the axolotl tumbled from his dead hands and rolled into the pool of blood. My eyes darted away.

When he was out past his shoulders, Earl leaned in to grab his hands. Except for the lumps, the guy was just skin and bones. Between Earl and me, it was an easy lift to get him placed in the body bag. A red smear marred the white of Earl's Tyveks where the guy's chest had bumped against him.

As Earl bent to zip the bag, Decker said, "Wait." He frantically pushed his way past us and leaned dangerously far into the bloody tent. He appeared with the plushie and then tucked it into the body bag. "Now you can close it," he said mournfully. A set of tears streamed down his cheeks, and he stepped back.

Earl's lips drew into a firm line.

I tried not to look at the body as Earl zipped up the bag, but my eye still caught a flash of pink just before it was swallowed by the darkness.

That stupid axolotl. I knew images of the plushie would be there when I closed my eyes tonight. Right along with those of the damn pink toenails with painted flowers.

We lifted the body, hauled it to the truck, and slid it into the bed.

Walking back to the camp, Earl carried the spray paint, and I had the pump sprayer. I wasn't sure how effective it would be on the water-drenched streets, but I let some of the bleach loose on the smear of red on the sidewalk.

Decker had sat back down on the edge of the curb and looked lost. His bloody pike dangled from his hands.

Earl ignored him. He sprayed the outside of the tent with the usual encircled L and the date. I followed behind, spraying the dude's spilled blood with the disinfectant. I wasn't sure it mattered; it was a mess in there. I figured they might even have to close down this section of street for a bit while they waited for all of the infected cells to die. I wondered how they'd go about it with all the needles and broken glass around. It was a risky site.

Decker finally got his shit together enough to stand. His head turned to look beyond us to the other side of the overpass. "We got company," he said, voice hushed.

My back straightened, and my head whipped around. Four skinny adults huddled under the bus stop about twenty feet on the eastern side of the overpass, smoking cigarettes. Every single one of them watched us.

Even from where I was, I could see their threadbare clothes. One of them had a cheap flannel Christmas blanket thrown over his head and shoulders with only a dark, matted beard poking out. One of them had bare feet.

Even though I hadn't been on many runs, I'd sat through my fair share of lockdowns. People just didn't go out when the sirens rang. They hunkered down until the lumper was popped. I wasn't used to seeing folks out and about. But on the last two runs, we'd had watchers, and it made me nervous.

I wondered why these folks hadn't been pulled into quarantine. It wasn't a big leap to think they'd been sharing this humble abode with Mr. Lumper. With him that far gone and all the needles lying around everywhere, surely, they'd been exposed. I found myself squinting, trying to identify any shit growing on them.

"What about them?" Decker asked softly, jerking me out of my thoughts.

"What about them?" Earl parroted back. "Not our fucking problem. Let's go."

"But..." Decker started and turned his head back toward the group. "Should we make sure they aren't sick?"

"Fuck that noise," Earl grumbled. "They're not my problem until BCB calls me out to put a pike in 'em."

Decker's eyebrows furrowed, and he folded his lips in. "But why aren't they in quarantine?"

"Probably don't want their nasty asses in with the normal folk," Earl snapped.

I frowned at his response.

Decker chewed his lower lip and lifted a polite hand toward the group.

"Thanks for taking care of Paul," a skinny woman called out across the space. Her voice was gravelly from years of smoking.

Paul.

The guy we'd piked had a name, even if the paperwork hadn't given us one. And the people living here cared enough about him to know it.

Earl sucked his teeth and turned his back on them, stomping back to the truck.

Decker followed, shoulders sagging and face turned away from the rain.

I took one last look at the small group huddled in the shelter of the bus stop. My eyes scanned over the tents and along the piles of stuff. I saw the broken broom for what it was: a tool to try to keep the camp clean. And the milk crate was there so they could sit by the fire. And the bike parts were to help them get around this sad fucking city.

That was when I finally *saw* them.

Sure, I'd ignored my fair share of homeless dudes begging at stoplights or in front of stores. They stank. They made everything they touched look like a fucking rat's nest. But the guy we'd popped today had also treasured a pink axolotl plushie. He had friends who cared enough to stick around, too. Cared enough to even thank us for putting him out of his misery.

When was someone not good enough to warrant being cared for by the state? Not good enough for quarantine? And who decided where that line was drawn?

I turned my back on the camp and trudged back out into the rain.

CHAPTER
FIFTEEN

Decker held himself together until the showers at Decon; then, he lost his ever-loving mind.

As soon as the water hit his back, he let out a mournful wail that set the hair up on the back of my neck. I froze mid-wash and stared at him.

Decker slid down the wall and curled into a ball with his ass on the cement. His knees folded in, and his hands cradled his face. The bones of his spine poked through the skin down his back. His shoulders shook with silent sobs.

Earl watched him with a deep frown. His hands were still busy lathering soap on his legs. He caught my eye and said, "Leave him be and finish up."

It was enough to shake me right, and I finished washing up, keeping Decker in my peripheral vision. I didn't know why I was so freaked out, but I didn't feel comfortable letting him slip from my sight.

The three-minute buzzer sounded. Earl and I shut the water off and moved toward the exit.

Decker was still curled in a ball, water pouring down his thin, white skin.

I took a risk and caught Earl's arm. He tensed but didn't throw a punch or shake me off. Releasing him, I nodded my head back to Decker with my eyebrows raised.

"Just leave him be," he repeated softly. "The guards will take care of it."

I wasn't sure how I felt about that. Decker was part of our crew, and we were the ones who should be watching out for him. I couldn't imagine a guard doing any "taking care" of anything other than making sure the animals stayed locked up in the cage and didn't eat each other.

I frowned and glanced back at Decker, reluctant to leave.

"Come on, man," Earl said under his breath, pushing the door open into the next room.

We stepped through, and I lost sight of Decker when the door closed behind us.

"Where's the rest of your team?" the guard asked, tense.

"He needs a minute," Earl said. He kept his eyes cast down and grabbed a towel to dry off.

The guard frowned, debating his options. He must've decided to ignore the slight breach in protocol because before I knew it, he told us to stand in the yellow circles for inspection.

Once we were cleared, he waved us on to get dressed. I slipped a fresh pair of coveralls and tight-fitting boots on, all the while watching the door for Decker to come through.

We made it all the way outside without catching a glimpse of him.

The rain drizzled down, and everything felt damp and cold after the shower. We moved to a table under an overhang to wait for the truck.

Earl took a seat, looking stony and far away.

I ran my fingers through my wet hair, trying to untangle everything, and wishing like mad for a hair tie. Leaning forward, I rested my forearms on my thighs. I snuck a glance at Earl, who was still avoiding all human contact.

I was really starting to worry that Decker wouldn't be coming back with us. The guards hadn't seen him freeze with the grannie or freak out with the junkie, so no one with any power knew how fucked up in the head he was. But that shit in the shower—there'd been cameras on for that. There was no hiding that mess.

What happened to guys who flipped out like that? Would they switch him to burner duty? Put him in regular prison and give him extra time? They sure as hell wouldn't give him counseling to help him work through his feelings.

Just when I was about to get up and ask the guards about him, Decker clanged through the exit doors. His head was down, hiding his eyes. His hands clenched in his pockets. The muscles in his arms and back were strung tighter than a guitar string. Instead of taking a seat with us, he stood by the door, looking lost and alone.

Before I knew it, a burner pulled the truck up, threw it in park, and killed the engine. After slamming the door behind him, he headed back the way he came without a word.

Earl got up first. "Let's get out of here."

Decker and I followed, and a thick cloud of silence filled the space around us.

Earl fired up the truck, and the windshield wipers screeched back to life. Without giving either of us the time of day, Earl fiddled with the radio, and rap music filled the truck.

Decker didn't say a word. He sat there like a zombie, and his face was expressionless. It was like the part of him that could actually feel shit had been locked away. I wondered if being a thumper was too much for him.

My mind flashed back to the look in Earl's eyes after the grandma, and I wondered if being a thumper was too much for any of us. I'd only been around for three kills. What would I look like when I really started racking up the lumper kills like one of the OGs?

I shook off the thought.

Decker was probably going through a kind of delayed shock, something he'd shake off in a day or two. Hopefully, he could get it together before our next run. I was a little nervous bringing a shambler like him along; that was how people got hurt.

My eyes bounced to the rearview mirror, and I risked a look at Earl. The muscle in his cheek bounced as he ground his teeth, but he kept his eyes locked straight ahead.

By the time we returned to the Home, it was after lunch. The rain had picked up a bit, and Earl and I hustled inside. Decker trailed slowly behind us, rain plastering his crazy hair to his gaunt cheeks.

We clanged through the door and found Ramos at the front desk. She was a stern woman, and I'd only seen her once or twice. She wore her black hair slicked back in a neat bun, tidy as a pin. Even though she looked to be in her mid-thirties, there wasn't a hint of gray. Large glasses were perched on her nose.

She gave Earl a sad, knowing look when he passed our ID cards and the truck keys through the window.

Jackson sauntered out for the pat-downs. He was standing tall with his back straight. He had one hand on the butt of the baton hanging from his waist. The other had a thumb hooked loosely in his pocket. A smirk twisted his lips.

"Everything go alright, boys?" he asked. With his nasty grin, I knew someone from Decon had called over. I wasn't sure what the process was on the administration side of things; they had a habit of leaving inmates in the dark about all sorts of stuff, including what might be said about us behind the scenes. But if there was such a thing as a red flag on a file, Decker now had one.

Earl scowled.

Jackson snickered and said, "Stand in the circles. Arms up. You know the drill."

We complied.

He patted us down, humming merrily as he did so. I kept sneaking glances at Decker, but all he could do was follow simple commands with his eyes unfocused.

"You're all clear. Move along," Jackson said, still grinning like a fool.

Earl pushed his way through the last set of doors with enough force that they clanged back against the stopper.

"Watch it, inmate!" Jackson called after him.

Jackson turned toward Decker and me with a sneer.

I stalled a bit, letting Decker go ahead of me. With the look on Jackson's face, I didn't want to leave Decker alone with him. I followed Decker's shuffling footsteps through the door, keeping my eyes down.

Jackson huffed a low, mocking laugh.

Decker made a beeline for our room, ignoring everything around him. He quietly folded himself onto his cot. Lying on his side, he pulled his knees to his chest and wrapped his arms tightly around them. I could hear his spirit crying out into the abyss, hoping someone would listen.

Earl stood by his own cot, watching Decker with a worried expression. He swept his hand over the top of his head and sighed heavily.

Decker was in a real bad way, and neither of us knew what to do. A part of me hoped Cockroach would make an appearance. Maybe the sight of him would be enough to pull Decker out of the dark spiral he was in.

My jaw clenched.

The assholes running BCB assumed that, because we were felons, killing would be easy. The normies didn't think nothing of what we were forced to do either. They just sat back, ignoring us, as we cleared the trash and slowly lost a piece of ourselves with each kill. Some shiteaters, like Jackson, even mocked us for coming back a little fucked in the head. I'd like to see Jackson pike a grandma or a sad dude with an axolotl plushie and walk away with his brain still working right.

Each death weighed heavy on all of us, and there was no getting around it.

I stood in the doorway to our room with my hands fisted at my sides. There was a dangerous roaring in my head, and my chest grew tight. An angry tide swept in. I could feel it coming, but I couldn't move.

From far away, I heard Earl's voice repeating the same word. Finally, a stern "Bear!" bit through the fog.

"Breathe, man," he said in a low, even voice.

I turned to him, my mind finally able to see everything else in the room as I took a shuddery breath. Earl's expression was cautious. He was positioned just close enough to pin me down if he needed to.

I finally registered the bite of my nails in my palms and looked down at my hands. Despite my nails being clipped short, there were little red crescents dented into the surface. I blinked a couple times, trying to get back into the moment.

"Bear," Earl repeated, softer this time, like he knew I'd come out of the dark place. "Let's go get something to eat."

All I could do was grunt a reply and numbly follow his command. I slowly turned and drifted out of the room and into the breezeway. Earl followed me in silence.

I took a few deep breaths of the damp air, trying to focus.

When we entered the gym, lunch was long over. Earl leaned over to talk to one of the staff members who was wiping down the counters. Somehow, he sweet-talked her into giving us a few generic protein bars. That was twice now that they'd looked out for us.

Earl pressed one into my hand as he walked past. The wrapper crinkled when I clenched my fist. Even though I was hungry, the adrenaline still buzzed through me. If I tried to eat just yet, I might barf everything right back up, my body readying itself for a fight.

Earl had his bar open by the time we got back to the room. He tossed the third one onto Decker's cot. Decker didn't even twitch, and I had a sudden urge to check for a pulse. I pushed the feelings away and slumped down onto my cot.

I took a few deep breaths, feeling the tingle of the adrenaline fade. The shakes came next, and my hands bounced as my fingers fumbled with the wrapper. The fake blueberry smell hit me, and I felt a wave of nausea. I fought past it, knowing I needed the calories. The first bite was awful; the bar was dry and grainy with a flavor that was almost like plastic. I choked it down in four bites and went to the water fountain, chugging down gulp after gulp to chase the nasty taste away.

By the time I returned, Earl had finished his bar. He was on his back with hands folded on his chest, staring up at the ceiling.

Cockroach wandered in and hopped on Decker's bed with an inquisitive *meow*. Cockroach sniffed the bar lying on the bed, batted it with his paw a couple of times, and then curled up in the crook of Decker's knees.

Decker didn't move a muscle. I couldn't tell if he was asleep or still awake, but lost to the world. Either way, it didn't sit right.

I sat on my cot and leaned back against the wall. I pulled my sketchbook out, fully intending to draw. But all I could do was stare at the blank page.

The rain pattered softly outside. A faint sound of music mixed with occasional loud chatter drifted into the room. A booming laugh bounced across the courtyard.

My eyes shifted to the ceiling tiles. There was a grey dampness at the edge of the brown stains. I wondered if there was enough water leaking through that it would drip on my cot tonight. I thought about moving my shit, but the effort seemed like too much.

Somehow, I fell asleep like that, considering the damp, rotting tile, and the dinner bell woke me a few hours later. I blinked my puffy, dry eyes open. I shifted my feet to the ground and rested my forearms on my thighs. My hand went to the back of my neck, trying to work the kink out.

"Rise and shine," Earl said flatly from his cot. His eyes were cast down on a round of one-handed solitaire.

Decker still had his back turned to us. The slow rise and fall of his chest told me he was alive.

Cockroach was gone.

Earl swept all of his cards back into one pile. "Let's grab dinner," he said in a soft, resigned tone.

To my surprise, Decker slowly rolled over and swung his legs over the edge of the cot. His face was twisted in agony, and he still wouldn't meet our eyes. But he'd somehow managed to get up, and I figured that was something.

Earl led us out with Decker coming in behind him, and I pulled up the rear. Even though the rain had stopped, the courtyard was still damp, and the sky was a grumpy gray. We kept to the breezeway as we made our way to the chow hall.

We slid into the end of the line. Chatter swirled around us, but we waited in silence. The staff spooned food into the trays with clanking sounds. Dinner was something trying to be macaroni and cheese. A slab of cornbread and soggy canned carrots filled the smaller compartments. We took our trays and slumped down at our usual table.

A guy at the table next to us was squirting a couple of Tapatio packs over his meal. The bright red sauce splashed across the mac and cheese in thin streaks. I wasn't huge into hot sauce, but a part of me wished I could get some just to make the meal taste like something other than cardboard. To make me feel less gloomy and numb. Maybe if we'd been able to finish that game of Spades with Mateo, we'd have some.

Decker poked his food with a dull expression. He hadn't lifted the spoon to his lips once. He didn't have an ounce of fat on his body to draw from, and I wondered how many more meals he could miss and still stand.

Earl noticed, too. And even though he chomped through his food like he didn't have a care in the world, his shoulders were tense, and he watched Decker from his peripheral vision.

After we finished, we waited a bit for Decker, who still stabbed at his mac and cheese. Without looking up, Decker palmed the cornbread and rose to bus his tray. I glanced at Earl to see what was what, but all he did was follow Decker out.

I cleared my tray and trudged behind them.

Back in Room Four, Decker set the cornbread in an empty yogurt container. He sat on the edge of his cot, leaned his elbows on his thighs, and rested his face in his hands.

Earl and I took a seat on our own cots. I watched Decker carefully.

"Sorry," Decker finally murmured.

The apology surprised me more than anything. I wasn't sure what he was sorry for. He'd done his job today and piked the dude. Sure, he'd lost his marbles for a bit there. But Earl and I were on clean-up duty, and Decker hadn't pushed any more work on us.

Earl seemed to understand, though.

His face softened with a look of empathy I'd never seen on him before. He walked over to Decker and placed a hand on his shoulder. He gave it a light squeeze. Without a word, he went back to his cot and started rolling a cigarette.

Feeling a bit like I was watching a moment that I wasn't a part of, I turned to fidget with my meager stash. I fished out a hair tie and pulled my hair back into a tight braid. I felt cleaner that way, almost normal again.

I leaned back on my cot and laced my fingers behind my head. The wet spot on the ceiling felt ugly and depressing, so I turned to watch Earl finish rolling his stick.

Cockroach slipped through the window with a *meow*. The white part of his hair was damp with brown-tinged water, and he left fading wet prints behind him as he hopped onto Decker's cot. Decker reached out absently and scratched his scruff.

Cockroach's purr rumbled through the room. Decker placed the square of cornbread on the bed next to Cockroach. The cat purred around each bite as he wolfed it down.

There was a *click, click* of the lighter, and a deep exhale as Earl took his first puff. He held his cigarette out to Decker. "Want one?"

Decker looked up and shrugged. "Sure, I guess."

Earl stood and passed him a rolled stick and the lighter.

"Thanks," Decker murmured as he lit up.

Decker shucked his slides off and scootched back on his cot. He leaned his back against the wall and folded his knees to his chest.

Cockroach had finished up and swiped his paw across his face. Decker reached out with his free hand to pet his back.

After a couple of puffs, Decker sighed. He flicked the ash and looked up at Earl, finally making eye contact. "Sorry, man," he repeated.

Earl pressed his lips together and tipped his chin down once in acknowledgement.

"That guy should've been put down a couple weeks ago," Decker said sadly as he watched the smoke rise from his cigarette. "That was some fucked up shit back there."

My eyes darted to Earl, who, in turn, studied Decker silently. He seemed to know that Decker needed and gave him the space to do it. I wondered how many times Decker had lost his shit before I'd joined the crew. I had a feeling Earl had done this with him before.

I didn't like having someone so jumpy on the team. Decker was always crying over this and that, preventing us from just going in, doing our job, and getting out. His emotions spilled all over the place, making it hard for me to keep my own in. Part of me hated him for it.

"It isn't right letting someone suffer like that," Decker continued, picking absently at his arm.

"Yeah," Earl agreed, voice low. "That's the worst case of Lumps I've seen."

My eyes jumped to Earl. He'd been at the home for a long time and had been out on a shit-ton of runs. I was pretty damn sure he'd seen it all.

Earl took his last drag and stubbed his cigarette out. "But I ain't ever put down no bum either. It's probably because he was living on the street."

"But he was in a camp. With other people," Decker insisted, teetering on the edge of what sounded like a whine.

Earl shrugged. "No one wants to see bums, so they don't."

"But they're *people*," Decker said emphatically. "They wouldn't let someone from East Sac or Land Park get like that. It's inhumane."

Earl sucked his teeth. "People living in those neighborhoods are the fucking royalty of this city. The bums, the druggies, people in the projects, you, me…shit…we're the fucking *serfs*, man. We don't matter. We're like the roaches living in the walls or the rats in the sewer. Best for the richies to pretend we aren't there and set traps to make us go away."

Decker's face folded into a frown, and his eyebrows scrunched together. "That's dark, bro."

"It's the truth," Earl grumbled bitterly.

Silence spread through the room.

Decker rested his legs down, holding his cigarette just over the edge of the cot. Cockroach climbed into his lap.

"How do you keep doing this shit, Earl?" Decker said in a voice so low it was practically a whisper.

Earl shrugged. "Don't got a lot of options."

"The way they send us out like we're delivering a fucking pizza, it's fucked up. Like it ain't a big deal that we're going to kill someone." Decker's face folded, and his eyes filled with tears. "We should at least get longer breaks between runs."

"This ain't a fucking job like out in the world. You ain't got no union or HR or someone taking care of your mental health and shit." Earl's face had grown stone cold, and his voice was stern. "You're doing fucking time, man. And you're doing it for some fucked up shit *you* did. You just gotta suck it up."

"We have rights," Decker offered weakly, a tear streaking down his face.

Earl snorted. "You ain't got shit, fool."

Decker swiped at his face.

Earl's expression softened a bit, and he said, "Look, man. You gotta find a way to block that shit out. Just lock it away and do your time. If you lose it like that again in front of 'em, they're gonna put you on burner duty. You think it's bad being a thumper? Try working Decon, bro."

Decker chewed on his lower lip.

"Here," Earl said, tossing him another protein bar he'd pulled out of fuck knows where. "You need to eat. Your scrawny ass can barely hold a pike, bro."

It was enough to make Decker drop the subject.

Earl had a grin on his face. But his eyes were far away, dealing with his own shit.

CHAPTER SIXTEEN

The next morning, the rhythm of the Home helped us focus on the here-and-now. Decker ate all the food on his tray and even tossed a couple jokes back and forth with Earl. I thought we'd somehow made it through the dark space and to whatever fucked up version of normal we had.

And I was right. For about four hours.

After lunch, the sun was out, but the courtyard was still muddy from the day before, so we headed to the rec room. Al was in his usual seat, but this time, it was *Wheel of Fortune* on the screen. The bright colors, flickering light, and fake smiles were almost too much.

Earl breezed into the rec room, wearing an unusually cheerful grin. He took an empty seat next to Al and asked in a bright voice, "How you doing, Al?"

Al didn't offer a response.

Earl relaxed back into his chair, still smiling. Decker folded himself into the chair next to Earl, slouching a bit. I capped off the row at the end, stretching my legs out in the open space of the aisle.

"Mind changing the channel, bro?" Earl asked not unkindly. "Vanna White is hot and all, but those sparkling lights and that spinning wheel are gonna give Decker here a seizure."

Decker made a noise that was part huff and part snort. The smile tipping his lips told me Earl was full of shit. But it was a good teasing, the kind that told me things might be okay.

Al surprised all of us by holding the remote out to Earl.

"Well, shit," Earl exclaimed, grinning. "Thanks, bro."

Earl took the remote and started flipping through stations. He landed on *All My Children* and passed the remote back to Al.

At the first commercial break, Earl stood and said, "Be right back." He had a mischievous grin. I didn't have a clue what he was up to.

Before the commercial narrator had made it all the way through the laundry list of side effects of some new drug, Earl was back, clutching a bag of chips. It was an honest-to-goodness sharing-size bag of Fuego Takis.

"What the actual fuck is that?!" Decker asked, eyes wide.

I was right there with Decker, shocked by the sudden appearance of a magnificent bag of crunchy, spicy chips. I wondered what magic hat Earl had pulled that out of. It was an unwritten rule to stay the hell out of each other's stashes, but we shared a room, and it was easy enough to see what another dude had lying around. I was sure I would've noticed that giant purple bag.

Decker couldn't take his eyes off the thing. "Where did you get those from? They don't have Takis in the commissary, and you got no money in there anyway."

With a huge shit-eating grin, Earl popped the bag open and said, "I got my ways." He surprised me again by turning the opened bag to Al first. "Want some?"

And, since everything invariably comes in threes, I got another shock when Al actually turned his head to look at Earl and then at the bag.

I hadn't really *seen* Al before. It was hard getting past the patch on his neck and the puckered scar behind his ear.

Al's eyebrows were dark streaks of black on an otherwise clean-shaven face. The skin around his eyes had the wrinkles of late middle age. Three faded, solid teardrop tattoos were folded into the creases, and I knew that they'd been there for ages. His eyes were dark, almost black, and they shone with intelligence.

The hair on the back of my neck went up. I'd thought Al was as dumb as a lumper. With that one look, I knew the bullet hadn't taken a single lick of his mind away. He was sitting there like a rattlesnake, and I hadn't even picked him out.

The crinkle of the chip bag shook me out of my thoughts as Earl shook it a couple times, waiting. Al reached into the bag and pulled out a small handful. He snapped his chin up sharply to indicate his thanks. Earl turned the bag to Decker and me, and we each grabbed a handful, before Earl finally helped himself.

The orange-red powder on the chip rolls dusted my fingers. I crunched into one, taking a moment to appreciate the texture. There wasn't much in prison food that really crunched, except maybe burnt toast, and just that single snapping feeling was utterly satisfying.

On the TV, Erica Kane snarked at some poor soul within her orbit. We all just sat back and watched, enjoying our Takis in slow, measured bites. The only thing that would've made it better would be having a cool beer to wash it down.

When the bag was empty and we'd all had our fair share, I sucked the salty powder off each finger, enjoying the lingering spicy flavor.

"Thanks, bro," Decker said with a sigh. "I haven't had chips in fuck knows how long. It's weird what you miss."

Earl's only reply was a small, self-satisfied smile. His shoulders were relaxed, and he'd kicked his legs out in front of him.

He interlaced his fingers over his belly with a look of contentment.

I wish I could've taken a snapshot of that moment and held onto it. Because everything that came after was fucking terrible.

And it all started with that asshole ball-grabber, Mike.

We'd moved past *All My Children* and switched to *General Hospital* when the shithead walked in.

"Look-ee here!" Mike chirped loudly as he sauntered in. One of the dudes in his crew followed behind him.

I turned over my shoulder to watch him. At the sight of his shit-eating grin, the muscles in my back tensed, and my feet shifted underneath me.

"Another slow day," he huffed dramatically and flopped into the chair in front of Earl.

He was a big guy—maybe six and a half feet or so. Muscles pulled against his pale skin, and I knew he wore the wife-beater just to show them off. I wondered if he was just a lifter or if he actually knew how to use that strength.

Decker shifted nervously next to me, not liking the fact that the dude was sitting one up and over from him. Earl looked unfazed, even though the guy's bulk was crouched right in front of him. I wondered how Mike felt safe enough to put his back to a guy like Earl.

Mike leaned back, threw his arm over the empty chair to his left, and crossed his ankle over his knee. On the surface, he looked relaxed. But there were small tells: his tense shoulders, the purposeful placement of his loose left hand near his pocket, and that damn spooky grin.

I shifted my weight, put my feet flat on the ground, and turned slightly toward him. He was just far enough away that I'd have to jump the chairs to get to him, but I would if the asshole did something stupid.

Mike looked over his right shoulder at Decker. A nasty light danced in his eyes, and I could see the whole thing spool out in front of me from a mile away. I leaned forward, resting my forearms on my legs, and balled one fist into the other.

"Heard you were crying like a baby when you popped a homeless lumper, Deck," Mike said with a smirk. "Being around a garbage junkie a little too close to home?"

Fucking guards, I thought.

They were the only ones who could've been talking shit about what had happened to Decker over in Decon. Later, I'd wonder why they'd given Mike that info, and a twisted part of me would think maybe BCB wanted Mike to put Decker out of action and chalk it all up to a prison fight. All those thoughts came afterward, though. Just then, my sights were locked on Mike, and I was only seeing red.

"What the fuck's your issue?" Earl said in a voice laced with warning.

Mike shifted a bit to see Earl sitting behind him and smiled. "I ain't got a problem, bro. You do. How can you even ride with that limp-dick piece of shit?" His eyes swept up and down Decker. "Gotta watch out for junkies, bro. Having someone like that on your crew is gonna get you killed. Just a little scrambled up there, you know?" He tapped his temple and turned back to the TV.

The guy next to Mike huffed a laugh. There was a nervous edge to it, like he knew what was coming.

If Mike was gunning for Decker, I wondered why he'd decided to pick a fight when Earl and I were there. It was also stupid as fuck to choose the row of chairs that put his back to us if he planned on starting some shit. It would've been smarter to catch Decker alone on the john.

Decker curled up into himself, watching Mike with a fierceness that was borderline dangerous. What did it look like when someone like Decker finally lost his shit? Would he lock his mind away, ball himself up tighter, and take the punches? Or would he come at the dude like a rabid dog and claw the fucker's eyes out? I didn't want to find out.

Mike swiveled his head back around to look at Decker, a crazy flicker in his eye.

A dump of adrenaline swept through my body. I knew that look.

"So why did you cry like a little bitch in Decon?" Mike said slyly. "That lumper remind you of your pops? Or...hmm...let me see...maybe all you druggies stick together, and he was a buddy you knew from before. Someone who jumped you in with a needle. Like a homeless gang." He barked a deep belly laugh. "Yeah! That's it! And instead of flashing colors, you got those thick rubber bands tied around your arms, and instead of a patch, you got tracks."

The whole monologue was a surprisingly creative leap for someone so stupid.

Mike laughed again, watching Decker closely.

The dude next to Mike snickered along, eyes dancing around nervously. He was small and held his body loosely. I instantly dismissed him; he'd probably piss himself if it came to blows.

"Whatcha say, Deck?" Mike pushed again.

"That's about enough of that," Earl said firmly. "Turn the fuck around and watch the show."

Mike's grin widened, and his perfectly aligned teeth flashed brightly. His eyes bounced from Earl to Decker and back again. Then, he turned his head toward the screen.

There was a brief, tense moment where no one spoke. The only sound in the room came from the conversation on the TV, which was frantic and a bit whiny. I couldn't pull my eyes from the back of Mike's head to watch the show, and I didn't care enough to try to place the actors by their voices.

This wasn't over, and something was coming. I didn't know what it was or when it would happen, but it was coming. And sure enough, when the commercial break hit, Mike turned his mug around and gave Decker a look of feigned consideration.

"I was thinking...." He tapped his chin dramatically. "Maybe you just wish you were dead. And every time you go out and don't get taken down, you cry yourself to sleep knowing you have to spend another day in that shit-heap of a body."

A sharp screech interrupted him.

Mike dropped his arm off the back of the chair and shifted his body toward us.

Earl had stood so fast I'd missed the whole thing. One moment, he was sitting there, clenching his jaw, and the next, he was towering over Mike.

A millisecond after seeing Earl pop up, I was next, knocking my chair over in the process.

Mike let out a slow, controlled laugh. He turned his back to Earl—which was either really brave or really stupid—and stood slowly. He swung to face Earl, the chair between them keeping them about three feet apart. His triceps flexed dramatically as he straightened his back to look down at Earl.

"You got a problem, old man?" Mike growled.

If it weren't for the real anger coming off Earl in waves, Mike's whole schtick would have been comical. But one honest look at Earl, and I could tell he was about ready to kill this guy. It was clear that Mike was blindly stumbling into a place he'd never been before, and he was a hair's breadth away from getting his ass handed to him.

"Yeah, I got a problem," Earl said coolly. "You buggin' me. Now, either sit down or get the fuck out of here."

"Or what?" Mike snorted. "You ain't gonna do shit." He lifted a hand to his wife-beater and pulled down one corner to show a tattoo with the letters "PB" surrounded by a laurel wreath.

Several possible scenarios sped through my head in snapshots. Mike's chair sat between him and Earl, and it was just enough space that it would be hard to get a good punch in. Earl could pull it to the side, but that would be just enough time for Mike to launch the first hit. Earl could pick the chair up and use it as a weapon, but there wasn't a lot of space.

I moved nice and slow into the aisle, giving myself a straight path down the row to Mike's crewmate. I felt the red edge in, and my focus narrowed. My heart drummed in my chest like a call to action.

Earl tucked his chin, and his eyebrows dropped low over his eyes. "Fuck you. Acting all tough. You don't know shit, motherfucker. Now, get the fuck out of here."

Mike shifted forward, and his leg bumped the seat of his chair. "What the fuck you say?"

There was a loud *clang*.

My head snapped toward the sound, and I saw Al's chair had hit the floor.

At this angle, I could see the "XIV" tattooed in bold across Al's throat. But it wasn't the patch that caused the hair on the back of my neck to go up. It was the crazy look in Al's eye. Even though he stood about a foot shorter than Mike, that look told me all I needed to know; Mike would be a red smear on the ground after Al was done with him.

Al tilted his head up so that he looked down his nose at Mike.

"What, *ese*?" Mike snarked, drawing out the last word with an exaggerated accent. "You gonna do something, you fucking gangbanger?"

In a flash, Al grabbed the back of the empty chair in front of him and yanked it to the left, where it fell on its side. Al swept right over the chair's legs to deck Mike in the face.

From there, everything happened at lightning speed.

Mike let out a squeaky yell of surprise and fell back against the chairs in the front row. He lost his balance, falling on his ass and tipping the chairs over. Al jumped on top of him and balled his left hand around a wad of Mike's shirt. His right fist swung over and over. Mike flailed at Al, trying to brush him off.

Mike's crewmate stumbled down the now-open end of the aisle in shock and ran out the door.

Earl grabbed Decker's arm, pulling him to the back of the room, away from the fight.

Al seemed to be doing just fine turning Mike's face into hamburger, so I moved to the door to make sure Mike's guy didn't come back with more dudes and change the odds. My heart pounded in my chest, and my skin tingled with the rush, ready for a fight.

Within seconds, Brown and Garcia ran into the room. I let out a whistle, hoping Al could hear me through the fog of his fury. I stepped back as the guards pushed into the room.

Al stood and stepped back from the mess he'd made of Mike, chest heaving. His back was toward the door, and his hands were clenched at his sides, blood dripping from his right fist.

"Hernandez!" Brown shouted and pulled a taser out. "Step back from Jansen and put your hands up."

Al's chin dropped to his chest, and he held his hands up over his shoulders.

"The rest of you, on the ground," Garcia barked.

Earl, Decker, and I dropped down, bellies flush with the floor.

Brown and Garcia circled Al, coming down opposite ends of the aisle cautiously. Al stood still, Mike's blood dripping down the arm of his raised hand.

Jackson and Jones appeared at the door.

"Jeeesus," Jackson said, drawing the word out quietly. His eyes darted around the room. He stepped to the side and pulled his baton out.

Jones's eyes swept across the room, and she tensed; then she moved to stand guard just outside the door.

Even though Earl, Decker, and I had been told to hit the deck, I was surprised they hadn't called "yard down" for the entire Home. There was something about the smell of a fight in the air that tended to trigger people.

Brown stopped a few feet away from Al, taser ready, while Garcia moved in to cuff him. Garcia twisted one arm down with gloved hands, snapping a cuff over his wrist, and then brought the next one down. Before I knew it, Al's wrists were locked behind his back.

"Come on, Hernandez," Garcia said. His eyes looked sad, and his tone was ever-so-slightly disappointed.

Al had accomplished what he'd wanted to do; Mike was now an unmoving, bloody lump on the ground. Al didn't have a beef with the guards, and he let himself be led through the room. The glazed look that he often wore had dropped back over his eyes.

Brown moved to check Mike's vitals with gloved hands. Mike groaned at the touch and shifted. I couldn't see much from where I was on the ground at the back of the room, but I did see red. Lots of it.

"You three," Jackson snapped at us. "Get up. Go to your room and stay there."

When we stepped out into the breezeway, it was empty except for Jones. Even though the alarm hadn't been pulled, the guards had managed to get all the residents into their rooms. Curious faces peered out.

As we moved through the breezeway to our room, I watched Garcia buzz Al through the doors into the cop shop.

With an uncomfortable feeling of loss, I wondered if I'd ever see the guy again.

CHAPTER SEVENTEEN

By the time dinner rolled around, everyone in the Home knew Al had put the demo down on Mike. Even though we weren't part of Al's crew, we'd been in the rec room when shit had gone down, and the other residents gave us a wide berth.

Things were powder-keg tense.

Mike wasn't well loved, and I wasn't expecting to get jumped. But fights tended to put everyone on edge. Even the smallest slight—a bit of side-eye, an accidental bump in line—and someone was liable to get beaten.

When it came time to grab food, Earl held us back with an unspoken command. I wasn't sure if he was just trying to lay low for a bit or if he was protecting Decker from the gossip. Inmates were worse than old biddies when it came to talking trash. Who knew what the rest of the guys in the Home were saying?

We caught dinner right before things shut down. All the other guys had finished up, and the gym was pretty much empty. We slid right through the line, collecting our trays. The hamburgers were sad-looking: a slab of something that was trying to be meat topped with an unmelted slice of plastic cheese. The rest of the tray was filled with a handful of soggy tater tots, some dry baby carrots, and a sickly-sweet fruit cup.

We took our seats without saying a word and went through the motions of getting our calories. The only sound came from Decker as he chomped at his food. When we finished, we bussed our trays and went straight back to our room. The evening count came at nine, like it always did, but then something different happened.

They locked everyone in their rooms.

Though the routines could get boring sometimes, they were also reassuring in their own way. We knew what to expect, even if it did feel like rinse-and-repeat. That small change messed with my head, and I felt like a trapped animal. Which was weird, considering the ankle tracker and all the other locks between me and the outside world.

The lockdown must've bugged Decker and Earl, too, because none of us could sleep. The three of us lay quietly on our cots, eyes wide open in the gloom of the city's streetlights, lost in our own thoughts. Cockroach had made an appearance, been fed, and was now the only one sleeping.

In those dark hours when the world felt like it wasn't real—like an old black-and-white photograph that could be a fake—that was when Decker finally spoke up.

"What's going to happen to Al?" Decker whispered. His blankets rustled and his cot creaked as he rolled over.

A thoughtful silence followed before Earl replied. "I don't know. Depends on how bad Mike got fucked up."

"Will he get more time?" Decker asked.

"Al's a lifer, man." Earl shifted in his bed and put an arm across his forehead. "No. It won't be more time they give him."

"You don't think they'll switch him to burner duty. Do you?" Decker's voice was hushed with worry.

"Don't know," Earl replied curtly.

"But he was defending me," Decker said, and it sounded kind of petulant.

At that moment, I felt like smacking him. I knew he'd seen his own version of shit, and putting down that lumper yesterday had been rough, but sometimes he could be such a whiny, naive ass. The world didn't give two shits about why Al had pulled Mike's punk card and beat the hell out of him. Sometimes people stood up for others and still got the ass end of the stick.

"Could we go tell the guards what happened?" Decker continued. "Maybe they'll just give him a night to cool down or something?"

Earl sighed. "The guards don't care, man. Just let it go."

"I feel bad, is all," Decker said, his voice edging on a sniffle.

Earl's silhouette leaned up on one elbow and turned toward Decker. I couldn't see his expression in the low light, but his voice was stern when he said, "Look, man. Al knew what he was doing and what would happen. He's been here longer than I have, and he'll be locked up 'til he dies. He normally doesn't stir up any shit, and the guards don't mind him. Plus, he's piked a fuck-ton of lumpers, and he's good at it. My guess? He'll be back tomorrow with a slap on the wrist, and his crew will be the first one out on the next call."

There were a few beats of silence as Decker took it all in.

"This is all so fucked up, man," Decker muttered.

Earl twisted back to lie flat on his cot. "Yup. But it is what it is."

Decker sighed heavily, then asked, "Think Mike'll come back?"

"Fuck if I know," Earl answered.

There was another long stretch of silence.

"If anything happens to me, will you take care of Cockroach?"

Decker's question came out in a cautious half-whisper, like saying the words out loud might make them come true.

There was something tragic about Decker worrying about the cat more than himself. It was like he'd been told he was a worthless piece of trash so often that, now, even he believed he was disposable. The BCB and the rest of the normies treated all of us that way. It was hard to think otherwise.

I wondered if the cat was the only thing keeping Decker from totally losing it.

Decker's question must've bothered Earl, too, because he grumbled, "Shut the fuck up. Ain't nothing gonna happen to you. Stop worrying about that damn cat and go to sleep."

The conversation ended there, but my mind was wide awake. Decker's words bounced around in my head, making a mess of things.

There was the surface worry of getting jumped by someone once we came out of the smash. I didn't think anyone else in the Home rolled with the Proud Boys other than Mike, but they might work connections to have someone inside paint us. Earl acted like we didn't need to worry about retaliation, but I couldn't relax. Something told me it wasn't over.

Below the surface, I couldn't shake the uneasiness over all of Decker's talk about something happening to him. Was he worried about getting yanked out of the Home for losing it in Decon? BCB hadn't taken him off thumper duty yet, but it could be coming. If that happened, where would he go? Burner duty? Back to regular prison? He'd get eaten alive.

There was another reason he could be leaving: the one that none of us wanted to talk about. That was the one that slithered round and round in my head, leaving a trail of black slime until I finally fell asleep.

CHAPTER
EIGHTEEN

When the bell rang the next morning, I woke up feeling like I'd been run over by a truck.

My nightmares had been filled with pink toenails, grannies, and axolotls. My mind was stuffed with every lumper death I'd been a part of. They were stacked in my brain like infected sores, smarting every time I tried to get some real sleep.

And the dead look in Al's eyes. That haunted me, too.

I rolled onto my back and rubbed my dry, puffy eyes. Even though I hadn't jumped into the fight, my muscles ached like I had. I dropped my hands across my chest and stared up at the stain on the ceiling.

With a sigh, I twisted out of bed, slowly realizing the guards had already unlocked and opened our door. A slim, filtered band of sunlight stretched across the threshold.

There was a shuffling sound from Decker's direction. He twisted to sit up on his cot, grunted at me in greeting, and ran his hands through his tousled hair. Cockroach was MIA.

And so was Earl.

A quick shot of adrenaline raced through my system, and I slipped my slides on. "Where's Earl?"

Decker looked up and blinked like he was just now registering the room. A flitter of panic crossed his features. "I...I don't know," he stammered.

I pulled a T-shirt over my head and headed out into the courtyard, not caring if Decker followed or not. In a place like the Home, routine was king. When something shifted out of place—like locked doors or Earl not being around at morning bell—it was time to start worrying.

As soon as I crossed the threshold of Room Four and out into the breezeway, I caught sight of Earl, and I could breathe again.

He leaned against the courtyard wall, casually talking to one of the guys from Room Two like it was no big thing to be up and about before morning bell. The other dude was one of the OGs who played dominoes in the rec. I couldn't remember his name.

Earl noticed me and tossed his chin up in greeting.

I felt Decker behind me, looking over my shoulder, but didn't want to take my eyes off Earl.

"What's Earl doing with Jorge?" Decker asked, sounding half awake.

I didn't answer; I was still trying to figure out what the fuck was going on.

After the shit had gone down yesterday, I didn't know how the other guys in the Home were going to respond, and I didn't like Earl going out by himself. Jorge seemed chill enough, but I couldn't shake the uneasy feeling.

My eyes raced around the courtyard. Even though all the doors were open, none of the other residents were out. All the guards were tucked away in the cop shop. I still felt nervous, and my eyes shifted back to Earl.

Earl gave Jorge a smile, dapped him up, and headed back across the courtyard.

There was a loud crackle over the PA system, and a guard announced, "On the count."

Earl joined Decker and me as everyone lined up outside their rooms.

The guards moved around the breezeway with their clickers. The other residents tossed us looks. Some of them were curious. Some of them were cautious. None of them were hostile.

My shoulders relaxed slightly.

After the all-clear, Earl said, "Let's go get food." He turned to the chow hall, assuming we'd follow.

I glanced at Decker.

He shrugged, frowning.

Unsure of what to expect, we left our room and trailed after him. Earl was a hard read from behind. His body looked relaxed, like it was just another day. Just another meal. It wasn't until he glanced toward us that I saw a flicker of tension behind his eyes.

We shuffled through the line in silence. Most of the other residents chatted about dumb stuff. We'd get the occasional appraising glance, but I didn't feel like we had targets on our backs either.

Breakfast was cold cereal with a banana and an orange. I ate my meal in silence. After I finished my food, I still felt hungry. Earl and Decker were unusually quiet. When our trays were empty, we bussed them and went back to our room without a word.

It wasn't until we were safely back and resting on our cots that Earl filled us in. "Mike went to the infirmary," he announced casually.

I felt a jolt of surprise.

Al had done a pretty good job on Mike's face, but I'd expected bandages and ice packs would be enough to patch him up. Going to the infirmary meant a trip back to prison, the kind with bars and shit. I wondered if he'd gone to Folsom or somewhere else for treatment. I figured wherever the asshole went, he'd probably get eaten alive, and part of me felt a bit happy about that.

"He ain't coming back, neither," Earl added. "Guards say he's gone for good."

Decker looked too stunned for words.

Earl caught his expression and shrugged. "Serves him right for being such an asshole."

"I guess..." Decker said softly, feeding bits of dry cornflakes to Cockroach. His eyebrows were twisted in knots, and he looked shattered. The only thing grounding him was that damn cat who left crumbs scattered on his blanket.

Earl pulled his playing cards out and shuffled them for a game of one-handed solitaire. "Al's coming back," he added conversationally, not looking up.

Decker's face lit up. "Really?"

Earl folded his lips in and nodded. "Got twenty-four hours in Seg. He should be back this afternoon."

I was surprised they even had Seg in the Home. I'd thought I'd seen all the rooms this little rundown school had to offer. It wouldn't have surprised me if they'd stuffed Al in a janitor's closet. I could practically see a hand-written sign on a piece of printer paper taped to the door with "SEG" scrawled out in Sharpie pen. Wherever Seg was located in this shit heap, it was probably janky as fuck.

I had mad respect for the guy, and I hoped his night in Seg hadn't been too rough. Part of me wished I had the connections to get the man a bag of Takis.

CHAPTER
NINETEEN

The following week moved slow as molasses. I should've been grateful, but being in a cage is rough.

After the fight, things had been tense around the Home for about a day. Everyone seemed bent out of shape about the lockdown that night. Even though guys usually stuck to their rooms at night, the rumple in the normal routine had a weird effect on the residents. I figured most of us were carrying around some serious trauma, and predictability made life run a bit smoother for everyone.

Lockdown aside, nobody shed any tears over losing Mike. Most of the folks bouncing around the Home—guards and inmates alike—didn't dig him too much. The residents liked to keep things mellow, and Mike had always been dramatic and tried to stir up shit. With him gone, everyone could relax a bit.

Al returned the day after the fight and slipped right back into his silent flow. We found him in the rec room, remote in hand, watching *Jeopardy*. With Earl leading the way, we took the seats next to him, filling up the row like nothing had happened. Earl didn't even ask him to change the channel. It was enough to pull Decker out of his shell, and he murmured most of the answers before a contestant could hit the buzzer.

The days dripped by like a leaky faucet. There was laundry day. There was cleaning day—we got put on bathroom duty. A crew went out. All of them came back. We got our three meals.

We played a shit-ton of cards. We gambled when another guy joined us. We lost some shit and won some shit. We also started spending more time in the rec room. After everything had gone down, sitting with Al in the morning became part of our daily routine.

It's weird how being out in the world means all sorts of bad shit, like having to kill people. But when you're inside with the same guys, spinning your wheels, going out to pop a lumper starts to seem not so bad. Riding in the truck and sitting in the bitch-seat eating my knees might be worth it just to feel the breeze from a lowered window and watch the world sweep by. It's nice seeing other people, even if they don't want to see us.

A couple days after the fight, Mike's replacement showed up. He was an older Filipino dude named Jacob with short black hair and a dusting of a goatee across his face. There had been whispers and eye-hustling when his giant frame had first walked in; he was big enough to give me a run for my money. But it turned out the guy was cool. He minded his own business and pulled his weight. He eased right into the routine of the Home, and we all liked him better than Mike.

None of the inmates knew exactly how BCB picked guys for thumper duty. We all started out in the same place after our verdicts were delivered: crying ourselves to sleep behind steel bars, wondering if so-and-so would wait for us to get out. From there, it seemed random: a guy could be in for two days or two years before he was pulled out and moved to a Home. Sometimes, we'd know if he was just switching prisons or if he was going to work out in the world. Other times, the guy would just disappear.

Not knowing if or when someone might be moved was rough. Idle inmates were worse than old biddies in a knitting circle, and they were always getting each other riled up about something they might've heard the guards say. They'd place bets on who was next. When someone got picked, deep down in their hearts, those left behind didn't know whether to be jealous or happy. I guess it depended on the guy.

I'd been in prison for about three months before I got the golden ticket.

It was during rec time—that blessed period when the cell doors were open and we could move freely around the pod. I was in my bunk, sketching on a piece of scratch paper. My bunkie was out doing fuck knows what. The guy talked constantly, and I was enjoying the quiet time alone.

One of the guards walked up and stood just to the side of the cell door. "Castillo?"

I put down the sketch I was working on and peered down from the bunk. "Yeah?"

"You're being moved," the guard announced matter-of-factly with a neutral expression. "Get your stuff together. You'll go right after rec time."

I felt a tingle of apprehension.

At the time, I hadn't known what was going on. I could've been switching pods, moving prisons, or being pulled out for thumper duty. Even though I'd done something terrible, I didn't think they'd pull me for burner duty, but that possibility always sat there like a single bullet in the chamber. A part of me didn't want to know where I was headed, and I sure as fuck didn't want the assholes in my pod knowing either.

Instead of asking, I just said, "Okay, Boss," in a respectful way.

The guard drifted off, and I climbed down from the top bunk. Other than a total of three hair ties, I didn't have fuck-all to bring with me. The pencil and sketchbook were from the prison, and I was pretty sure I couldn't bring them, even if I was just switching pods.

I pulled the linens off my bed, folded them, and stacked them neatly on one end of the bunk. I knew I'd be walking out with those in my arms, the guys in the pod hollering like they always do when someone shuffled out.

I had a few sketches stashed under my mattress. I wasn't sure what I wanted to do with those, but I didn't want to leave them for Mr. Chatty. I took the thin stack and placed it on the linens. After a brief moment of indecision, I added the pencil and sketchbook to the top, figuring it never hurt to try.

Less than a minute later, all my worldly possessions were ready to go.

The buzzer rang, and inmates flowed back into their cells. Mr. Chatty noticed the stack of linens and immediately barraged me with questions. I ignored them, standing to the side, waiting.

After the doors were locked, they came to get me.

Hands through the slot. Cuffs on. Cuffed hands back through the slot. Grabbed the stack of linens. Ignored the shocked look on Mr. Chatty's face. Ignored the jeers as I walked the breezeway and out of the pod.

It wasn't until I was having my personal items checked that they finally told me where I was going.

"You're headed to the Midtown Home for thumper duty."

I was surprised more than anything else. Considering what I'd done to get in there in the first place, I wasn't expecting to get pulled out. I figured I'd be spending every second of those ten years behind a set of prison bars.

When they announced I was going for thumper duty, I couldn't do anything but nod.

A couple days of bogus training later, and I was sharing a room at the Home with Decker and Earl. And even though thumper duty was some of the worst shit I'd ever done, it was nice not looking at bars all the time.

About a week after the fight, Decker, Earl, and I sat on our cots, relaxing after dinner. It had been some sort of sweet mush they called beans and franks. Decker had pulled out all the bits of hotdog and brought the sticky mess back to our room. He'd put the pieces in a rinsed applesauce cup, and Cockroach happily munched away at it.

We hadn't been called out during that whole time, and the days had seeped by. I rested my back against the wall, slung my arms across my bent knees, and watched them. Earl perched on his cot, playing one-handed solitaire.

The weather was comfortably warm, and we were in our T-shirts. A gentle breeze drifted in through the door. It had dried up enough outside that the wet-foot smell had gone away. A few guys were in the courtyard, chatting away, and the scent of cigarette smoke trailed in.

"You know what I could totally go for right now?" Earl said wistfully. "A big fat steak."

Decker snorted. "You just ate."

Earl dropped his hand in his lap and looked up from his cards, incredulous. He nodded his chin to the dog barf that Cockroach was lapping up. "You call that food?"

"Cockroach likes it," he replied.

Earl picked his hand back up and started shifting cards. "A big steak. Nothing fancy. Just salt and pepper. Done medium rare on the barbecue."

"Just the steak?" Decker asked.

"Mmmhmm," Earl answered, practically salivating.

I was right there with him. A steak sounded pretty fucking amazing. And even though I'd cleared my tray in the chow hall, I'd find room for it.

Decker looked up thoughtfully. "I'd want some potato salad with it. The kind my nanna used to make with the dill in it."

"Dill?" Earl snorted. "What the fuck, man?! Who puts dill in potato salad? That's a travesty, bro."

"What?" Decker replied somewhat defensively. "The way my nanna made it was delicious."

I thought back to the lumper we'd piked from Seavy Circle: the old lady in the nightie with the small blue flowers with pink dots. I imagined her making potato salad and serving it up to her grandson. I wondered who was making him potato salad now, and if they put any dill in it.

Earl had finished the round, and shuffled the cards. "I don't need no potato salad. Just the steak."

Cockroach had finished his second-hand meal and swiped his paw across his face.

Decker reached down to pet him and said, "You know what I *really* want? Ice cream. From Vic's."

Earl snorted. "Of course, your bougie Land Park ass would be going to Vic's."

Decker lifted one shoulder. "Meh. Their ice cream is nothing special. It just tastes better in a legit malt shop."

I'd take it all right about now: the steak, the potato salad, and the ice cream. I wouldn't care one way or another about the dill. And I wouldn't give two shits about where the ice cream came from. Though if I had my druthers, it'd be that little shop on the corner of 34th and Broadway. The one that had fancy ice cream names, like "Kitty, Kitty, Bang, Bang" and "Fat Elvis."

I hoped the place was still around when I got out.

There'd be none of that shit for me until then, though. I'd given into the rage, and now I wouldn't be getting anything like a steak or ice cream for another ten years. I thought about how many lumpers I'd have to pop over that long stretch, and then I wondered if I'd even be able to enjoy anything as simple as steak or an ice cream after that.

"What about you, Bear?" Decker asked.

The question surprised me. I wasn't one to speak up. Plus, Decker and Earl usually kept a conversation going well enough without me.

"Hm," I replied, trying to buy myself time to think.

There were a lot of things I missed, and most of them weren't food. But what I really hankered for bobbed right up to the top of my thoughts.

"Tacos," I said. "With carne asada. From that truck that's always out on Martin Luther King and 6th."

"Oh, tacos," Decker moaned wistfully.

"With those small, handmade corn tortillas and that crumbled white cheese," Earl added. "That's some good shit."

"And fresh pico," Decker slipped in.

I nodded. "Tacos," I repeated in a half-whisper.

I could see myself standing in line at the truck after a long day on the construction site. I'd still be in my work clothes, dusty from handling the rebar. My arms would be tanned dark brown from the end of my shirt sleeves to the cuff of my work gloves. My hair would be braided back, and there'd be a dent where my hard hat had pressed against my sweaty head.

Maria or one of her daughters would hand me a little paper boat holding four tacos and a beer. I'd sit at one of the plastic tables they set out in the empty lot and enjoy every single bite.

In ten years, maybe I could go back. If they were still around.

If *I* were still around.

Decker shifted back onto his cot with a creak, pulling me out of my thoughts. Cockroach jumped up next to him and curled into a meatloaf. Decker ran his fingers along Cockroach's back, and then there came a low, rumbling purr.

"You and that cat," Earl said, not unkindly.

"You're just jealous," Decker teased.

"Psht," he snorted. "Jealous of you or the cat?"

Decker huffed a laugh. "Couldn't it be both?"

"Fuck no," Earl replied.

Decker made a *hmpf* sound.

I wondered what Decker meant by the question. It was hard being in a place where no one loved you. And though the three of us had a friendship of sorts, we were nowhere near a brotherhood that would be strong enough to last outside of prison.

I wasn't a cat man myself, but there was something about the way Cockroach always showed up for Decker that made me a bit jealous. Of course, Decker fed him all the time. But Cockroach always decided to stay for snuggles after, and that had to mean something.

It seemed Decker didn't have anyone outside of prison who cared about him anymore; Cockroach was probably it. Decker was clearly all Cockroach had. I wondered if Cockroach had ever had a real home with fancy cat litter, a fluffy cat bed, and genuine cat food instead of hotdog slices fished out of sticky-sweet sauce. Then, I wondered if it even mattered. Decker took good care of him, and he looked happy. All those trappings of a cushy life didn't mean shit without a buddy, and Decker was just that.

Decker still had over a year of time, and who knew if Cockroach would even make it that long. Living on the streets had its risks. But once Decker's time was up, I couldn't help but wonder what would happen to the little guy.

CHAPTER
TWENTY

It was a beautiful Friday afternoon when everything went to shit.

We spent the morning watching soaps with Al. Lunch had been limp microwave burritos that were bland but not awful. The warm air of spring made the courtyard half-decent, and the perfect temps seemed to cheer everyone up.

An hour or so after lunch, Brown found us in the courtyard. His dark hair had been freshly buzzed into a high-and-tight haircut. Even though he'd surely shaved this morning, a shadow of a beard started to peek through. His uniform was on point, as always. He held his hands loosely at his sides in a non-threatening way.

"Team Four, you're up," he said in a monotone.

My gut clenched.

I was up next for piking duty, and the thought of popping a grandma or a sad homeless guy made me sick. The thought of those damn pink toenails was even worse. They still haunted me at night.

Earl tossed his hand on the table with a *thud*, and the cards fanned out. "Well, shit. I was winning."

Decker smirked. "Yeah, right."

Decker and I put our cards down, and Earl swept them into a pile before putting them away.

"Hurry up, boys," Brown said, casually. "Central wants this taken care of before everyone gets off work."

Earl sucked his lips but obliged.

Decker and I trailed behind Earl. Brown followed us back to our room and waited outside the door, facing the courtyard, while we sifted through our clothes to find a set of coveralls.

Once dressed, I sat on the edge of my cot and pulled my boots on. A moment of hesitation preceded every movement. I was starting to understand how Decker felt. I didn't want to kill someone today. I'd be just fine never killing anyone again.

I knew Earl didn't like killing either. But he was able to go someplace else while he did the dirty deed and still come back acting normal. I wondered how he'd sectioned himself off like that and how hard it was to do. If I were going to make it through my sentence, I needed a place like that in my head.

Earl had practice, though. It was obvious he'd seen some shit in the service. No one had shared the details, but I figured it had been pretty dark based on that faraway look in his eye when he'd piked that grandma.

After we'd changed into our coveralls, we followed Brown to the front office, my feet dragging on the cement. I'd do anything to have them say it was all a mix-up and send us back to our room, but I knew that would never happen.

Brown buzzed us in and announced, "Team Four." He held the door for us as we passed through.

Ramos was behind the counter. "ID cards, please," she directed.

Each of us obliged, passing them over for her to scan. After three small beeps, she passed them back through. Earl returned them to us, and we clipped them on our chest pockets.

Decker and I hung back as Earl waited at the counter.

Ramos grabbed a slim stack of papers, tapped them once on the desk, and put a staple in the top before sliding it over. "1407 11th Ave."

Earl looked up from the papers. "Isn't that Land Park?" he asked, looking a tad incredulous.

Ramos pushed the truck keys across. She caught his eyes and frowned slightly. "Yes, that's Land Park."

Decker shifted next to me and started rocking slightly. His hand jumped to his cheek, and he started picking at his skin. He glanced at me, and his face crumpled with worry.

It hit me that I'd be piking a posh person today. I wasn't sure how I felt about that. I hated the high-and-mighty rich folk, always thinking they were better than us and having no problem earning money while riding on our backs.

Hating them was different than killing one of them, though. And I wasn't sure how the richies in Land Park would feel about two brown dudes and a white-trash tweaker rolling into their la-dee-da neighborhood with pikes in their hands.

Ramos interlaced her fingers and rested her hands on the counter in front of her. She locked eyes with Earl. "Look. Be careful today, alright?" Her voice was earnest, and it sent gooseflesh up and down my arms.

Earl frowned deeply, his lips pulling down to his chin. "Whatchu mean?"

Ramos sighed and shook her head slightly. "This one hasn't been confirmed."

"What?" Earl blurted, eyebrows shooting up. He gestured to Decker and me before turning back. "We can't go into Land Park of all places to pike an unconfirmed lumper. What the fuck?" His voice was loud and agitated.

"Watch yourself, inmate," Jackson called from behind Ramos.

"Sorry," Earl said quietly to Ramos.

"You'll need to confirm she's infected before you put her down," Ramos said. She leaned forward and spoke softly so Jackson couldn't hear. "Just be careful. Something doesn't smell right with this one."

"But...." Earl's eyes flicked down at the papers and up to Ramos. "This ain't never happened before. We need to know what we're walking into. Are there pictures at least?"

Ramos nodded to the packet. "Pictures of the woman are on the second page. But none of the lesions."

"What the fuck?" Earl said, voice hushed. "We're not being sent in to murder someone, are we?"

"We're always being sent in to murder someone," Decker murmured under his breath.

Ramos heard and practically rolled her eyes. "It's not murder when it's a lumper." After a beat, she added, "Somebody probably pulled some strings so they could skip the confirmation step. Not sure why, but something's off."

"Fuck," Earl said and started sifting through the papers.

"There's supposedly a dog, too," she added. "The husband was explicit about not hurting the dog."

Earl looked slightly offended. "We don't kill dogs."

Ramos shrugged. "Just passing on the message." She nudged the keys closer to Earl. "Better get going. They want you out of there before five."

"They? They who?" Earl asked.

"Good luck out there," Ramos replied with sincerity, not answering Earl's question, and turned back to her computer.

Earl palmed the keys and snatched up the packet. He turned to us, lips folded into a tight frown. Deep furrows creased the skin between his eyebrows.

We passed through the doors, and the cheery afternoon sun danced across our faces. If I hadn't been going out to pike some rich lady, I would've stopped for a moment to enjoy it. Now, all I could do was pile into the bitch seat and wait for Earl to fill in the blanks.

Earl rubbed his fingers between his eyebrows as he read through the packet.

"What is it? Anything else in there?" Decker asked nervously, sewing machine leg bouncing.

"Forty-three-year-old white female. Name's Olivia Kingston." Earl turned to show us the picture.

The woman's blond hair was styled in an elegant bob. I was pretty sure she probably had some gray, but the dye job was good, and no one could tell it was fake without knowing her actual age. She'd also either had some work done or the picture had a filter, because she didn't have enough wrinkles to be forty-three.

"Damn," Decker said in a half whisper.

I wasn't sure if he'd said that because the woman had a beautiful smile of perfectly straight, pearly white teeth and crystal blue eyes, or if he was exclaiming about the delicate diamond necklace laced around her neck. That thing was probably worth more than a house. Decker came from rich folk, though, and I figured seeing a string of ice wouldn't elicit such a response.

Then, I wondered if maybe he knew her.

Earl pulled the papers back. "Says here that her husband is out of the country on a business trip, but his wife had complained about headaches. Contact tracing put her in proximity to her maid, who was infected. The maid was put down a month ago."

"A month? That can't be right," Decker mumbled nervously.

I quickly did the mental math and agreed with a slight nod. The Lumps blasted through a body like wildfire. Within a day or two of exposure, the first mass would spring up at the site of contact. From there, it spread easily across other parts of the skin. Once it hit the bloodstream, it started feasting on the brain.

I wondered if the woman had somehow bypassed the strip-search required by the contract tracers. I knew rich people bent the rules all the time, but this was a fucking public health issue. Surely, the only accommodation she should've gotten was letting her private doctor have a look. How much would it cost to pay the contact tracers off?

More than that necklace hanging around her neck, I bet.

I also wondered who she'd exposed while swimming in her ocean of privilege. How many more people would we have to pike because she was a selfish bitch?

A slow-burning hatred for the woman built in my stomach.

The sound of a flipping page dragged me out of my thoughts.

"She walks the dog every day in the park, and the neighbors haven't seen her leave the house in a while," Earl continued. "Husband said he had a video call with his wife and thought he saw a lump above her eyebrow. No pictures of it, though. Said she got really angry when he asked her about it. She hasn't answered any texts or calls in three days."

"Maybe she faked it to leave him," Decker offered, sounding bitter.

"And go completely off the radar?" Earl scoffed. "Yeah, right. I'm sure she wouldn't want to miss the country club luncheons with her girlfriends."

"Maybe he beats her or something. Threatened her," Decker replied somewhat defensively.

Earl sucked his teeth. "Nah, she didn't run away. She's got the Lumps."

"Then why didn't the team confirm it? Something ain't right, man. I can feel it." Decker looked at the window and started chewing the nubs of his nails.

I didn't like it either.

I knew richies didn't have to go through the same shit normal people did. But too many things weren't sitting right. First, the tracers had somehow missed her. Then, the husband called her in to BCB based on something he thought he saw on a video call. And now, they were sending us out to pop her when she hadn't been confirmed. It was fucking weird.

"Why do they want us out of the district so fast?" Decker asked the window.

Yeah, that's bugging me, too.

Maybe the husband wanted to spare the neighbors the sight of watching the messy cleanup. Maybe he wanted to keep the whole thing under wraps. But someone couldn't just hide the fact that there was a lumper in their house. We'd be spraying the fucking "L" on his door like we did all the others.

Earl looked over his shoulder to make eye contact with me. "We gotta take this one slow, alright? Make sure we do everything by the book. I don't want to kill some rich lady who ain't sick."

I nodded slightly and looked down at my hands, thinking about how I really didn't want to kill *anyone* today, even if she was some privileged little shit with the Lumps who bent the rules and probably fucked over a handful of people in the process.

Earl turned back to the papers. "Watch out for the dog. The paperwork doesn't say what kind it is, but it could cause us trouble."

"It's been a month since she was exposed. It's probably dead. I bet she forgot to feed it," Decker said morosely.

"Fuck, Decker," Earl growled. "Would you stop?"

Decker looked up, and a flash of hurt crossed his face. He hunched his shoulders and turned back to the window.

Earl's eyes darted to me in the rearview mirror and then back to Decker. The pinched look around his eyes showed how pissed he was getting.

"Look, fuckers," Earl barked. "This is bad. We know it's gonna be bad. So, we do everything by the book. Got it? And we don't touch the fucking dog." His eyes caught mine in the rearview mirror again. "And no matter what, confirm it first. Got it? If we go in and pike some rich white lady who ain't a lumper, we are *fucked*."

My stomach clenched, and I nodded.

"Decker?" Earl said, turning to him.

He didn't respond, so Earl nudged him with his elbow. Decker jumped and faced him.

"Decker?" Earl repeated, voice stern. "Got it?"

"Yeah," he replied softly. "Got it."

Earl sighed heavily, fired up the truck, and pulled out of the parking lot.

CHAPTER
TWENTY-ONE

As we passed through the city, the knot in my gut just kept getting tighter. I wondered how many more of these fucked up drives I'd be taking before I was released.

Would I even be the same person when I got out?

I didn't think so. I'd started to think that piking lumpers was just as bad as clearing fucking buildings in Fallujah. There was some shit that just couldn't be unseen. It was hard to be "normal" after something like that. I figured I'd be carrying this shit with me to the grave.

We wove through midtown at an even twenty miles an hour, and the buildings sailed by. Sacramento's midtown skyline was mostly one to two-story buildings. On the north side, there was a mix of hundred-year-old Edwardian and Victorian-style homes. As we moved closer to the capitol building, more restaurants, coffee shops, and bland office buildings appeared.

The sweep of the capitol lawn passed on our right. Two small kids played tag in the rose garden, and an older woman kept a close eye from a park bench. At the red light, people in business suits swept past in the crosswalk, busy on their phones.

It all felt so normal.

The truck rumbled forward when the light turned green. We passed an open checkpoint and through the rest of midtown. On the south side, the houses were smaller and stacked tightly together, interrupted by stretches of new condos that would pop in and out.

When we passed under the shadow of the freeway, my pits started to sweat. I kept wishing Earl would slow for the yellow lights. I wanted to spend just a few more moments feeling as close to normal as possible. I kept wanting to delay whatever fucked up mess was waiting for us at 1407 11th Ave.

After we drove through the next checkpoint, I watched the people in the other cars while we waited at the reds. I knew it was a bit creepy, but I was trying to take a sip of what it felt like to be free again. Every once in a while, someone would catch me looking. Then, they'd see the BCB logo on the truck, and their eyes would dart away. They treated us like shit floating in the toilet bowl. We were a necessary part of life that they'd try to ignore. They'd hold their breath and look away while they flushed us down. It made me feel dirty and unwanted.

The street ended at the intersection with Broadway. To the left, the iconic spire of the Tower Theater reached above the trees clustered around the adjacent cafe. Even at this time of day, there was a line out front.

Earl turned the car in the opposite direction. We hit Riverside Blvd. a few blocks down and turned south.

We passed a familiar old cemetery. My mental map placed Seavy Circle less than half a mile west of here. The kids from that neighborhood probably had to walk through the snazzy streets of Land Park and past all of these richie houses to get to the high school on Freeport.

What's that like for them? The thought chafed, and the rage bubbled up.

Ahead, the sweep of the infamous Land Park trees spread out before us like a deep green shroud. The small homes turned into mansions, and the housing prices instantly jumped up to the stars. The richies were out, jogging in spandex and pushing strollers in their yoga pants.

We passed an ice cream shop on the left, and with a start, I realized it was Vic's. I could see what Earl had meant about Decker being posh if he were getting ice cream there. It was like a tiny little piece of the 1950s, perfectly preserved and surrounded by multi-million-dollar homes.

I couldn't watch anymore. I looked down at my hands, opening and closing my fists and trying not to think about how I'd gotten myself into this mess. Trying not to think about what I'd look like on the other side of it all.

The checkpoint for District 7 sat just past the intersection of Riverside Blvd. and 8th Ave. I figured it was strategically placed there to keep the real richies separate from the upper middle class. The latter group could serve as a buffer between the public housing projects and bums who shuffled along Broadway.

The slow fire of anger burned in my chest.

Earl pulled the truck up to the checkpoint gate. He rolled his window down, pressed the buzzer, and waited for the guard to come out.

District 7's checkpoint was a world apart from any other checkpoint I'd passed through. High stone walls topped with decorative spikes stretched in both directions.

The guard post was slick. It was constructed in the same fancy stone as the walls and was painted with a flashy white trim. A rainbow of carefully selected flowers graced decorative planters. It was entirely enclosed and appeared to have a working HVAC. Six monitors filled one wall. A second guard rested in a chair in front of them. I'd never seen a guard post like it before.

The first guard slipped through the door and stepped onto the curb. "Yes?" he asked with a scowl.

He didn't look like the guards at the other checkpoints, and he clearly didn't work for the city either. He wore a private security uniform. He was slim and well-groomed. I figured he must have a gun on him somewhere, but I couldn't see it from where I sat. I was sure it was discreetly tucked away so as not to ruffle the feathers of the richies.

"Team Four from BCB," Earl said as he passed our ID cards through the window.

The guard scanned them and handed them back to us. "Know where you're going?"

"Yes, sir," Earl said. Though he tried to be polite, I could tell he was irritated.

The guard studied us for a minute, not moving to open the gate. "You need to be out of here before five."

Earl's shoulders stiffened slightly. "Yes, sir."

"Stay on Riverside and 11th," the guard said. "If you turn down any other street, I'm calling you in."

I took a hard look at the scrawny piece of shit who was talking to us like we were dirt, and was just about ready to push the door open and beat his face in. Since I didn't want to be piking lumpers for another three to five years, I clenched my fists and took a few deep breaths instead.

"Just so you are aware, we have a full inventory of the Kingstons' home. If anything is found to be missing, it will be reported," the guard added.

"You fucking kidding me?" Earl growled, just as offended as the rest of us.

The guard took a step back. "Do I need to call you in now?"

"Open the gate," Earl replied, cranking the handle to roll up his window.

The guard frowned and hesitated before turning back into his cushy post to open the gate. It slid wide smoothly and silently.

Earl drove through without giving the guy another glance. "Fucking asshole," he muttered.

Decker was pale and unusually silent. I wondered what it was like for him, being on the other side of all that shit. To be one of the richies and then be one of the dregs. That was a long way to fall.

The blinker made a *tink, tink, tink* sound, and Earl turned onto 11th Ave. Mansions passed by on the left. The sprawl of William Land Regional Park, with its perfect landscaping and thick tree cover, sat on the right.

The expansive 160-acre park was bordered by a well-kept running path. Large swaths of perfectly mowed lawn stretched from 11th to a large playground. Further down, there was a baseball field, and beyond that, a pond. The trees were old, so much so that some of them were probably here when Sutter first placed his dirty boot on the neck of the locals. The redwoods had trunks so big that I could stretch my arms around them and still be a good three or four feet from being able to touch my hands together. Large oaks, pines, and sycamores were intermixed. Squirrels hopped between trees, enjoying the emptiness of the space during the lockdown.

Earl pulled over to the right and parked opposite the home.

Our destination loomed across the street: a two-story colonial. It had a brick face with bright white columns that supported the roof as it hung over a large porch. The windows were bordered with bright white trim and decorative forest-green shutters.

The garden was immaculate. Topiary framed the house. Camelias heavy with dark red flowers crouched in a tidy row parallel to the porch, leaving an opening for a delicately paved pathway that stretched a good twenty to thirty feet from the sidewalk to the home. The driveway slid down the right of the house to a three-car garage that was tucked discreetly in the back. A fancy spring wreath hung from the front door.

Earl turned off the engine and stared at the house. "Fuck," he muttered. "That's gonna be a bitch to clear. How many bedrooms do you think it has? Four? Five?"

Decker's eyebrows furrowed, and he started to fidget. "Who knows how that space is divided up? There might even be a mother-in-law's suite in the backyard."

The place screamed money. The main home had to be pushing four thousand square feet. I was pretty sure the house had been there for more than fifty years, but I bet it had been renovated to a nice open floor plan. If so, that would make it much easier to clear.

It was still a fuck-ton of area to cover while we looked for a woman who may or may not have the Lumps in a home where a dog of unknown size and temperament may or may not still be alive.

"Welp," Earl said, sounding a bit disgusted. "Time waits for no man. Let's get this shit done and get the fuck out of here."

CHAPTER TWENTY-TWO

There was no putting it off any longer. We had to face whatever was inside the home at 1407 11th Ave., regardless of the feeling in our guts.

With my heart thumping and muscles tense, I climbed out and followed Decker to the back of the truck. Earl was already there. He dropped the tailgate and pulled out the gear.

There was an eerie absence of human sound. Despite the many freeways that laced though the city, the usual background hum of traffic was absent this deep inside Land Park. There were no gardening crews with leaf blowers or lawnmowers. No slapping feet and puffs of breath as someone ran the jogging path. No casual conversation between retirees dressed in respectable athletic gear as they made their afternoon loop through the park. The only sound was the twittering of some finches and the occasional chitter of a squirrel.

I zipped up my Tyvek suit and took a deep breath of the rich air.

Even though we were deep in the city, the tree canopy over the park cleared all the grime away. It was a fresh, earthy smell. This close to the park, I could practically close my eyes and pretend I was away from all this mess. I could pretend I wasn't going to have to pike a richie in about ten minutes.

The house crouched across the street must be worth a pretty penny since it faced the park. The view was something special, especially since this was the only park in the city without homeless camps mucking it up. I figured Cowboy Joe and his crew up at the guard post made sure only the "right" people came through that checkpoint. Part of me wondered if those gates were always closed.

Fairytale Town and the Sac Zoo were on the other side of the huge swath of green—far enough away that I couldn't see either of them from 11th Ave. I figured the district's fences probably carved right around them, locking them and all the families who went there out of this paradise. It disgusted me that the richies could just lock people out of a public park because they didn't want to look at them.

"Bear," Earl said, pulling my thoughts back to the present.

I nodded my chin in response.

"You're on piking duty today. Get your head in the game," he grumbled.

Earl and Decker had already geared up. I quickly pulled on my shoe covers, gloves, and flimsy, disposable face shield. Wisps of hair got stuck in the janky foam band, and for the millionth time, I wished I'd worn a hair tie.

We moved to the left side of the truck and faced the house sitting on the other side of the freshly paved asphalt.

A curtain fluttered in one of the first-story windows on the home next door.

"We got an audience," Earl said in a hushed voice. "We gotta assume they're watching us. Plus, I'd bet money they're gonna have cameras on us, too. Keep your cool, alright?"

Earl turned to us, his face serious, and we nodded.

Earl folded his upper lip in and considered the house. "Looks like a heavy door. We're gonna need the ram." After a moment of consideration, he continued, "Okay, let's run through this. Everything has gotta be by the book. I'll announce us. Bear, you ram the door since Decker here can't even lift the fucking thing."

"Geez," Decker interrupted, looking a tad hurt at the slight. Earl shrugged, unabashed. "It's the truth."

"I guess," Decker replied doubtfully.

"Bear, you'll ram the door," Earl repeated. "As soon as the door opens, drop the ram and grab your pike. Got it?"

I nodded, feeling the tingle of anticipation same as right before a fight.

"I'll take point," Earl continued. "We ain't splitting up today. Stay together to clear the rooms. Understand?"

"Shouldn't Bear be on point? He's piking today, ain't he?" Decker said, worried. "The person piking is the person on point."

For as many times as Earl had said "by the book," I was also a bit surprised that he was doing the exact opposite. But I'd grown to trust him.

"Look," Earl said, voice hushed. "Something ain't right. I don't know what it is. But I've cleared more rooms than anyone in the Home if you count the shit I did before thumper duty. I want to suss things out before one of you dumbasses puts a pike in something you shouldn't. I'm clearing today."

The last sentence was said firmly and brooked no argument.

Decker and I nodded.

"Once we've found her, we all got to get eyes on a lump. Clear? I don't want no one saying we killed someone who ain't sick. All of us gotta see it. Got it? No arguments. No pussing out, either."

"Yes, sir," Decker said.

I nodded, trying to keep my heart rate in check.

"And keep your voices down." He pointed his chin in the direction of the twitching curtain. "I don't want that bitch telling everyone at the country club what we were saying when we popped this chick. Got it?"

Decker and I nodded again.

Earl took a deep breath and pulled the walkie from his belt. "Team Four reporting. Arrived at District 7."

"Roger that, Team Four," someone replied. "It's three thirty. Make sure to clear out by five."

Earl gave us an exacerbated look and shook his head in disgust before pressing the button on the walkie and replying, "Roger."

Earl clipped the walkie back on his belt and finished zipping up his Tyvek suit. He reached into the truck for the ram, lifted it out, and handed it to me. I tested the weight, thinking it wasn't all Earl made it out to be. Decker pulled out the three pikes.

We turned to the monster of a house. Earl led us up the path, head down, ignoring whoever watched us from the home on the right. Decker was next, twitchy as fuck, jumping at every little sound. I took up the rear, trying my best to get my head in the game.

Earl stood just to the left of the front door. Decker stood to the right. I took center but back a few paces, ready to step forward and ram the door.

Earl knocked three times. "BCB. Anyone home?" he called out.

Decker's eyes darted to me and back to Earl as he shifted on his feet.

"Calm the fuck down, Decker," Earl hissed without looking at him.

I expected Earl to step back and let me ram the door. Instead, he rang the doorbell and knocked three times. "BCB. Anyone home?" he called again.

A crash echoed from somewhere toward the back of the house, followed by silence.

"We going in or what, Earl?" Decker whispered nervously.

I knew why Earl hesitated. If three felons bashed in some rich white lady's door without cause, we'd either get shot or strung up. He was making sure that all the cameras and the eye-hustlers knew we were giving her ample opportunity to come forward before we rammed the shit out of her Norman Rockwell door.

Earl stepped to the side. "Go for it, Bear," he commanded, voice low.

I stepped forward, positioning myself on the hinge side of the door. I pushed my right boot up against the threshold and squared myself to the opening. I grabbed the handles of the ram with two hands, swung it back, and let the momentum push it forward between the knob and the deadbolt.

The ram hit with a loud *smack* followed by the sound of crunching wood.

The door held.

Another crash sounded from somewhere in the house. I looked back to Earl. He was in the zone, body tense. Without looking up, he commanded, "Again."

I swung again, and with a booming *thwack*, the door splintered open around the deadbolt.

Stepping back, I dropped the ram to the ground and grabbed my pike from Decker in a fluid motion.

Earl was already moving in. He held his pike by two hands at waist level, half crouched and at an angle, every muscle tense as his eyes scanned the room.

Earl's head turned to sweep the room. "Clear," he said loud enough so only we could hear. He stepped in and moved to the left as I followed in behind. "Dead dog on the right. Blood is from the dog."

"What?" Decker whispered nervously from behind me.

I caught the dog out of the corner of my eye. Goosebumps traced up my arms. "Earl," I said, wanting him to stop. Wanting him to give me a second to get my shit together.

Earl ignored me and swept the entryway. Stairs arched up on either side, bracketing a large chandelier that hung from the second-story ceiling.

Decker stepped through the door and caught sight of the dog. "Oh fuck. Oh fuck. Oh fuck. Earl?" It came out in a low, panicked murmur, and he froze.

"Stand watch. Checking the center door," Earl commanded quietly. He moved to a small door tucked under the staircase. "Closet is clear."

"Bear," Decker whispered to me. "The dog...it's...what the fuck, man?"

Without turning around, Earl said, "Decker, watch the stairs and the door on the right. Bear, you're with me."

"I thought we weren't splitting up?" Decker said, looking a bit frantic.

"Too many access points," Earl said, voice like a robot, and started moving to the next room.

Decker looked like he might piss himself as he tried to process the mess of slashed white hair and congealed blood on the entryway floor. His knuckles were bone-white from gripping the pike. He turned his back to the front door, eyes darting between the sets of stairs and the door on the right.

I followed Earl through the door on the left into a large sitting room. Our fuzzy reflections flashed across the blank screen of the large TV mounted between the windows on the left. He moved around the plush couches and fancy chairs, checking behind each of them. I wasn't sure if he was looking for another dead body or what.

Adrenaline raced through my system.

"Clear," Earl said, voice low and mechanical. "Moving to the next room."

The room toward the back of the house was a large dining area. I took in all of the details in seconds: a broad mahogany table with eight cushioned chairs, a minibar in the far corner, and sweeping glass doors that opened to a backyard with a pool.

After checking behind the bar, Earl repeated, "Clear, moving to the next room."

We passed through large double doors into an expansive kitchen. To the left, there was a small kitchenette table with four chairs and a bay window, complete with a cushy window seat. The kitchen itself was huge and sparkling clean. A large island sat in the center with a bowl of rotting fruit.

Two smaller doors broke up the wall on the right, and both of them were closed. Earl stood to the side, swung one open, and then peeked in. "Bathroom clear."

He moved to the next door and repeated the movements. "Pantry clear."

His eyes swept once more across the kitchen.

"Clear, moving to the next room," Earl repeated quietly as he moved around the island to the rooms on the opposite side of the house.

We passed through another set of doors and into a library. Bookcases were stuffed from floor to ceiling with fancy books. A large desk sat near a window straight ahead of us. A wood-burning fireplace crouched to the left.

Earl leaned to peek over the desk. "Clear."

I wondered why he kept looking around the furniture. We almost always found lumpers in their beds. Every once in a while, they'd be slumped on the couch or shuffling around.

Then it hit me, and I realized he was looking for a dead body. Just like the dog.

Who the hell had done that to the dog?

My pits started to sweat, and my heart rate sped up again. If I didn't do something with all this adrenaline soon, I'd get the shakes. And, even though Earl was checking the ground for a dead body, there was still a pretty good chance that I'd have to pike someone soon.

"Moving to the next room," Earl said.

The set of doors on the right was closed. Earl knocked lightly, and stepped to the side. He nodded his chin to me and then to the door.

I stood to the side, back to the wall, waiting for his cue.

He held up three fingers and silently counted backward, dropping each finger until he made a tight fist.

I quickly reached forward with my free hand, twisted the knob, and pushed it open. Earl moved smoothly through.

He disappeared quickly, and I followed him in. The last room was another sitting area. A grand piano took up one corner. The rest of the space had tastefully arranged chairs with color-coordinated pillows that looked like they'd never been used.

"Clear," Earl said. He dropped his pike to his side and turned to me, frowning. He nodded his head to the closed door on our right. "Decker should be on the other side of that. The lumper must be upstairs."

He moved to the door on the right and tapped it with the tip of his pike. "Decker? It's us. Coming through."

"Okay," he responded weakly, voice muffled.

Earl passed through the door, making sure to keep the front of his body turned toward the stairs.

"Nothing?" Decker whispered nervously. He chewed at his lip, and there was a small flash of red where he'd nipped a piece of chapped skin away.

"She's probably up there," Earl said quietly. He sighed heavily and folded his lips in.

"What happened to the dog, Earl?" Decker asked, voice low and shaky. His eyebrows were crunched together. "This is fucked up, man."

Earl frowned at him. We all knew something was off about this run, but Decker's jumpy ass only made shit worse.

"Cut it out, would ya?" Earl hissed. "Get your shit together, bro."

Decker's eyebrows wrinkled with hurt.

We looked back to the sweep of the stairs, and a hush settled over the house. The upstairs rooms faced the landing in a large U-shape. The doors of the rooms yawned open. Ornamental tables pressed against the wall of the landing and were decorated with picture frames and vases. Even from the story below, I could tell the sagging flowers were brown; they'd been dead for at least a couple of weeks.

The hair on the back of my neck went up, and it took everything in me not to look down at the dog lying in a pool of dried blood a few feet away.

"I'll go first. Bear, you're second. Decker, you take the rear. Stagger yourselves up the stairs, got it?" Earl commanded in a hushed voice.

We nodded as he looked to each of us.

Earl moved slowly up the steps, eyes darting between the open doors on the second floor. He turned into the room on the right, pike in front of him.

I swept behind him, moving to the left of the door, holding my pike in both hands. I turned to do a visual sweep of the landing, and my pike caught an empty vase. It crashed to the floor.

Earl turned his head and hissed before turning back to clear the room.

I released the pike into a one-handed hold and reflexively crouched to pick up the broken vase just as Decker put one foot on the top stair.

That's when I first saw her.

In my mind, everything slowed to a crawl, and each millisecond was a snapshot. But when I tried to react, everything around me moved at lightning speed.

The woman streaked out of the room at the far end of the landing. She made a shrieking sound that was something halfway between a moan and a scream. Her blond bob was a rat's nest. Her pink, satiny robe fluttered behind her like a cape as she flew past.

I tried to stand, and my pike caught on the leg of the table, jarring me and knocking a few of the pictures down. The butt-end of the pike stuck in the legs of the table and had me half-pinned against the wall.

She sped right past me, wailing like a banshee. She gave Decker just enough of a bump to send him sprawling down the stairs with a cry.

She leapt like a fucking leopard through the door and onto Earl's back. He let out a surprised "Oof!" and there was a booming *thud* as they both hit the floor.

I forced myself to stand, yanking my pike and dumping the table over with a loud *crash*. I swiveled around to face Earl.

He was down, stomach pressed to the ground, arms and pike trapped beneath him. The bitch lay spread-eagle across him, snapping at the back of his neck and side of his head. His face shield had twisted to the side, flat against the ground, and his face was exposed.

"Ah! Fuck! Get it off me!" Earl blared. He bucked and managed to get one arm free. His hand swatted toward his back.

With a quick snap, she took a solid bite out of his flailing hand.

That's when the screaming started.

I sped into the room and kicked her, trying to get her off him.

"Stab her! Fucking stab her!" Earl's scream gurgled with blood as he tried to push himself onto his side.

Blood was fucking everywhere, and I had to fight through the rising panic. I stabbed the pike down hard, trying to get an angle that wouldn't pierce straight through to Earl. But everything was happening so fast, and I didn't have time to do fucking trig or some shit to make sure my angle was right. I just wanted to put the bitch down and get her off him.

She was still chomping at his neck when I pulled the pike out of her side and struck her again. With that, she started to lose steam, and Earl finally managed to crawl free. She rolled on her back, gasping and grunting, blood streaking down her cheeks. I piked her a third time, feeling the metal hit bone, slide to the side, and into her chest with my full weight behind it.

She emitted a loud groan, and blood bubbled up from her mouth.

I released the pike and stumbled back, panting, and fought the racing adrenaline.

Her body went limp, and her chest went still. She was finally fucking dead.

Earl had crawled a foot or so away and was lying on his back. He'd somehow managed to get his face shield all the way off. He huffed for breath, and his eyes stared up at the ceiling.

Blood was everywhere.

"Earl! Fuck! Earl!" I rushed to his side.

His head rested in a bright pool of blood. A piece of his ear was missing, and a large bloody crater filled his cheek. The bite on his neck was the one I was the most worried about. Instead of oozing, the blood rhythmically pumped out. I pressed my gloved hands over it.

His eyes shifted to my face, unfocused.

"Fuck, man," I whispered, watching the blood pulse through my fingers.

I knew he was dying right there in front of me.

A fucked up part of me thought that was a good thing. Even if he survived the blood loss, she'd surely infected him, and he was fucked either way.

"It's alright, man. I got you," I whispered. I took one hand off his neck and slipped my palm under his. His fingers were limp in mine. I watched the pulsing blood slow to a trickle.

A deep gurgling exhale escaped, and I knew he was gone. I didn't know fuck-all about medicine and shit, but I pressed my fingers where I thought I should on the intact side of his neck, checking for a pulse. I didn't feel anything. His chest wasn't rising either.

I stood, felt the wooziness of a head rush, and stepped back.

"Decker!" I called, unable to take my eyes off the shitshow in front of me. "You alright, man?"

I was met with silence.

I backed out of the room, covered in blood, unsure if it was Earl's or the woman's, and figured it was a bit of both. Bloody footprints followed me out.

Decker was at the bottom of the stairs. His left leg sat at an odd angle, and blood soaked around a tented structure in his thigh that could only be bone. Blood seeped from his head and onto the marble floors. He'd lost his face shield and one of his shoe covers on the way down.

I stumbled down the stairs, holding the banisters with both hands. Even with the carpet, my feet were slippery.

I crouched a few feet away from Decker.

"Decker?" I wanted to give him a shake, but I was covered in blood.

His eyes fluttered open. He tried to turn his head slightly, and a low, painful moan escaped.

"Hold on, man. Okay? I'm gonna call for help."

I ran back up the stairs.

Facing the two dead people a second time made the bile crawl up my throat. I tried to ignore the tangy smell of blood and shit.

I fumbled around Earl's waist for the walkie. Smears of blood coated his Tyvek. I unzipped it and fished around blindly. When my fingers found the walkie, I unclipped it from his belt and held it away from my lips. My mind raced, and I couldn't remember what to say. But I knew that Decker needed help right away, or he was going to die.

"Team Four. Someone there?" I said in a shaky voice.

There was a scratch of static and then a responding "Go Team Four."

I moved out of the room, trying to escape the gore. "I got one man dead and another down. I need an ambulance right away."

A beat of silence.

"Say again?"

"Fuck, man! Earl's dead. Fucking rager chewed him up! And Decker's lying at the bottom of the stairs, all busted. Send a fucking ambulance!" I was shaking now, and all the anger and fear that I'd kept inside finally boiled to the surface.

"Is the lumper cleared?" the voice asked.

"Are you fucking kidding me?" I hissed back. "Yes, the lumper is dead! Send an ambulance or Decker's gonna die!"

"Has anyone been exposed to the infected?"

Gooseflesh traced down my arms, and the arm holding the walkie went limp. With those words, I knew exactly what was going to happen.

I still had to try. I held the walkie back up. "Decker didn't touch the lumper."

"Does he have any open wounds?"

I glanced over the rail to the floor below, looking at the blood pooling around Decker.

"No," I lied.

"Okay, we'll send an ambulance. It's after four. You need to clear the bodies, tag the door, and get out of District 7."

My entire body froze.

Are you fucking kidding me? I just watched a man get his face chewed off!

I felt like punching a hole in the wall.

"Team Four?"

"Yeah," I replied, barely holding my shit together.

"Clear the bodies. Mark the door. And leave the district before five. Now, confirm receipt of orders."

Fucking heartless bastard.

"Roger."

The rage boiled to the surface, and I threw the walkie over the edge of the landing. It shattered on the tile floor below in a satisfying crunch.

I sped back down the stairs.

"Bear?" Decker gasped through panting breaths.

"Yeah, man. I'm here. They're coming with an ambulance. Just hang on."

It felt like a lie, but I hoped it wasn't.

My Tyvek was covered in blood, and the last thing I wanted to do was get Decker sick. I moved a few feet away and tore off my splattered face shield, Tyvek suit, and shoe covers. My gloves came off last, and I dropped them on top of the pile.

I couldn't see any blood on me, but I was so panicked, I could've easily missed some. "I'll be right back," I called out.

I raced to the kitchen, scrubbing my hands, arms, and face in the sink with dish soap. Strands of my hair got wet with the last splash and stuck to my face. There was a trace of pink in the water, but I was too worried about getting back to Decker that it didn't fully register. All I could think about was not having a hair tie. I wet my hair and pulled it back as best as I could so it wouldn't fall all over Decker. I jogged back through the posh rooms to the entryway and Decker's side.

My knees hit the marble as I crouched down to hold his hand. His skin was cool and clammy.

"Stay with me, man," I pleaded.

Decker breathed short, shallow breaths now, and his skin had gone from a pasty white to almost green.

"Decker?" I whispered.

A low *uhhh* sound forced itself from his chest and through his open mouth.

I felt utterly useless. I was scared to move him. I wasn't sure if lifting his head to put a pillow or something underneath him would make it worse. Seeing his broken body, crushed at the bottom of the stairs, and the bright red blood spilling from the back of his head—I couldn't do nothing except hold his hand.

Tears pressed in, and I wanted to fucking scream.

The minutes dragged by, feeling like eternity. I still hadn't heard any sirens. I wondered if the guy on the other end of the radio had even called it in. I glanced at the trashed walkie, broken into pieces on the marble floor. I was furious at myself for losing my temper.

It already felt like I'd been at Decker's side for hours, but the ambulance still hadn't come. The pool of blood under his head had reached the dried blood around the dog. I was still sitting there when he took his last breath.

That's when I finally let myself cry.

I dropped Decker's hand, feeling numb.

My eyes shifted to the dead dog. The fucking lumper had probably killed the dog, too. Here I was thinking we were being set up to murder a healthy woman, and she'd been a lumper all along.

Well...not a lumper, though...right?

My chest grew tight as all of the pieces fell into place.

A rager.

She'd been a fucking rager. And I was certain that someone had known. Someone fucking *knew* she was a rager and had sent us in blind.

I stood. A flood of rage zipped through my body, chasing the sadness away, and my muscles hummed. I looked at Decker again, crumpled on the floor like a skinny ragdoll. His eyes were half-lidded, and his mouth was slightly agape. The blood matted in his wild blond hair had started to thicken.

I stormed outside and jerked open the truck door, feeling the rage buzzing through my body. I yanked the hand mic from the cradle. "This is Team Four." My voice was shaky with anger.

"Go ahead, Team Four," a bored voice replied.

I gripped the truck door with my free hand so I wouldn't punch something. "Decker's dead, you fucking assholes. You can tell the ambulance to fuck right off, if you even bothered to call them in the first place."

There was a long stretch of silence.

Finally, the voice replied, "Roger that. Load all of the bodies in the truck and take them to Decon as quickly as possible. Mark the house and clean up. It's getting late. You need to clear out of the district."

Every muscle in my body went still, and a cool "Fuck you" slipped out.

I threw the hand mic in the seat.

A wave of rage overtook me—the dangerous kind, the kind that had gotten me locked up in the first place. I rested my head against the doorframe, closed my eyes, and took three deep breaths.

It didn't help.

I reached back and punched the quarter panel of the truck in three quick pumps. With the first hit, the metal bent and bit into my skin. On the third hit, I felt a crunch, and I knew I'd broken my hand. I turned and leaned against the truck, panting. Blood oozed from the cuts, and I knew my rage had just put me into quarantine.

I looked back at the house, that fucking perfect Norman Rockwell house, and wanted to punch the truck again.

There were three dead bodies in there now, four if you counted the dog. And all because of a series of small exceptions for the richies: side-stepping the tracer, skipping confirmation, and not letting anyone know that there was a fucking *rager* in there.

All the anger and frustration roiled deep in my belly.

I looked down at my bleeding hand, feeling like I was outside of my body, and wondered how the hell I was going to make it through the rest of this horrible day.

CHAPTER
TWENTY-THREE

The twitch of the neighbor's curtain jolted me out of my thoughts, and the pain in my hand reminded me of my stupidity.

The cuts stung sharply. Beneath that, there was the white-hot burn of the break. I could still make a fist, but it hurt like hell when I did. I held my hand up to inspect the red gashes. The flow of blood had stopped, and the drips had congealed down the tops of my fingers.

A distant part of me remembered the water, tinged with blood, streaming off my hands in the kitchen. I wasn't sure whose blood had snuck through the gloves and the Tyvek. I must've gotten some on me when I was scrambling to get my stuff off to check Decker.

In my mind, Earl barked at me to clean my shit. Unable to do anything but follow his imaginary order, I pulled the first-aid kit out of the truck and squirted the bottle of alcohol across my knuckles. It burned like a motherfucker, and I bit back a hiss. The pain was good in its own way; it kept me from thinking about what waited for me in that house.

I wiped away the blood with some gauze, careful not to brush the fresh clots from the tops of the cuts. I threw some bandages on for posterity. But I knew everything would come back off in Decon.

Fuck.

Decon.

I wasn't looking forward to that shit either.

A clock ticked away in my head, and I knew I needed to get moving. I thought about hopping in the truck and making a sharp U-turn to get the truck as close to the house as possible. But the keys were in Earl's pocket.

My chest felt tight. I rubbed the creases in my forehead, trying to pull myself together. A list of all the crap I needed to do swam through my mind: get the bodies in the truck, mark the door, spray the path, and get the hell out of here.

Come on, man. It was Earl's voice again.

My shoulders stiffened. I went to the rear of the truck for a new set of gear. The double set of gloves stretched painfully over my swollen pinkie as I pulled them on. A fresh Tyvek suit and shoe covers were next. I braided my hair, hoping it would stay laced long enough without a tie to get the bodies cleared. The open cuts on my hands meant I needed to be extra careful. Given the mess upstairs, it was gonna be hard not to get any blood on me, especially since I was working alone.

I grabbed the body bags and slumped back up the walkway, past the discarded door ram, and into the house. One body bag stayed in the entryway, and I tried not to look at Decker as I moved toward the stairs. It was important that I kept my shit together long enough to get the fuck out of this mess and through Decon.

Why the fuck weren't they sending another team to help? Piking and bagging a lumper was hard enough. Now, I needed to drag the bodies of my dead friends and load them in the back of the truck with the crazy richie who'd killed them. And all while fighting the rage building inside and trying to keep my head together enough to not get the rager's blood on me.

What would Earl do?

He'd get the rager first. Watch where all her blood went and change again before moving the others. I walked up the stairs, avoiding the bloody footprints heading down. I turned into the room on the right. The initial shock had worn off, and the sight of it all practically brought me to my knees.

Earl lay on his back in a pool of blood. His plastic face shield had been ripped off in the madness, but he still had his Tyvek suit, gloves, and shoe covers on. Large chunks were missing from his cheek, ear, and neck. A distant part of me wondered at how someone could be strong enough to tear a chunk off another person like that. It looked like a rabid dog had gone at him.

I turned to the woman—the rager—who'd been bouncing around this house for at least a few weeks, swimming in her privilege. A wave of disgust washed over me, and I felt like spitting on her. I couldn't see the woman she was before. I couldn't feel any pity. All I felt was a rising tide of anger at the situation. Wealth had allowed her and her husband a few loopholes. And because of that, she'd killed her dog and two of my friends.

And no one would fucking care.

Blood coated her face and congealed in her hair. A quarter-sized lump pressed against the skin on her forehead above her eyebrow, and my chest loosened a tad.

Based on her behavior, it would be almost impossible to say she hadn't been infected. But I could just see the richies concocting up some story about a home invasion and self-defense or some shit. A part of me was grateful to see that lump. Another part of me wished we were allowed cell phones so I could document it. I still wasn't feeling entirely confident I would make it through this shit without people pointing a finger at me.

I wasn't sure what I'd do if someone tried to weave a story that was anything but the truth of how these guys died. The easiest thing would be to bash the fucker's face against the nearest solid object. But that was assuming I'd be close enough to do something about it. Even if I could get my hands around someone's neck, all I could do was feed the rage. Painting some fucker wouldn't change whatever bullshit the richies might put forward on paper.

I tossed one body bag to the side and laid the other one parallel to the rager.

During the fight, her robe had opened to reveal a silk sleeping shirt that exposed her bloody midriff. Another lump was poking out above the waistband of her silk sleeping shorts. Lumps coursed down her legs and peppered her hands; she even had one pressing against her manicured nail. I reached down and tied her robe closed. It felt weird otherwise.

She was light enough that I could pick the top half of her body up and shift it onto the bag. I moved to the bottom half, grabbed her ankles, and shifted the rest of her in. I stuffed her pink silk robe to the sides and zipped the bag up. A part of me was glad I wouldn't have to see the terrible thing again.

Ignoring the bark of my broken hand, I grabbed two of the body-bag handles and tested the weight. I'd be dragging her out for sure. There was no way in hell I would hoist her over my shoulder. Plus, she didn't deserve it.

Earl was big enough that I might have to drag him out, too. That simple fact just about crushed me.

Checking my grip, I started backing out of the room, pulling her along with me. I stopped as soon as we were out on the landing and dropped the bag. Getting her down the stairs was going to be rough. If I pulled her down, the momentum might be enough to push me over, and I could end up at the bottom like Decker. But if I tossed her down, that would batter her up even more.

Normally, lumpers were incinerated in Decon. But given that this couple had been given all sorts of exemptions, it was possible that someone besides the burners would get eyes on her before she was cremated. Plus, there was the added issue of my two dead crewmates.

"Fuck it," I muttered to myself. I grasped the body bag handles, gave it a sharp tug, and turned away as she tumbled down the stairs, hoping she wouldn't land on Decker.

When the thumping stopped, I peered over the banister. The bag rested in a sad heap next to, but not on top of, Decker. The outline of the body inside looked small and fragile down there. Even though she was right next to the man she killed, I felt a hint of pity for her.

Feeling a bit sick, I trudged back down the stairs, avoiding the blood smears. I paused at the bottom of the staircase and closed my eyes. I knew I had an audience and was likely being recorded. But I didn't pity her enough to carry her out respectfully.

I wondered why they made us drive pickup trucks and carry dead lumpers like trash. Surely it would've been smarter to use an old ambulance and tuck the body neatly on a stretcher. I didn't know if it was because BCB was run by a bunch of cheap fuckers or if there was something demonstrative about the whole process of lugging a dead body out and tossing it in the back of a truck. Like, "Look! This is what happens when you don't report!" It made me fucking sick.

I opened my eyes and turned to the dead rager.

I grabbed the handles of the bag and pulled her in a wide arc. Even though the bag wasn't leaking, I tried to keep the bag's trail away from anywhere I might need to go. Dragging the bag, I backed out through the front door, past the flowering camellias, and down the expertly paved walkway. Her body thumped lightly down the curb as I moved to the back of the truck.

At the rear of the truck, I paused a beat to catch my breath. Dead bodies were tough to move, and even with Decker helping, it had been rough with the grandma. I had no clue how I was going to get the rager in the back by myself.

Or Earl....

I felt like dropping to the curb right there and having a good cry. This whole thing was impossible. I pressed my eyes closed, trying to fight off the waves of frustration and anger. There was only one way to do this.

My teeth clenched.

I reached down and scooped her up, cradling her in my arms, feeling gross having her that close to me, but not knowing what else to do. She was lighter than I expected, and with my knees bent, I was able to get her into the truck as seamlessly as possible. I climbed into the truck bed and tugged her to the far end, knowing I'd need space for two more bodies.

More space for Earl and Decker.

My feet kissed the ground as I hopped off the tailgate. I gave myself a minute to catch my breath and did a quick inspection of my gear. My gloves had made it through without any tears, but they were still covered in blood, along with the shoe covers. My Tyvek also had a few smears. I decided to change all my gear again, careful to keep anything that was contaminated well away from the cuts on my hands.

I donned fresh gear for the third time today, ignoring the sharp pain in my broken hand, and headed back in. Sweat had soaked through my coveralls, and I was still breathing heavily from moving the rager. I tromped back up the stairs and stood on the landing, just outside the circle of blood, trying to figure out my next move.

I couldn't throw Earl down the stairs. I just couldn't. I knew he was dead, and it didn't matter anymore. He'd probably say the same thing and give me shit for breaking my back over a corpse, even his. But it still hadn't fully sunk in that Earl had been chewed to death by a rager, and I just *couldn't*.

I stood there for a good five minutes, wading through everything that whirled through my head, trying to figure out how to get Earl downstairs. The thudding in my chest slowly evened out, and my breathing returned to normal.

I took one last look at the strong man who'd led us through the dregs of being a thumper. The man who'd shared cigarettes and Takis. The man who'd helped Decker through his shit and kept him from burner duty. The man who'd held our group above water.

I was pissed the richies had taken this man from us. I wanted to grab one of those stupid decorative rocks and smash it through the windows of the nosy neighbor next door. I wanted to toss a pike through the window of the tastefully expensive SUV parked in the driveway. I wanted to let my rage explode from me. But seeing Earl's face held me back. Letting loose would solve nothing, and I could practically hear his deep voice barking that at me. Protecting me.

I opened the second body bag parallel to Earl's body.

Some of the blood on him was definitely from the rager; I'd piked her when she was still crouched on top of him. But at this point, I couldn't give two fucks about getting the Lumps. I needed to take care of my friend.

I slid my hands beneath him. He was a heavy dude, but I pushed with my legs and was able to shift him into the body bag. Blood smeared across my arms and down my chest.

I closed his eyes with a gloved hand and zipped up the bag. Tears threatened again as the zipper passed his sagging face and the hole chewed in his cheek. I'd be carrying him down; I had to.

Ignoring the blood on my Tyvek, I slipped one arm under the bag near his bent legs and the other under his back. I lifted with my knees, and through sheer force of will, I was able to stand. A grunt escaped as I adjusted his weight, rolling the bulk of him against my chest. Cradling him, I slowly made my way down the stairs, following the trail of bloody footsteps.

My arms and legs burned as I carried him all the way to the back of the truck. I laid him on the tailgate, almost reverently, wanting to say something over his body but not knowing what. I shifted him all the way into the bed of the pickup. That was when I realized he still had the truck keys in his pocket.

My chest grew tight, and my eyes filled with tears.

Feeling like a nasty rat-fuck, I unzipped the body bag just enough to fish through his Tyvek to the pocket of his coveralls. My eyes focused on the black plastic of the body bag as I tried to look anywhere but at his lifeless face. Metal touched my fingers, and I slipped the truck keys out and laid them on the tailgate. They were covered with blood.

I zipped the bag back up and rested my hand on his chest. "Hope you find some peace," I finally murmured and turned before the weight of it could crush me.

I sprayed the keys with disinfectant and let them sit on the tailgate. No one would be stealing this truck.

The adrenaline had worn off, and the exhaustion started to set in. I knew Earl would want me to change again. So even though I was wrung out and the pain in my hand screamed at me, I went through the motions. As I was pulling on a fresh pair of gloves—my pinky finger now twice the size it should be and turning a deep red—the radio cracked from the front of the truck.

"Team Four. Check in."

Every fiber of my being recoiled from the voice.

"Team Four. Check in," the voice repeated, more urgent.

I thought about ignoring it, but I knew it wouldn't do any good.

I reached in and grabbed the hand mic. "Team Four. Go ahead," I said, voice grave.

"It's five. Have you left the district?" The voice was annoyed.

I've got a fucking ankle tracker on! You know exactly where I am!

I wanted to pound the mic against the dashboard. I wanted to scream at the motherfucker. I wanted to tell him to shove it up his ass.

Instead, I said, "I've got three dead people to move. On my own. In a two-story house. No, I haven't left the district. And no, I don't have all the bodies in the back of the truck yet."

There was a beat of silence.

"Residents will be returning soon. You need to be out of the district *now*," the voice commanded.

I clenched my teeth, trying to quell the rising tide of anger. "I've got one dead body still in the house. Should I leave it?" I snarked.

Decker. Decker is still in the house.

There was a crackle followed by silence, like the guy on the other end had started to say something and stopped.

I wondered why they were pushing people back into the district so soon. I hadn't even sprayed the sidewalk with bleach yet.

Oh, yeah. Right. Because they're rich.

Of course, the richies wanted to get back into their homes to relax. They needed their nightly glass of wine after an exhausting day of cracking their whips across the backs of the employees they abused.

The privileged chatter of the richies echoed in my head: *Oh? And did you hear about Olivia? Oh, yes. A team of felons came in to clear her today. Can you believe it?*

There was a second crackle from the radio. "Follow protocol, Team Four. Hurry your ass up and get out."

"Roger," I bit out the word.

I tossed the hand mic on the seat and didn't wait for them to say any more of their dumb shit.

Decker was up next.

Though he was the lightest of the bunch, carrying his shattered, slight frame was the hardest. He was like a broken bird in my arms, fragile and bony. Once he was in the body bag, I crossed his arms and closed his eyes. I zipped him up into the darkness.

Decker had the biggest heart of anyone I knew, finding a place in there for just about everyone we shared this messy world with. He was like the moral compass for our crew, and I wondered who would keep my spirit grounded with him gone.

"Don't worry. I'll look after Cockroach," I whispered down to him, knowing it to be the truth as soon as the words left my lips.

It felt weird leaving the dead dog in the house all alone, like a discarded piece of trash. Poor thing was just as much a victim as Earl and Decker. Once Decker was in the truck bed next to Earl, I grabbed a plastic bag for the dog and the spray paint before heading back to the house.

The bright red paint of an encircled L dripped down the stark white of the fancy door. I added the date, knowing it probably meant nothing to the asshole who owned the place. I bet he'd have a cleaning crew out within an hour. That way, he could come home from whatever business trip he was on and pretend a massacre hadn't happened in this forsaken place.

I slipped the stiff, bloated dog in the bag, trying not to gag. It had clearly been dead a while, and I was surprised I hadn't noticed the smell when we'd first come in. I figured we were all so amped up from seeing the thing and clearing the house, we hadn't even noticed. I wondered if stopping to assess the dead dog would have helped us get a better read on the situation. Then, I kicked myself for even thinking that.

What's done is done.

I left the bag and the spray can by the door before going up one last time to collect our pikes. With all three pikes, the bag, and the can in hand, I dropped them off in the truck.

By then, my muscles had just about given up, and I was fighting a pretty good case of the shakes. The swelling in my hand was to the point where I could barely force it into a fist again. I bit through it all.

I grabbed the pump sprayer and blasted the dilute bleach across the asphalt, up the path, and to the threshold. The sharp chlorine smell stabbed my senses, and puke boiled up into my throat. I closed the front door as much as possible, grabbed the door ram, and dumped everything into the back of the truck. Another quick change, and I was back into plain coveralls and rubber boots. I grabbed the keys and closed the tailgate, trying not to look at all the bodies piled in the back.

My hair was plastered to my head with sweat, and the loose braid had come mostly undone. A quick check in the mirror confirmed that I'd somehow avoided getting blood on my face or in my hair. From what I could tell, my hands, coveralls, and boots had also somehow made it through the various changes of Tyvek suits and gloves without getting soiled. It was a damn miracle, all things considered, but I couldn't feel grateful. And I still couldn't be certain blood hadn't soaked through somewhere.

I climbed in—my first time in the driver's seat—and stuck the keys in the ignition. I adjusted the rearview mirror, feeling sick. Two of my friends lay dead in the back of the truck.

I heard Earl's voice telling me to man up and get the bodies to Decon. Barking at me to get my shit together so I didn't end up on burner duty.

I picked up the mic. "Team Four, here."

"Go ahead, Team Four."

"I'm leaving the district now," I said, and hung the mic up.

"Roger," the voice replied, but I ignored it.

The engine roared to life.

Earl's favorite radio station was already on. I turned the song up, stretching the speakers, and left that fucking piece of twisted paradise behind me.

CHAPTER
TWENTY-FOUR

It'd been forever since I'd driven, but holding the steering wheel felt all sorts of fucked up. I had a hard time getting my head in the game. I was deep in Land Park, and I wasn't sure how to get out.

I managed to find my way back to the District 7 checkpoint; it was just one turn, and I'd be stupid not to remember that much. The gate rolled open, and I slowly pulled through. Both guards eyed me through the glass windows of the guard station, not bothering to come out.

They must've been expecting only one person to be in the front of the truck. Otherwise, they'd be screaming bloody murder about two felons floating around in their gated paradise. I wondered why they looked at me so mean when they knew my crewmates were dead in the back.

As I pulled out, I noticed a fancy car parked to the side, waiting to come in. The guy behind the wheel wore a business suit. He had one hand on the wheel, fingers tapping impatiently, and his lips were pursed. It was all the confirmation I needed that this place was filled with assholes.

The anger at the richies burrowed itself in my mind like a thorn under my nail. I felt like roaring my frustration and despair at the sky. I felt like pulling the truck over, yanking that fancy car door open, dragging the guy out of his car, and beating him with my broken hand. Instead, I ground my teeth and continued north on Riverside, feeling all sorts of sick.

A red light stopped me at the intersection of Riverside and Broadway. The familiar cemetery loomed off to my left, and I realized that it was the last landmark I remembered. From here, I was hopeless when it came to finding my way to Decon. Earl had always driven, and I'd always been stuffed in the backseat.

I turned the music down, trying to puzzle my way through this. It was hard to think straight. Thoughts of Earl and Decker lying dead in the back of the truck pressed in. I spent most of my energy trying to push those thoughts right back out again. I was exhausted, and a numbness spread through me.

Decon was on the east side of the city, where the neighborhoods started trickling out and industrial buildings and swaths of pastureland took over. It was far enough out of town that the smell of burning bodies wouldn't piss anyone off.

The guys in Central could've helped me. But I couldn't make myself pick that mic back up and ask those fuckers for anything. I figured I'd head in the general direction and fuck anyone who tried to give me shit about the fact that my ankle bracelet was tracking all sorts of crazy ways.

The *tink, tink, tink* of the signal echoed over the music, and I turned right on Broadway. Within a few blocks, I passed the checkpoint at Franklin where we'd come to pike the homeless lumper.

Since District 3 wasn't in lockdown, the gate was sitting wide open, and the guard didn't even look up from his phone. Less than a minute later, I passed under the freeway. The tent we'd killed the thumper in was still there, the spray-painted flap waving gently in the breeze.

A few people sat by their tents on the other side of the street, doing their own thing. They didn't look up. They didn't see me pass, mixed in with the trickle of other cars. It felt weird knowing I'd been here just over a week ago, killing one of their friends. Now, I was driving back through with two of mine lying dead in the back.

I tried to remember the homeless dude's name, and all I could think about was that axolotl plushie.

I followed Broadway to the end of the road, turned north, and then turned east again on Folsom Blvd. I knew that road would take me out to the boonies, and I could try to figure my way from there. I breezed through three checkpoints, wondering if the guards in there even knew what I had in the back of my truck. I wondered if they even cared.

When I passed the Home Depot, things started to click into place, and I knew Decon would be just a few blocks down on the right. Soon, the building complex came into view, and my chest went tight. I'd been trying to fight back the thoughts of all the shit that had gone down. But it hurt like hell knowing I was here to drop off several bodies, two of them belonging to my friends.

The truck thumped into the driveway, and I pulled into the bay. I killed the engine and left the keys dangling. I half-slid out of the car, my muscles finally starting to complain about all the shit they'd been put through.

Fuck the pain.

My muscles could just stop their whining and be grateful I was still alive.

The bay was empty when I exited the truck, and I figured the burner was probably supposed to wait until the thumpers were inside to get the vehicle. I wondered at the fact that I'd never noticed this little detail before. Of course, this was only my fourth run.

My fourth run, and both of my crewmates have been smoked.

I took the long way around the truck, stopping at the back. I imagined Earl and Decker in those black bags, stiffening up, faces wearing weird, lifeless expressions, and part of me wished I hadn't come around this way.

I didn't know how to say goodbye to them, but I wanted to. I'd never done this shit before, and it felt awful just leaving them in the back of the truck to be hauled off and burned like fucking trash.

Part of me wanted to fold my arms on the back of the truck, rest my head, and hold some kind of vigil. Something to remember who Earl and Decker were. Celebrate their lives. But I was a felon, and they had been felons. There was no way the shiteaters would have enough compassion to let me take a moment to mourn. We were dispensable like the one-and-done disposable mops. We'd clean up the mess and get thrown away.

Plus, they probably wanted to speed me through Decon and clock out to go home.

The tide of rage pushed in and lapped at my heels. My chest grew tight, and I couldn't breathe. "Take it easy," I murmured, and forced myself to take a couple of breaths.

I put my hand on the tailgate and tipped my face down for just a moment. When I came back up for air, the numbness had returned, and I found I was somehow able to walk into Decon. With the swipe of my ID card, the door buzzed open. I stepped through the doors, like I'd done three times before. But from there, nothing else was the same; it was a fucking shitshow.

When I passed through the first set of doors, the guards stared at me through the glass windows with various degrees of scorn and pity. The intercom clicked on, and one of them said, "Proceed through decontamination and scratch check. A guard will meet you after for a debriefing."

My face twisted into an expression of disgust, and I snorted.

Debriefing. Yeah, right. More like interrogation.

At that moment, I wasn't sure how things would be on the other side of this. To be honest, I didn't fucking care. I'd seen two of my buddies killed by a rager. I'd stepped through their blood and held their limp bodies as I carried them to the truck. The same two guys I'd eaten microwave burritos and played cards with just a few hours ago.

I stared at the guards through the glass, feeling the rage sneak back in. When one of them put a hand on their weapon in response, I figured I must've looked like a crazy motherfucker. I almost laughed at the heavy sheet of bulletproof glass between them and me.

I pushed my way through the door into the decontamination room. It banged open, bouncing off the wall with a loud *clang*. My fingers scrambled at my clothes, eager to be out of them and wash this day off me. The back of my coveralls was damp with sweat. When I pulled my undershirt off, the strong smell of stale, panicked BO filled the room.

The bandages on my hand had started to peel, and I snatched them off the rest of the way, tossing them in the biohazard bin against the wall. My half-assed braid—the one I'd made to keep my hair out of Decker's face as I held his hand while he was dying—had come completely unraveled. Strands of hair fell across the skin of my shoulders and back like a shroud.

The cement was cold against my bare feet. I turned the shower on and stepped into the hot water. Like a robot, I went through the motions of washing myself from head to toe. My right hand was now so fucked up that I had to use my left to suds up my hair.

With a detached, almost scientific interest, I wondered briefly what they would do about my broken hand. I'd cut the fucker off if it meant getting Earl and Decker back. Thinking about my crewmates was like a punch in the gut, and my shoulders hunched as I tried to curl into myself. The lemony smell of the soap made me sick, and I fought a trickle of vomit.

After the three minutes were up, I stepped into the next room. A guard waited for me with thick, hairy arms crossed over his barrel chest. He watched me, face unreadable, as I toweled off.

I hadn't seen him before, but this was only the fourth time I'd passed through Decon. The name bar on his chest said "Lopez." He was a big dude—large enough to give me a run for my money. But he didn't have the cocky air of an asshole.

In a weird way, he was a steady rock, and his expressionless face helped me keep my mind on the task at hand. I wasn't sure if they'd sent him in special, but I appreciated not having a shiteater like Jackson walking me through this mess.

As soon as I tossed the towel into the bin, Lopez said, "Stand on a circle and put your hands up." His voice was calm and even.

I shifted my feet onto the faded yellow circles painted on the floor and did as he said. This was the normal process for scratch checks, but I'd never had open cuts before. I wasn't sure if they were gonna just wave me through or throw me on the ground, cuff me, and toss me into quarantine. I hoped it wasn't the latter; after all the shit I'd been through today, I wasn't sure I could hold the tide of rage back if they did.

Lopez circled around me. "You can drop your arms now."

I knew he'd clocked my right hand as soon as I'd walked through the door; it was so swollen and discolored it was hard to ignore. Sure enough, Lopez said, "Hold out your right hand."

He examined my hand without touching it, and grumbled softly, "What the hell happened?"

I didn't bother to answer, and he wasn't expecting me to.

He stepped back with a deep frown; it was the first hint of any emotion I'd seen on the guy's face since stepping out of the showers.

Lopez announced, "Three, roughly one centimeter cuts on the right knuckles. They appear fresh. No other cuts or abrasions." His voice was louder now, likely so the camera mics could pick it up.

I'd never had something like this happen before, but I figured someone must be on the other side of the cameras, typing all the information in. With a detached coolness, I couldn't help but notice that he didn't mention the fact that my hand was obviously broken. It was impossible to ignore with the deep purple puffiness spreading around the outer edge of my hand. The cuts were the most important thing for infection control, though. The Lumps could be setting up camp in those jagged tears right as we stood here, my wet hair still dripping down my back.

There was a clicking sound on the PA, and a voice said, "Take him to the clinic."

Lopez nodded once, and said to me, "Go ahead and get dressed." His voice was even, but his frown was still there.

Going through the motions, I stepped into a fresh pair of coveralls, careful of my hand as it passed through the sleeves. I pulled on a set of rubber boots, not even noticing the way they pinched my toes; it was the least of my worries.

Lopez buzzed both of us through. Normally, a crew would head straight out to the waiting area and hang out until the truck came back around. This time, the guard led me down a narrow, dark hall to the left. He was brave, turning his back to me. I wondered if he did it because he was stupid or if he didn't give a shit what happened. Maybe he thought I wasn't a threat.

He might think I was docile as a lamb, but the rage burned hot through my exhaustion. One wrong word or a bit of side-eye, and I'd be more than a threat. The numbness snuck in and out like sand peeking out between the waves of rage. Catch me at just the right moment and in just the right way, and I wasn't sure what I'd do.

We made a sharp turn into a room I'd never seen before. It looked like any other doctor's office. There was an exam table covered in paper sitting in the center. A computer and wheeled stool sat to the left. A counter with examination supplies sat to the right.

"Have a seat," Lopez said. "Doc will be in shortly." He closed the door behind me.

I moved over to the exam table and sat on the edge. My legs were long enough that my toes brushed the ground. My shoulders folded over, and I cradled my forehead with my left palm.

The suffocating silence of the room pressed around me. Horrible images of everything that had happened kept flashing through my head. The gurgled scream of the rager filled the empty space. Then, Decker's cry as he flew backward down the stairs. Earl's screaming, trying to get the rager off his back.

There was a gentle knock at the door.

"Mr. Castillo?" a soft voice spoke through the door.

"Yeah," I blurted gruffly, unable to get anything else out.

A woman in a lab coat entered, followed by Lopez. The small, dingy room was getting crowded. I was grateful for the distraction.

"I'm Dr. Singh," she said, introducing herself as she pulled on her gloves.

When she turned, I noticed she wore a pink blouse under her lab coat. I looked away. I wasn't sure I'd ever be able to look at that color the same again.

"May I see your hand?" she asked politely.

I held it out, still unable to look at her.

She took my hand in her gloved ones and raised it to inspect the cuts. She delicately pressed around the base of my hand. I welcomed the resulting pain.

"What did you hit?" she asked. It was a simple question without a hint of accusation.

"The truck," I grumbled.

"Hmm." She turned away to rummage through the cabinets. "Did you come into contact with anyone else's blood?"

I thought about the bloody footprints down the stairs and the smears across the white of my Tyvek suit. The trail of pink in the water when I washed up. The blood seeping through the first set of gloves. Then, there was the fact that I'd had so much blood on me that I had to change my gear several times.

I wanted to laugh in her face.

"I hauled three dead people and a dead dog out of a two-story house. So yeah. I got blood on me. But nothing on my skin," I lied.

She looked at me, eyes full of pity. Turning away, she opened the cabinets. She rested three individually wrapped swabs and collection tubes on the counter next to a small biohazard bag.

"Each of the cuts will need to be swabbed for PCR," she said all business-like, not bothering to explain what the fuck "PCR" meant.

She pulled open the first swab. "Hold your hand out for me, please."

I did as I was told.

With a bit of pressure, she broke open the cut on my last knuckle and swirled the swab around in it. She placed the swab in the collection tube, labeled it, and placed it in the biohazard bag. It was rinse-and-repeat with the other two cuts. The pain was so far away, it didn't even register.

"We should get the results back within twenty-four hours," she explained. "You'll be held in quarantine until then. If they come back clean, you'll be released back to the Home. You won't be completely out of the woods, and a nurse will continue to do daily health checks for the next week. But I haven't had anybody turn after the initial PCR comes back negative."

Turn. She actually said "turn."

She sighed. "You broke your fifth metacarpal bone. With the swelling, it's difficult to tell if it is displaced, and I won't know if you'll need surgery until I see X-rays. But they won't let me take those until you're fully cleared."

I wondered who "they" were, and figured it was some BCB bean-counter who didn't want to waste money on someone who might be infected.

"I'll send the nurse to put on a temporary splint," she said.

She turned to me and frowned. "Next time, don't punch anything. Try deep breathing or meditation to control your anger," she chided.

With that, I couldn't hold it back anymore, and the tide swept in. My head rose slowly, and every muscle in my body stiffened. I locked eyes with her, ready to fly off the table and punch her in the face. The tension instantly crackled in the room.

Dr. Singh took a step back, and her throat bobbed. "Okay," she said sternly, taking another step back. "We're done here." When she took her gloves off, her hands shook.

Lopez watched me cooly. His hands dropped to his sides, and he repositioned himself to easily intercept me if I went for her.

She slipped out of the room, leaving the two of us behind a closed door. Nostrils still flaring with unspent anger, I looked to Lopez, and he stared back. Neither of us knew what to do next, and I wondered if the nurse would still be coming.

A knock at the door a few seconds later answered the question. The nurse was a burly, older woman with her hair cropped close to her head. Her scrubs were a drab olive green with an ID badge clipped to the pocket. She carried bandaging materials and an extra-large hand splint.

She stepped in, laid the supplies on the counter, and pulled a set of gloves on. She rolled a stool over to me and took a seat.

"May I have a look?" she asked, holding out a hand.

I placed my injured one in hers, and she gently examined the cuts and the spreading bruise.

From there, it was a blur. She cleaned the cuts again, taped some gauze across them, and placed my hand in the splint, locking my fingers into position with the Velcro straps. She worked in a mechanical silence that was oddly reassuring.

I was grateful she didn't give me any shit about breaking my hand or say anything about taking deep breaths. I'd like to see the prissy-ass Dr. Singh haul her chomped-up and broken friends into the back of a truck without screaming or punching anything.

Once the nurse finished, she said, "There you go. Only take it off in the shower."

She sat a beat and studied my face. I lifted my head to meet her gaze. There was no pity there, just a sense of understanding. She reached over with a gloved hand and squeezed my left hand before turning to leave.

"Time to go," Lopez said, voice neutral.

He led me out of the room and through a labyrinth of hallways, buzzing through several doors. The final one read "quarantine." I passed through that last door, thinking I might never make it out again, and then wondering if I even wanted to.

CHAPTER TWENTY-FIVE

The quarantine cell was exactly like the ones that really fucked up prisoners were stuffed into on TV shows. There was a thick metal door with a slot for getting cuffs on and off. There was a bed that consisted of a flat metal panel with thick legs bolted to the floor and no mattress. A metal, lidless toilet sat in the far corner. There wasn't a sink or a mirror. And there damn well wasn't a window.

I stared down at the stainless steel of the toilet, my reflection a blurry mess, and couldn't help but feel like it reflected my soul. I figured if someone didn't want to kill themselves before they walked in here, they sure would when the door closed behind them.

Looking down at my splint, I wondered about the wounds buried deep beneath the bandages. If I popped with the Lumps, would they pike me in here or somewhere else? Maybe they'd pike me in front of the incinerator to make it easy to clean up.

Or would a guard just shoot me?

I sat on the edge of the metal bed and ran the fingers of my left hand through my hair.

Probably not worth the bullet in a confined space.

There was a clink as someone opened a small flap near the floor that I hadn't noticed. A tray slid in. Saying it had food on it would be a joke. Everything was a soft, bland tan color and virtually unidentifiable.

Even if a steak with a side of potato salad and a bowl of ice cream had magically appeared on that tray, I still wouldn't have been able to eat it. I'd worked my ass off and *should* be hungry. But I kept seeing the flashing images of blood, the pink streak of the rager's robe, Decker windmilling before he tipped over the stairs, and Earl thrashing with chunks taken out of his head. Anything I tried to eat would just come right back up.

I rested my forearms on my thighs, feeling the weight of it all. I needed a pencil and a piece of paper to take my mind off shit. But I only had the four concrete walls and my own thoughts. The rage slowly burned in my chest, and all I could think about was beating the shit out of the richies who'd had a piece in this mess.

Time slipped past with no way to mark it. After what could've been an hour or a day, there was a single rap on the door. "Castillo. Slide your hands through. Time for your debriefing."

I used the toe of my boot to slide the untouched food tray to the side. Facing the door, I held my hands through the slot, hoping they'd cuff me in the front. Sure enough, gloved hands slapped cool metal cuffs across my wrists, one a bit looser than the other as it clasped around the splint. I took a step back, and the door swung open.

Lopez stood there with his usual neutral expression, and part of me was grateful. There was something about his cool detachment that smothered the fire of my rage. If anyone else had opened that door, I probably would have lost it, pushed the guy down, looped my cuffs around his neck, and hoped I'd have enough time to choke him out before the other guards swooped in.

I wasn't in a good mental space.

"To your left." Lopez gestured down the hall. "Last door on the right."

It wasn't lost on me that he had me walking in front of him down that grim hallway. I suspected I probably looked like a caged animal, ready to bite, and he knew it. But that was his only tell, and I appreciated him keeping his emotions tightly wrapped up where I couldn't see.

He followed me into a small room and asked me to have a seat. I obliged, holding my hands up for him to uncuff me. He backed out of the room. There was the *click* of the bolt as he locked me in.

The room was tiny and painted in a neutral off-white. A bland, padded office chair faced a short shelf and a large window. On the other side of the glass, there were two people dressed in business clothes. Two cameras sat in opposite corners, with one positioned to catch my back and the other to catch my face.

The two-way mic clicked on, and the woman behind the glass said, "State your full name and BCB ID, please."

Her face was unreadable as she leaned back into her chair. She was average-looking with black hair laced with gray. She wore it straight, and the ends brushed the shoulders of her navy blue suit as she lifted her head to look at me. There were hardly any wrinkles around her dark brown eyes, and it was impossible to guess her age.

"Bear Castillo." My voice cracked with dehydration. "CA73363."

"Mr. Castillo, we're here to discuss the events that occurred earlier today," she replied and then rattled off the Miranda warning. She paused, waiting.

I could've asked for a lawyer, and maybe I should have. But I was so fucking exhausted. I just wanted to tell my story and try not to think about it ever again.

"Shall we continue?" she asked in a relaxed tone, not really expecting an answer. She rattled off the date and time, then added that we were being recorded.

"I'm Detective Kailani Hasegawa." She gestured to the man sitting next to her. "This is Detective Carl Silva."

Silva was a big dude, broad-shouldered but soft. His fingers were laced across a fairly generous middle-aged pooch. His dark hair was buzzed short. Acne scars marred the puffy, light-brown skin of his cheeks. He had his coat off, and there was a hint of sweat darkening the pits of his long-sleeve shirt. A far-off part of my brain wondered if he stank.

"You were sent to 1407 11th Avenue in District 7 to clear a lumper, correct?" she began, reading from a paper in front of her.

"Yes, ma'am," my voice croaked again.

Hasegawa pointed with a finger through the window and to my left. "There's water and a nutrition bar there for you, if you'd like. We can get you coffee, too, but that'll take a minute."

Silva studied me, face expressionless.

I hadn't noticed the stuff stashed to the side and felt a bit grateful. I reached for the bottle, the cheap plastic crackling under my fingers. I managed to twist the cap off despite the splint and took a sip. Even though the water was room temp, it felt cool going down. I left the lid off and placed the bottle on the small shelf between us.

When I'd finished, Hasegawa pressed on. "Walk me through what happened. Start from when you left the Home."

I rubbed my eyes and wondered where to start. Sure, she'd said "when you left the Home," but everything had started before that, hadn't it?

There was silence as I tried to get my messy thoughts in order.

"Was there anything unusual about the drive over? Any arguments?" Silva asked.

Surprised, my head jerked up. "No," I answered cautiously.

Hasegawa flashed Silva an annoyed look that was so brief, I almost missed it. She turned to me with a neutral smile, waiting for me to tell my story.

"Earl drove, Decker rode shotgun, and I was in the back. Same as always," I finally managed to get out.

But it wasn't the same as always. There was that warning from Ramos before we'd left. Things had smelled off from the start, and Earl had picked up on it. He'd been jumpy before we'd even left the Home, his sixth sense tingling. I wasn't sure if I wanted to share that.

"That would be Earl Williams and Decker Andrews, correct?" she asked.

I knew she was only doing it for the recording, but I still felt annoyed.

"Yes," I replied. I scrambled to get my thoughts in order and continued, "The guard at the checkpoint let us through. The house was only a couple blocks in, and we parked across the street."

"Then what happened?" she asked.

"Earl checked in with Central. We geared up. Earl said he'd take point. I was on the door ram. Decker took up the rear."

"What did you think about Earl leading the team? Ordering you around?" Silva asked.

I knew he was trying to make up some shit between us that wasn't there, and it rankled me. "Earl always led the team, and Decker and I were cool with that. He had experience."

"Experience?" Silva repeated.

I suspected the guy had already finger-fucked our files and knew exactly what kind of experience I was talking about.

Having to parrot everything out for damn cameras pissed me off.

"Military service," I replied, voice clipped.

"Team leaders typically don't take point, though, do they?" Silva challenged.

My annoyance was teetering on anger. "I don't fucking know, man. Alright? I've never been in the military. I trusted Earl. Something was off about the place. Decker was always jumpy, and today was only my fourth run. I'm sure Earl had a good reason for taking point."

Silva pressed his lips together.

I wasn't sure if I'd said the wrong thing, but I didn't much care. I was exhausted. And hungry. And my body ached. All things that I hated myself for feeling because I *could* feel them, and my friends were ash.

Plus, I was fucking pissed that this fat ass, sitting in his suit in his cushy chair, was talking shit about Earl.

Hasegawa watched me carefully. "How did you enter the premises?"

A sigh of annoyance escaped. I knew they had to have camera footage from the richie's place—likely had even more from all the other richies on the block—and I was irritated that they were making me relive the whole fucking thing.

"Earl knocked and announced us. No one answered. I busted the door open with the ram."

And then he called out the dead dog.

Bile rose in my throat, and I took another sip of water.

"There was no response?" Silva asked, looking doubtful.

I shook my head, remembering the crash and thinking about how we'd all ignored it. Lumpers could bump around if they were still walking. How could we have known that it had been a rager up there?

"The dog didn't bark?" Silva probed harder.

My eyebrows drew together in a scowl. "The dog was fucking dead, man. It had been dead a while. That fucking rager bitch probably killed the poor thing for making noise or some shit."

"Hmm," Silva said.

I wondered if anybody had even looked at the dog before they'd tossed it in the incinerator. Did they look at Earl and Decker? Did they see the chunks the bitch had chewed out of Earl's head and neck? Did they do autopsies in situations like this? Or did they just throw the bags in the incinerator and brush off their hands?

"How did you know the dog was already dead?" Hasegawa asked.

"It was just inside the door in a pool of blood. Earl called it when he cleared the entryway. It was all puffy and shit. Like it had been dead a couple of days."

I clenched my fists, my right hand straining against the splint.

"Then what happened?" Hasegawa asked, voice monotone.

"Earl told Decker to stay there and stand watch. We cleared the first story. The house was a U-shape, and once we cleared the first floor, we ended up back with Decker."

"And you didn't hear or see anything? Nothing at all?" Silva asked, practically sneering. "Mrs. Kingston—an alleged rager—didn't respond to three grown men moving through the house?"

My jaw dropped slightly before I clenched it back closed, muscle bouncing in my cheek. "No," I finally bit out. "Earl told us to be quiet."

Silva spun his hand in a keep-going motion.

I clenched my hands again, feeling the splint bend with the effort. A sharp pain stabbed in my right hand as the broken bones scratched against each other, and it brought a fresh breath of clarity.

"After the first floor was cleared," I continued, keeping my eyes locked on the smug bastard, "the three of us moved up the stairs. Earl was in the lead, then me, and then Decker. Earl went into the first room, and I stepped to the side to cover the landing."

And that's when I broke the vase.

I looked down at my fists, wishing I could rewind time. Wishing I could've held my spear just a little bit different.

"I broke something. The sound triggered the rager, and she came rushing out. She bumped Decker, and he fell backward down the stairs. Then she jumped on Earl and started eating his fucking face."

It all spilled out quickly; I didn't want to relive that shit.

"She ran right past you?" Silva asked, doubt lacing his words.

"Yes," was all I could manage.

"Walk me through this again," Silva barked. "You were coming up behind Earl. You reached the top. And you were standing where?"

Hasegawa rested her hand on the shelf between them on their side of the window. It was a soft gesture, but it was enough for Silva to shut his trap.

"And then what happened?" Hasegawa coaxed.

"The rager...she knocked Earl down, and his arms were trapped beneath him. He tried to get her off, but he couldn't. I piked her. I tried to stop the bleeding, but Earl died pretty fast." My voice caught, and I had to pause a second. "Then, I went to check on Decker. His leg was broke, and his head was bleeding bad. I called for an ambulance. Waited for fucking ages. He died waiting. Fucking bastards."

The rage had turned into the shakes. I felt a buzz of unspent adrenaline. Tears pressed in. I fought them with everything I had in me; I refused to let that fucker Silva see them fall. I clenched my fists again and heard the crackle of the Velcro on the splint as it strained under the pressure.

I thought about the rager and how she'd plowed through Earl and Decker. I saw that ball of white fur lying in a puddle of dried blood.

An image of the guy I'd killed in my own rage flashed through my mind. It was that moment that had led me along a dark path all the way to this seat across from this dipshit.

My vision narrowed, and I felt my head go light.

"Did you kill the dog, kill the woman, and then kill your buddies so they couldn't snitch on you?" Silva's voice was cool and his eyes narrow.

The anger boiled to the surface, and my head cleared with a jolt of adrenaline. "Are you fucking kidding me, man? Yeah. You fucking figured it out. I tore the dog to shreds and bit chunks out of my friend. Did you even look at those bodies?! That crazy bitch fucking chewed Earl to pieces! I was lucky enough to pike her before she laid into me and Decker!"

Yeah, lucky.

I didn't feel lucky. Part of me wished I'd slipped on the blood going down the stairs and ended this.

Hasegawa watched me intently.

I panted through the rage, chest heaving. I closed my eyes and exhaled deeply, trying to get control over my body.

"Look," I continued. "This run was fucked from the start. She somehow dodged the contact tracers. And when her dickhead husband finally noticed something was off, no one confirmed her. No one told us she was a rager. We went in blind. And when I called it in, no one came to fucking save Decker. Now, they're dead. And for what? So some richie didn't have to get her blood drawn? So some fucknut didn't have to have the confirmation team in his shit? What the fuck, man?!"

My throat hurt from all the talking. I embraced the pain.

There was a long stretch of silence as they watched me intently.

My breaths came out in puffs.

"I think that's enough for now," Hasegawa announced.

She pressed a buzzer on the wall and turned to study me.

I had no clue what she was thinking and if she believed me.

Whether my story would be the one that left the building and made it into the report remained to be seen. Part of me hoped the richies had nanny-cams in their home, and then another part of me wondered if that footage would somehow disappear so that they could change the narrative. The Kingstons were wealthy enough to spin whatever story they wanted.

I suspected Mr. Kingston would just want to bury it and forget the little mess ever happened. In that case, I'd go back to my cell and avoid additional murder charges. But the husband had been so damn specific about not killing the dog. I wondered if he'd blame me for that mess, and come after me with a bucketful of wrath and a fistful of dollars to pay off the DA. Who cared about a felon anyway?

I didn't even feel the cuffs when Lopez snapped them back on. I just followed him back to the quarantine cell like a sacrifice at the altar of a rich man.

CHAPTER TWENTY-SIX

One sleepless night and two ignored meals later, they came to get me.

There was a knock, and someone called my name. I stood and moved to the door. I reflexively held my hands through the slot.

"You can pull your hands back. We won't be cuffing you," a feminine voice replied.

I didn't know what to think of that. My brain was too foggy to do more than hear the words. I slid my hands back in and let them hang at my sides.

There was a *click* as the door was unlocked, and it swung open.

The light in the hallway seemed too bright, and I blinked a couple of times. I reached to rub my face with my right hand, saw the splint, and stared at it stupidly.

A different guard stood in front of me. She was a woman of medium build with surprisingly muscled arms. Her brown hair was in a neat bun. Her uniform was crisp and ironed. I was with it enough to register the letters on her name bar: "Ferreira."

"You're going back to the Home," she said matter-of-factly.

Despite the exhaustion, I felt a flicker of surprise. Somewhere, my brain was telling me that I shouldn't be going back to the Home. That something was wrong. But I couldn't do more than stand there like an idiot.

"Get your boots on," Ferreira said and stepped back to wait for me.

I looked down at my feet, surprised to find myself shuffling around in my socks. Usually, when there was a knock, we knew to put shoes on before we were cuffed. I rubbed my face again, trying to clear the fog in my brain. I figured I might as well do as I was told. I was too tired and depressed to really care what they did to me next.

Returning to the steel bed to sit, I pulled the boots on. The usual pinch on my feet grounded me somehow. With my boots on, I passed through the door and into the hallway, uncuffed and confused.

Are they taking me somewhere to snuff me?

If they kept me calm, it would be easier to get me to come along without a fuss. They could lead me to whatever room they used to put down lumpers in this godforsaken place and slaughter me like a steer.

Ferreira gestured down the hall, and I headed in that direction, docile as a lamb. She followed behind me, only speaking to tell me when to turn through the maze of hallways. We made several turns, and soon, I faced the doors to the outside. My feet stopped, and I turned to gape over my shoulder at the guard.

"Truck should be waiting for you with the keys," she said, sounding bored.

"I'm just...supposed to go back?" I stammered stupidly, my brain still trying to catch up.

"Yes," she replied.

"I...."

I couldn't finish the sentence.

Through the reinforced glass doors, the sun hit the cement. The rickety table and mismatched chairs sat outside the door and to the left. We'd sat just right there when we waited for the truck to be pulled around after a run. Earl, Decker, and me. Now, my friends were ash, and I was pounding pavement back to the truck with nothing more than a broken hand.

When I pushed through the doors, the guard didn't follow. My eyes squinted in the bright light. I didn't know what time it was, but it felt like late afternoon, and the sun was hot against my skin. My mind fumbled around, trying to figure out what it all meant, trying to process me walking out of Decon like it had been any old run. My brain was running on fumes, and I couldn't shift it into gear.

Get to the Home ran on repeat through my mind.

The truck waited in its usual spot. I felt a sliver of hate looking at that thing. I'd carried my dead friends in the back of it. I never wanted to see it again. And now, they were making me drive it back to the Home like nothing happened.

Not really knowing what else to do, I climbed into the driver's seat. After the shock of yesterday, it felt dirty sitting in that spot. That was Earl's seat. I should be riding bitch.

A shuddering sigh escaped, and I turned to look at the back seat. I wondered what Earl must've thought, looking at my big ass folded into that tiny space. He probably had a chuckle the first time I clambered in.

Will I be driving from now on?

With a heavy dose of bitterness, I decided I'd probably be behind the wheel until my release date. Unless I died some fucked up death like Earl before then. Then, someone else would slide right into that spot. Rinse and repeat.

"Fuck," I murmured.

I wanted to scream. I wanted to rip my splint off and punch the dashboard. I wanted to feel the bite of physical pain so I didn't have to feel the pang of my crushed soul. I wanted to rest my head on the steering wheel, close my eyes, and have a good cry. Instead, I turned the key in the ignition, silenced the radio, and shifted the truck into gear, knowing that was what Earl would've wanted me to do.

CHAPTER TWENTY-SEVEN

When I left Decon, it was just like any other day. The guards scanned my ID card, the gates opened, and the truck dipped through the driveway and out onto Folsom Blvd.

My mind was still stuffed with wool, and I had a hard time focusing my eyes. A distant part of me wondered if I should be driving. At a red light, I rubbed my eyes with the palm of my hand until a honk informed me that the light had turned green.

That was when I realized that I didn't know the way back to the Home. I remembered it was somewhere on the north side of town before the blocky city buildings met the sweep of the river. I also knew it was in the light industrial area that capped the start of the alphabet streets. But somehow, I couldn't even remember the name of the street the Home was on. I wondered if I'd ever known it.

I figured I'd head down Folsom until I hit 16th, turn north, and hope I'd recognize some landmarks before I reached the river. Sure enough, about fifteen minutes and a couple of wrong turns later, I finally found the Home.

I parked the truck out front and killed the engine. Part of me wanted to turn into ash right there in the seat and say "fuck it" to all this noise. But I knew I couldn't just sit there. Powered by some unknown force, my hand found the door handle, and my feet found the asphalt.

I was glad it was Ramos at the desk when I buzzed in. She scanned my ID card, took my keys, and even did me a solid by coming out to pat me down herself.

It was a good thing it wasn't that shiteater, Jackson. As tired as I was, I knew the rage crouched on the periphery, ready to rise up and sweep over any motherfucker who jacked his jaw. Given the headspace I was in, I might've even killed him. Another death hanging around my neck like a noose.

After Ramos finished, she buzzed me through with a look of sympathy that almost crushed me right there.

I barely registered the looks from the guys in the yard. But there was a palpable shift in the air when I entered the breezeway. I knew word had spread about what had happened. I briefly wondered what version of the story had made its way through to the residents and then realized that I didn't really care.

I shuffled to Room Four, eyes held firmly away from the two empty cots. I collapsed on my cot face down and turned away from the rest of the room. Sleep took me before another dusty thought could circle through my head.

***

When I woke up, dim light filtered through the windows.

I rolled over onto my back, feeling each tired and achy muscle grumble with a dry sort of heat. My eyes and face felt puffy, and I couldn't focus. When I went to rub the sleep from my eyes, I managed to smack myself with the splint.

Seeing that thing strapped to my wrist brought everything back. Every second of that horrible day spun through my mind in bright flashes. I rolled to a sitting position, unable to help the moan that snuck out. When my feet touched the floor, a distant part of me realized I still had my boots on.

The analog clock on the wall read 6:32. I'd somehow managed to sleep all the way through to the next day. A part of me wondered why no one had come in to check on me. Then, I remembered that the only people who'd ever shown me an ounce of care in this fucked up place were dead.

My eyes betrayed me and drifted over to Earl's cot. It was neatly made, and if I didn't focus too hard, I could pretend he'd gone to the chow hall before me. But there weren't any thumper boots lined up neatly next to it. They'd probably burned his boots along with his body in Decon.

His stash was neatly organized beneath his bed, and I wondered why no one had rat-fucked it. There must be some unspoken rule about not touching the stash of someone who'd been chewed to death by a rager. Maybe it was a superstition. I wondered how many residents had even seen a rager before; the chances were pretty slim, all things considered.

The pain of looking at Earl's things was too much, and I tore my eyes away. I tugged my boots off and set them to the side. I pulled off my damp socks and shucked on my slips, still feeling numb.

As I stood, my eyes flicked to Decker's cot. His blanket was still rumpled and messy, like the man who'd slept there. Deep in the blanket, there was the smooth rise of white hair interrupted by brown tabby stripes.

My chest felt so tight I couldn't breathe.

There was a scuffing sound as my slips shuffled across the floor. I felt heavy, like I was wading through quicksand. When I reached Decker's cot, Cockroach looked up from his spot, blinked once, made a small *merf* of recognition, and then tucked his nose back under his tail.

The tips of my fingers brushed across his soft hair. My knees felt wobbly, and then every muscle locked up tight. My breathing sped up, and I felt a rush of protectiveness. A certainty washed over me: I would do whatever it took to keep that damn cat safe.

Still wearing the coveralls from Decon, I started toward the door in a daze, thinking I needed to get to the chow hall to get Cockroach some breakfast. The morning bell hadn't rung yet, and a distant part of me said I should wait for the count. My body halted just outside the door. I tried to blink through the fog in my mind. I stood there until the morning bell and then through the morning count, like a statue.

When they called out "Count cleared" over the PA system, I shuffled to the chow hall, slipping into line with everyone else. I kept my head down. I still felt the edginess that always swept over me before a fight, and I wasn't sure what might set me off. Also, I wasn't thinking right, so I tried to focus on getting Cockroach some breakfast and getting the fuck out of there before anything could go down.

The hair on the back of my neck went up, and adrenaline dumped into my system. I could feel people watching me. The normal chatter had died down to a whisper. It wasn't silent in the room, but all the attention had turned toward me.

I let my hair fall over my face, trying to block everyone out. Trying to keep all the boiling emotions tamped down.

I wove through the line. Breakfast was a large spoonful of oatmeal, two hard-boiled eggs, an orange, and a carton of milk. As I reached the end, one of the ladies made a point of asking me to wait, and a few seconds later, she passed me a container of plain yogurt.

No one else had gotten yogurt, and my eyes lifted up slowly. But before I could catch her, she'd turned away to help the next dudes in line. All I could see was the curve of her broad shoulders and her gray hair wrapped up in a hair net.

My chest tightened.

I dropped my head, letting my hair fall back into place.

Though the guards would tolerate us palming the occasional item back to our rooms, we weren't allowed to take the trays there. I knew this in a small corner of my mind somewhere, but there wasn't even a whiff of a shit to give. I shambled back to Room Four, holding my tray. I didn't even have enough energy to be surprised when no one stopped me.

Back in the room, I set the tray on the floor and curled into a sitting position, back against the wall. "Cockroach," my voice croaked.

Cockroach lifted his head and slow-blinked from Decker's cot.

"Come on, kitty," I called softly. I pulled the thin lid off the plain yogurt and leaned forward to set it about two feet in front of me.

Cockroach stood and stretched languidly, arching his back. There was a slight *thump* as he hopped off the bed. His tail was high, and the tip flicked back and forth slowly. He sniffed the air and then moved over to the yogurt. He crouched in front of it and slowly lapped the contents.

So many emotions spun through my head that I couldn't keep up. My stomach was audibly growling now, but that base need was so distant—so buried in the fog—that I couldn't be bothered to touch the tray lying next to me. I just sat and watched the cat lick the yogurt cup clean before sitting back and swiping his paw across his face.

After a few last licks across his whiskers, he paused and looked up at me. His eyes pierced through me like it was the first time he really saw me. I felt a reflexive desire to curl away and hide my sins. Cockroach moved suddenly, as if he'd made up my mind, and climbed right into the curl of my legs like he owned the place. A slow purr rattled against my leg.

Everything swelled up at once: so many emotions that I felt like they'd burst through my skin. I leaned my head back against the wall, closing my eyes. I wasn't thinking about any one thing. There was just the press of the cat on my lap and the wet streaks down my cheeks.

CHAPTER
TWENTY-EIGHT

I wasn't sure how long I'd been lost sitting there with Cockroach in my lap. It was long enough for him to fall asleep and my joints to complain.

I shifted slightly, trying to get the blood back into my legs. Cockroach rose from his spot, stretched, and stepped lightly onto the ground. He sniffed the tray with the congealing oatmeal and sat, watching me. I knew I needed to eat, and some distant part of me knew that the cat was telling me that.

I shifted the tray onto my lap and went through the motions. Nothing had a taste, and I wasn't sure if I really wanted anything to. After the last bite was down, Cockroach drifted over to me, arched his tail against my arm. With a *merf*, he sauntered across the room and leapt out through the window. There was a tug in my chest, and a part of me hoped he'd come back tonight. I found myself hoping that dinner would have something I could bring back for him.

The empty cots stared back at me, and I just couldn't take it anymore. I wasn't sure what was worse: looking at the empty coffins or being around other people.

I rose and crossed the yard, head low and hair hanging down. There were guys around me; I could feel them. But I couldn't bear looking at anyone. And I certainly didn't want to talk.

In the rec room, Al sat in his usual spot, all alone, loosely holding the remote. The dull noise of *The Price is Right* filled the empty space. It was an oddly comforting buzz of fake cheer, and a small part of me realized why Al liked watching it. There was a numbness to it.

I took the seat next to him and swiped my hair back with my left hand.

For the first time ever, Al turned to look at me. I watched him from the corner of my eye, unable to face him. His deep brown eyes were full of intelligence and understanding. I felt *seen* in a way I hadn't ever been before.

Part of me wanted to flinch away. It was hard when someone saw all the messiness and broken bits. It was hard to let them see that everything inside was being held together with duct tape and baling wire—just enough to get by. Another part of me felt relief. That part of me *wanted* to be seen, wanted someone to understand and accept me for all the fucked-up mess that made me who I was.

There was no judgment in Al's eyes. And no pity, either. It was the look of someone who'd seen some shit. It was the look of someone who'd had to do some dark things and sometimes went to dark places. But it was also a look that offered hope, a look that said, "I see the baggage you carry, my friend, and you can make it. Just hang on."

I finally met his gaze, feeling every single piece of bad shit shifting in the backpack of life I lugged around. All the scars, and the ugliness, and the darkness.

Al's eyes softened. He tipped his head in a single nod.

With that look, I knew I could keep walking the path no matter the load.

ACKNOWLEDGMENTS

The seed for this story came from the mind of Tyler Smith. While on a run for art supplies, he shared an idea for a D&D campaign based on prisoners forced to kill lumpy zombies. We spitballed ways in which people might become said lumpy zombies, and my veterinary brain went straight to transmissible venereal tumors in dogs. Yes, believe it or not, transmissible cancer is a thing. And if you choose to look it up, check out devil facial tumor disease, too. Veterinary pathology is the coolest shit ever.

From there, we built the characters, breathing life into them using bits and pieces from our own experiences. When I was a little girl, I was left to wander around a prison farm while my dad worked. One of the inmates at the farm took me under his wing. He made sure no one messed with me, taught me how to play dominoes, and kept me out of the "adult" bathroom. Looking back, some scary stuff could've happened during that time, but it didn't because of one amazing guy who looked out for me. I wish I could tell him how much he meant to me, but he's been lost to time. Instead, I tried to capture a bit of his caretaker soul into Earl's character. Decker is inspired by a childhood friend. His dad regularly beat the living crap out of him, and the constant abuse sent him straight into a lifelong struggle with drug addiction. He's been in and out of prison his entire life. I don't know where he is now, and my heart aches for him. He's a good guy and deserved better, just like Decker.

With every story I write, my hope is that people walk away with something to think about. With this book, I hope readers take a moment to consider the labels we place on each other and how hurtful those labels can be: junkie, bum, welfare queen, gang banger, felon.

Those labels only divide us.

We are more than those labels. The dude who looked out for me at the prison farm was more than his felony. My childhood friend was more than his drug addiction. We all make bad choices in life, and we all have the opportunity to do better. There's a living, breathing person under that label. I challenge you to see the person behind it.

If you want to learn more about the lived experiences of people who have served or are currently serving time, I strongly recommend visiting the Prison Journalism Project's website: https://prisonjournalismproject.org/. The stories published on that website helped guide the vibe of prison life in this book. There's some powerful stuff there.

Two wonderful beta readers also helped shape the heart of this book. Kashawn Taylor ensured the story accurately reflected the daily life, personalities, language, and different emotional experiences in prison. Derek Smith helped tighten up the pacing, found the plot holes, and guided the story to a deeper emotional resonance. The story is better because of their thoughtful input, and I appreciate both of these guys immensely.

And now to thank all of the lovely people who helped get this book polished up and ready for print. Oodles of appreciation go to my copy editor, Caryn Pine, and my proofreader, Yasmine Bonatch. I've worked with them on many books, and they always get things just right.

Finally, the most thanks shall be heaped upon Tyler Smith. The story began and ended with him. In addition to providing the seeds for the story, he designed the cover, a true work of art, combining many elements of the story into a single image and capturing the vibe of everything happening in Bear's mind. Thank you for breathing life into the world, Tyler.

ABOUT THE AUTHOR

Catherine Sequeira was born and raised in the Bay Area. She obtained her BS and DVM from UC Davis and completed an anatomic pathology residency at Cornell. Throughout her career, she has lived and worked in Switzerland, New York, Oklahoma, and Scotland before returning to California. With over twenty years as a veterinary anatomic pathologist under her  belt, she now writes and teaches. In her spare time, she enjoys reading sci-fi and fantasy, playing tabletop games, and gardening. She lives in northern California with her partner, cat, and dragon (the bearded kind, that is).

She can be found online at www.catherinesequeira.com.

www.ingramcontent.com/pod-product-compliance
Lightning Source LLC
LaVergne TN
LVHW091630070526
838199LV00044B/1010